# MISS

HARLOE RAE

*Miss*
Copyright © 2018 by Harloe Rae, LLC
All rights reserved.

No part of this publication may be reproduced, distributed, or transmitted in any form or by any means, including photocopying, recording, or other electronic or mechanical methods, without the prior written permission of the copyright owner and the publisher listed above, except in the case of brief quotations embodied in critical reviews and certain other noncommercial uses permitted by copyright law.

This is a work of fiction and any resemblance to persons, names, characters, places, brands, media, and incidents are either the product of the author's imagination or purely coincidental.

Cover Design:
Talia's Book Covers

Cover Photographer:
Sara Eirew

Cover Models:
Alex Boivin & Carolyn Seguin

Interior Design & Formatting:
Christine Borgford, Type A Formatting

This book is dedicated to Harloe's Hotties.
Each one of you makes a difference. Thanks for your part!

# PLAYLIST

"Closure" by Rachel Wammack

"Perfect" by Ed Sheeran

"You Got 'Em All" by Trent Harmon

"No Stopping You" by Brett Eldredge

"Mercy" by Brett Young

"Photograph" by Ed Sheeran

"All of You" by John Legend

"Can't Help Falling in Love" by Haley Reinhart

"Born to Love You" by LANCO

"What About Us" by P!nk

"Shoot Me Straight" by Brothers Osborne

"I Will Wait" by Memford & Sons

# ABOUT MISS

Delilah Sage was my comfort within all the pain.

A saving grace when I needed an escape.

The only one who understood me.

But our dreams were doomed from the start.

And I left her clinging to false hope.

Regret has plagued me for years.

Each second of every day, I want to claim her as mine.

But I won't ruin her life.

And she's better off without me.

When a job lands me in town, I plan to keep my distance.

My scars are mine alone.

Dredging up the past will only cause deeper damage.

But Delilah has always been my weakness.

And resisting her isn't an option.

This time around, we won't miss.

# PROLOGUE

## GONE

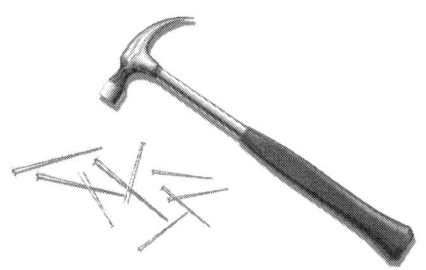

## ZEKE

I STORM OUT OF MY father's house for the final time, ignoring the burn blazing up my side. I'm more than ready to get gone and wrench open the truck door. As I toss my duffle across the seat, soft steps sound behind me. I know it's her without turning around. My heart beats wildly, even faster than when he was threatening my life a few moments ago.

Will she understand? Here's hoping.

I turn slowly and my breath falters at the sight of her gorgeous face painted with worry. My beautiful girl looks scared and I'd do anything to wipe the concern away. But I can't stay.

My feet shuffle toward her and piercing pain radiates from my ribcage. I do my best not to wince. He got me good tonight, but never again.

"Where are you going?" she whispers.

"Away. At least for a while."

A quiet sob hiccups from her throat. "W-why? I don't want you to leave."

I cup her jaw and tilt her face up. My eyes devour her porcelain perfect features. "The last thing I wanna do is be without you, Trip. But staying in that house, with him, is ruining me. I don't wanna go but if I stay, there won't be much of me left. He won't stop until he's destroyed me."

"Take me with you," she pleads. "I can't make it without you, Zee."

My shoulders sag under the pressure of her green stare. I hate disappointing her. "You gotta finish school, Trip. And you're so strong. I'm holding you back, feeding off your goodness. You'll do better without me, at least how I am now."

Her bright gaze is fierce and pins me in place. "You take that back. If I'm strong, it's only because of you. Having you here with me is the greatest gift."

I stroke her velvet skin, letting her kindness sink into my soul. I let the memories of simpler times rush in, easing the agony slightly. Our younger selves were full of so much happiness.

"Remember the day we met?" I ask into the darkness.

She nuzzles deeper into my touch. "How could I forget? I still sleep in that ridiculous shirt."

"And you stumbled in the grass rushing over to me. My little Trip." She laughs, and a hint of a smile tilts her lips. "That's right. Think of the good."

"I know what you're doing," she murmurs.

"Is it working?"

Moisture coats her lashes as she blinks rapidly. "No".

"Should I try harder?"

"Does that involve you sticking around?"

I don't respond. Words can't express the war waging in my heart.

Trip sighs. "Okay. I'll be strong. For you."

"For you too. Don't let them win. Keep your head up," I demand. A loud bang shatters the calm around us. I glance at house before focusing on her. "He'll be looking for me soon. I gotta go now."

My fingers twist a few locks of her blonde hair, committing the silky texture to memory. Her bottomless green eyes are shining with emotion, and nothing I say will stop her tears.

"No. Please, stay," she cries and clutches onto me tight. I suck in sharply when her fingers dig into the fresh bruises on my torso.

"Trip, baby. I can't. He's gonna kill me if I don't get to him first." I brush away the tracks streaming down her cheeks. Her tears slam into me harder than his fists ever have. With regret pooling in my gut, I lay out the truth. "I can't survive there another minute. But know if I could, I'd do it only because of you."

She stays silent because she knows it's true. Living next door, she hears the constant fighting. When Trip clings to me harder, my teeth grind to force the ache away.

"Where will you go?"

"I have distant family spread all around. No one stays in contact with my dad, but they'll take me in."

"Are you going far?" Her lip wobbles, and my thumb presses against it.

I shrug, helplessness soaking into my bones. "I'm not sure. We'll see when I get there."

"Will you call me? Tell me where you are?"

"Of course. You're all I'll think about. You know that, right? I've always loved you."

She sniffles and wraps tighter around me. "I love you so much, Zee. It hurts knowing you won't be here tomorrow."

"But it's only temporary. We'll be together again soon."

"O-okay," Delilah stammers.

I clear the tightness from my throat and whisper, "Knock, knock."

Her head moves against mine. "I'm not in the mood, Zee."

I'm desperate to dry her tears. "Please humor me?"

Her body quakes with a shuddering exhale. "Who's there?"

"Butch and Jimmy."

"Butch and Jimmy who?"

I nuzzle into her neck. "Butch your arms around me and Jimmy a kiss."

Delilah laughs, but it's forced. She snuggles closer and I grip her harder. Silence envelopes us, but my mind is screaming, and time has run out. I can't leave her with nothing but a faded shirt and cheesy jokes. I fiddle with the chain looped around my neck. As always, my mother's ring hangs from the center. I pull it off and place it over her head.

Delilah gasps and clutches the silver links. "No. I can't accept this. It's all you have left of her."

She's right, of course. That necklace is the only possession I've ever cared about. I tug on the metal strand and tell her, "It's to keep you safe. Like it has for me all these years. I don't need it now that I'm leaving. Wear this and know I'm always with you."

She's crying openly, the tears pouring freely without pause. "I'll never take it off."

"That's right. Hold on to it for me."

Trip nods. "And I'll wait here until you come back."

A knot pulls tight in my stomach at her words. Why does this seem like a gamble? I don't want her betting on false hope, grasping at a future that might not come, but damn, a life without her isn't one at all. So, I let us both believe.

"I'll come for you soon. Don't worry, baby girl. I'm gonna get a job and save up every penny. I'll get us a cute little place we can share. And when it's ready and you've graduated, I'll come for you."

"I believe in you. I know you'll make this happen for us."

I'm counting on her having enough faith to keep our love burning bright.

# ONE

## TIME

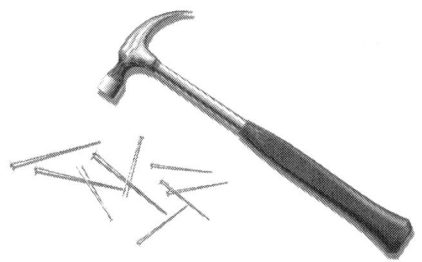

## ZEKE

THE ALARM BLARES FROM THE speakers outside, signaling quitting time. I pack up my tools and join the others gathering around the water jug. After guzzling a few glasses, my throat stops burning and the strain from a full day's work ebbs slightly.

I glance around, taking in my dusty surroundings. Only a few other buildings occupy this corner of Hacken. The saggy roofs and peeling paint beg for attention, calling out to anyone within earshot. Apparently, no one is listening. A resonating pang echoes in my chest because I often feel the same way. Forgotten to rot, left out in the sun to fade away.

Even at twenty-four, I feel old as fuck.

A hand comes down on my shoulder, yanking me from the dreary daze. "Long fucking day, huh? I'm damn glad we're almost done. Three months in this shithole is far too many," Lewis says.

I glance over a him and nod. He's the closest thing I have to a friend, but it's mostly out of convenience. "Yeah, this sleepy town isn't much to look at."

"I have no idea what the draw is," he replies with a yawn.

"Apparently the owners of Excel Entertainment keep this place on the map. Devon told me they get a lot of traffic from big wig musicians and artists passing through. Not that we got to see anything with all the shows on hold. Makes it hard to picture a lively crowd, I muse.

He snorts. "We could have used a few backstage passes. I'm done being bored. They need more than one rundown bar to keep people happy."

I roll my eyes at him. Lewis has nothing to complain about. "Hopefully this pays off for them. Gutting this disaster was a pain in the ass. That concrete fortress definitely needed an overall."

"Still not sure why this company didn't relocate elsewhere, whether or not Hacken went under without them. How can they be successful out here in the fucking sticks?" he asks.

I wipe sweat off my forehead. "Sentimental value? Who knows. Caring about that shit isn't part of our job. So long as the check clears, right?"

Lewis laughs. "Just follow directions and stay on schedule."

"Exactly."

"That's why you're Devon's favorite." He drags a hand through his hair.

I grunt. "Shut the fuck up."

"You're meant for this life, Zee."

"Zeke," I grit. Acid churns in my gut each time he calls me that. It's the biggest fucking trigger and never fails to ignite the fire in my blood. It doesn't seem to matter how many times I correct him. Not sure how much clearer I have to be.

He holds up his palms. "I always forget. Sorry, man. My cousin doesn't mind the nickname."

"Do I look like your fucking cousin?" My voice lashes across the space between us. I should feel bad for snapping at him, but he needs to cut that name from his vocabulary.

"Uh, no?"

"Try to remember that."

"You ever gonna tell me why?"

"No," I spit. "I don't owe you an explanation."

Lewis winces. "Jesus, dude. Chill out."

I grind my molars. "I will if you stop calling me that."

"Right, I got it."

"Good."

"Bad day?"

I glance at him from the corner of my eye. "Wasn't too shabby until a second ago. Now it all went to shit."

"Yeah, yeah. I won't make that mistake again. Gonna take it out on the bag later?"

Lewis has seen my bruised hands and busted knuckles enough to know how I release excess toxins.

"Probably," I reply.

"I always appreciate your one-word answers," he chuckles.

"We can't all be chatty like you."

His feet shuffle in the gravel. "Wanna grab a drink tonight? Before whatever else you've got planned. I think a few guys are going to that dive down the street. Even if it's lame as hell." Lewis gestures aimlessly over his shoulder.

"I'll pass," I say. But then add, "Thanks for the invite."

"You sure? Might be nice to—"

The badgering from him makes me lose what little control I was grasping to. This is what I get for not being a total dick.

"I said no," I growl.

Lewis doesn't seem put off by my tone. "Pretty sure you need one. Or five," he mumbles.

"What was that?"

His eyes widen. "Nothing." Lewis takes a few steps back, as if sensing the tension boiling within me. I'm thankful for the much-needed distance between us, but don't comment. He lingers for a few moments before saying, "Gotta meet with the boss. Catch you later." Lewis offers a jerky wave before spinning on his heel.

I blow out a forced breath and tip my chin to the darkening sky. Soon the stars will come out and dot the black with light. The sight always reminds me of . . . better days. Fuck, I've been traveling down that road more often lately. Probably has to do with the lack of sleep. But thinking of her won't bring peace, not like it used to. I rub my tired eyes and head toward the pickup. I toss my box in the truck bed and sit on the bumper, waiting for instructions from Devon.

As the foreman and owner of Big Rock Builders, he's got a ton to manage daily. I do whatever possible to make his job easier and return the favors he's always offering. Lord only knows where I'd be without his help. I'll never take it for granted. So long as he needs me, this is where I'll be.

As if hearing my thoughts, Devon ambles over. He crosses his burly arms and rests against the tailgate. "You good?" He offers me a fresh bottle of water.

I take it and unscrew the cap. "Yeah, sure. Ready to move on," I tell him honestly.

"Getting sick of being shacked up in Bumfuck, Nowhere?"

"You could say that," I grunt. "But I'm thankful for the steady work."

"I know you are. No doubts there. And the next city should have a bit more action. Pretty sure we all need it," he chuckles. A disbelieving noise escapes me and stops his humor. "Maybe not everyone," Devon amends.

I take in his wary expression, but look beyond that. He's in his late-forties and still a lady-killer. I'm sure they love his hard-earned muscles and tattoos. "You can take 'em," I offer.

He laughs again. "No play for you?"

"Not really my style."

"Everyone needs to blow off steam sometimes. Even you need to relax and take a load off, Zeke."

I give a limp shrug, not wanting to discuss this shit again. I lift the bottle to my lips and swallow some cool relief, silently telling him to drop the subject.

He elbows me. "Maybe your tune will change when we hit Garden Grove."

I choke on my sip of water and cough. "Excuse me?" I must be hearing things.

"That's our next site. Heard of it?" Devon asks, oblivious to the chaos erupting in my brain.

"It's almost three hours from here," I sputter, ignoring his question.

"And?"

"That's further than we normally travel. Hacken is already beyond our typical limits."

"I've gotta follow the money. If there's work, I find it for us. They've got some bar that needs restoration. Willing to pay top dollar."

Shit. I never expected to be in this predicament. This has to be some sort of test to my strength and loyalty. Maybe my sanity, too. When I signed on with Devon's crew, it was fairly safe to assume Garden Grove would never be on our list. Guess I was dead fucking wrong.

"But there was a contract in Bulten lined up. Figured that's next," I say. Even I hear the plea in my pathetic voice. That town is across state in the opposite direction, far from my demons.

Devon scoffs. "Bastards pulled out of the deal. Screw them. Nah, this new spot will be a great change of scenery for us. It'll be nice to settle in for a bit and meet some local tail. This joint has been a real bummer," he says and glances around the empty lot.

My stomach sinks. Fuck, this keeps getting worse. "We'll be staying there for a while?"

"Sure. Probably at least six months. Same as usual," Devon says.

A blast of expletives dance on my tongue, but only one escapes. "Shit."

"Thought you'd be pleased with the additional hours and overtime. What's eating you?"

I feel my face heat, and it isn't the oppressive summer humidity. I pop my jaw and attempt to keep shit locked down. "Uh," I start, licking my dry lips. "I used to live in Garden Grove."

His dark eyebrows furrow. "Yeah? What am I missing?"

I kick some rocks and watch them bounce along the ground. "There's a lot of history wrapped up in there."

"Seems you're not too thrilled about that," Devon points out.

"Didn't end well." Understatement of the fucking year. I force my features to remain void of emotion, refusing to give anything away. "Anywhere else you can send me instead?"

He blinks slowly, like he can't process my words. "The fuck? You go with the crew."

"Can there be an exception? Just this once?"

"No way. I need your dedication and skill to get this done right. Most days you do more than two others combined."

I want to be pleased with his praise, but can't summon the strength for that now. "Appreciate that, boss. But—"

He cuts me off by slashing the air. "Stop bullshitting. Tell me the issue."

I yank on my hair as frustration builds. "Too many memories. I don't wanna go back to that place," I admit.

"There's shit in your past, that much has been clear since we met. You don't have to tell me anything. All I expect is you show up to work and get the job done," he says with a dismissive snap of his fingers, like it's always that easy.

But Devon has no idea what he's asking. I gulp down the bellow desperate to release. After taking a few calming inhales,

I manage to ask, "When are we starting?"

"Early next week," he replies easily.

My pulse spikes and pounds through me. "Are you fucking joking? We just finished this gig," I say and hitch a thumb toward the looming building.

"You better watch it," Devon booms. "I'm still your boss, Zeke. Just cause I like you, and have a soft spot, doesn't mean this shit will fly."

My guard slams down at his callous tone. Visions of brutal fights and losing battles flicker in front of me. The grip my father kept on me has long been released, but I still feel his threatening presence. The scars littering my skin begin to itch as an unnecessary reminder. I scratch my arm, trying to rid the fire below the surface, but the damage is too deep. There's no chance of breaking free, so the struggle is pointless. The anger will pour out later when no one else is around. That's the way it has to be.

I continue to quietly stew in my self-deprecating misery. I glare at the expanse of nothingness in front of me, which seems ironic and stupid at the same time. I'm over this town.

Devon must pick up on my mood because he straightens off the truck. He turns to face me. "Don't let me down. You're always saying how much this crew and opportunity means to you. Prove it," he demands.

"It isn't that fucking simple."

"I can tell. Whatever you're fighting must be fierce, but that garbage can't win. You're stronger than that, Zeke. Better, too. Never forget that. I'll let you think shit over tonight, but there shouldn't be a choice. Just give me your decision tomorrow," he says with an edge of finality.

He's backing me into a corner, but that's his job. Devon needs reliable men on his payroll. Not whiny bitches afraid to face the past. I scrub down my face and begin to mentally prepare for this epic disaster.

"Fuck," I mutter. "Fine, I'll go."

Devon smirks and raises a knowing brow. "Was that so fucking hard?"

"Yes," I lash back.

He shakes his head. "Such a mystery. One day you'll spill the madness in there," he says and points to my temple.

"Doubt it."

Devon doesn't argue further. Instead he orders, "Finish the clean up tomorrow and Wednesday. Take a few days off. Then we're off to Garden Grove. Good?"

I lock my jaw to keep the truth from spilling out. I offer a single nod, which he accepts. After a jut of his chin, Devon wanders off.

When I'm alone, the weight of my situation collapses down and it's suddenly hard to breathe. Blonde hair, green eyes, and a river of broken promises rush over me. The five-year separation I've shoved between us has never felt so daunting. I can't stop the onslaught of regret stabbing into me, like her small fists beating my back. It would be best to stay gone and leave the hurt buried. The time away has changed me for the worse. I'm ashamed of the man in the mirror, and Delilah's reaction is bound to destroy me. Showing up in town is going to revive unbearable shit I can't handle. But there's no avoiding this.

Dammit, looks like I'm heading . . . *home.*

# TWO

## SPIN

## DELILAH

THE WHIR OF THE COFFEE grinder pierces through my pounding skull. The rich scent from the fresh grounds wafts over me, but I'm not getting the usual jolt as it reaches my nose. I silently curse my inability to get a decent night's sleep. Between the nonstop heatwave and longer hours at work, I can't seem to relax. I rub my swollen eyes, desperate for a machine that can instantly insert caffeine into my veins.

If I'm being honest, there's something . . . *weird* happening lately. I haven't given voice to this feeling yet because it seems too farfetched and beyond belief. But once again, the familiar prickle of awareness sneaks up my neck. I look around Jitters, taking in the bright light and low buzz of morning activity. Nothing appears out of the ordinary. A few regulars sit at tables, sipping from steaming mugs while munching on breakfast.

What the eff is wrong with me? If I don't get more rest soon, I'll probably start seeing things.

Raven ducks behind the counter and slides in next to me.

My college-bestie saved my ass by moving to Garden Grove earlier this year. Having her around has been a serious blessing. It definitely doesn't hurt that she's got master baking skills that elevated my shop to another level. Jitters, and me, would be lost without her. I give Raven's disheveled appearance a once over and send her a smirk.

"Cooking up a storm back there?" I question lightly.

She shrugs. "You could say that. I've got cookies, muffins, and cupcakes in the ovens. Do you think we need more scones?" She peers into the display case.

"I think we need more ovens," I reply.

Raven laughs. "There's already three."

"And you're always using them." I sweep a loose tendril from my sticky forehead. "It's really hot in this joint. The air conditioning can't keep up."

"Are you complaining about my master baking?"

I indicate a pinch between my thumb and finger. "I mean, you go at it all day and night. Doesn't Trey get jealous?"

"Oh, he gets plenty. Don't worry," she volleys back.

"So sassy. He's rubbing off on you."

"And I love it," she purrs.

I shove her shoulder. "Gross."

Raven bites the air. "Don't be jealous."

"Yeah, yeah." I wave her nonsense away, but a hollow pang settles in my chest. Pretend as I might, loneliness has been creeping in more and more lately. A heavy sigh deflates me.

Her brows crumple. "You okay?"

I nod. Before I can respond, the door chimes. I plaster a smile on my lips and twist to the register. I hold back a groan as Marlene practically prances toward me. A trail of potent perfume accompanies her and intensifies my headache. Her grey hair is styled to perfection, as always. Too bad she can't keep the lipstick off her teeth. She's the worst gossip Garden Grove has to offer and based off her gleeful expression, she's got something extra juicy to share. This should be a splendid combination of tedious and interesting.

"Good morning," I greet.

"Hello, Delilah," she chirps. Marlene sets her sights on Raven beside me. "And hello to you, dear. I'm so happy you worked things out with Trey." Her grin is more fake than the plastic pearls around her neck.

"I bet you are," Raven mumbles. I peer over and catch the curl of her mouth. Trey is definitely influencing her, and it's amazing.

Marlene doesn't seem to find the humor. "What was that?" She leans closer.

Raven smooths her features. "I said that's very nice of you. We appreciate your concern."

I cough into my fist hearing that pile of bullshit. These two make quite a pair. Raven pats my back, as if I'm actually choking. I can't help a giggle from bubbling out. I wipe under my eyes and straighten, facing Marlene head-on.

"I hope you're not sniffing around for trouble, Marlene. You've caused enough of it lately," I tell her.

"You girls need to be more professional. This is your place of business," she scolds.

"Is our behavior stopping you from dropping by more often?" I ask. If the answer is no, we need to step it up another notch.

She tsks. "Don't be a brat, Delilah. Your mother raised you better."

My teeth clack together and I bristle at her tone. But I should probably mind my manners with customers. No matter who they are.

"You're right. I apologize," I grind out. I elbow Raven, shooting her a look.

Her sneakers scuff the floor as she fidgets. "I'm sorry, too."

The older woman nods, her features stern. "That's better. I'll turn you two into respectful ladies yet."

I almost snort, but hold the noise in. "Don't hold your breath. Let's move on, yeah? What can we get you, Marlene?"

Before she answers, Raven pipes up. "Did you hear that? I think the cookies are done. Better go check on them." She begins to shift away, mouthing a silent apology.

I glare at her retreating form, not believing she's sorry for a moment. Marlene interrupts my chance at a rebuttal.

"She's a sweet one. Trey is a lucky guy," she comments. Marlene studies me with a slight tilt of her head. "How's your dating life?"

I rub my temples. "That's not why you're here. How about some fresh banana bread instead? Raven made it fresh a couple hours ago. I just brewed some hazelnut coffee, too. Would you like to try some?"

She allows me to change the subject, but purses her lips. "I do love that recipe." She taps her wrinkled chin. "I'll have two slices of cake and a large light roast. *To go*," she says with emphasis.

After pouring the coffee, I wrap the baked goodies in pink wax paper and place everything on the counter. Marlene's hand rests on the bread. Her eyes suddenly sparkle brighter, an obvious tell that she's got something more to share. The news might as well be scrawled across her flouncy blouse because the evidence is obvious.

Shit, I can only imagine. I tap my nails on the glass top, encouraging her to spit it out.

Marlene's wide grin lifts her wrinkled cheeks. "Have you heard about the renovation at Roosters?"

I sigh, disappointment settling in at her lame topic of chatter. This story is bound to be dull. "Hasn't everyone? Mary Sue and Bob have been talking about fixing their bar up for years. It's about damn time."

She edges closer, as if this is a secret. "But have you seen the construction site? Or better yet, the men they've hired?"

My brow rises at that. "Ah, even more cocks in the henhouse?"

Marlene's fingers flutter to her chest. "Delilah Sage, must you be so crass?"

"I think by now this type of language is expected from me. Can we keep things rolling?" I make a motion for her to continue.

Marlene scrunches her nose. "What's the hurry?"

"I'm working. This isn't Sunday tea time."

She huffs. "All right, fine. Have it your way. So, the renovation started earlier this week. I've made my way down there a few times. To check on progress, you know?"

"Uh huh." The boredom is heavy in my voice.

"One of the guys was particularly recognizable, and the years have been good to him. This fellow has always been a looker, but now? He's very handsome," Marlene explains.

"Really? How nice," I respond dryly.

"It sure is. He's grown up mighty fine since I saw him last."

"Are you going to fill in the blanks? Or is this a guessing game? Because I don't really want to play, Marlene. I've got to start doing inventory."

"Go visit the site and see for yourself," she urges.

I cross my arms. "And why would I do that? I know what that place looks like. Right now, it's just a gutted version. Pretty sure I can wait until they finish."

"You're wro-ong," she sing-songs.

I comb through my long hair, tugging at the ends. This crazy old bat is losing her marbles. "Why don't you let me be the judge of that, yeah?"

"They tore it all down," she adds.

"What's that?"

"Bob convinced Mary Sue to start from scratch. This burly crew came in and bulldozed the building. They'll have a brand-new bar in a few months. Isn't that exciting?"

"Huh," I say. "Didn't know that. Guess you're sharing something relevant after all."

"But it's more than that," she whispers.

"Yeah, yeah. The piece of man meat that caught your eye. I get it," I groan. I'm ready to be done with this little exchange.

Marlene winks. "I believe you'll be super glad to see this fella. Pretty sure he'd love to catch up with you. Take a walk down memory lane," she coos softly.

I give her a flat stare, but something jolts inside of me. I trace a line over my torso, following the tingling path. When she says shit like that, only one name comes to mind. Her hints are general and ominous, so I shove the possibility away. Zeke is long gone. Why I'm even thinking about him now is beyond me. That liar hasn't stepped foot in town for years. I swallow hard when unwarranted emotion stings my eyes. I'm unsure if anger, sadness, betrayal, or a twisted version of relief is the root cause. Probably a combination of them all. A wild, erratic beat kicks up in my chest. My heart is a traitor. And so are the memories constantly assaulting me.

I bite my lip, making sure this inner turmoil stays hidden. The last thing I need is Marlene catching wind of my stupid feelings.

She dips into my distracted line of sight. "Have I convinced you yet?"

I shake my head, sweeping away all that ancient history. "Not really." I shrug.

"Sure," she drawls. "We'll see about that."

"Great," I agree for the sake of ending this exchange. "Anything else today?"

Marlene gives me a once over, her gaze far too knowing. She pats the banana bread and picks up her coffee. "This should do it for now," she says.

I wave, but really want to shoo her out the door. "Thanks

for coming."

"See you soon, Delilah. Tell Raven tootles from me." She turns and sashays out.

I sag against the wall, thankful for the reprieve from her prying stare. A shiver creeps up my spine, but heat spreads all over me. I rest a palm on my forehead, checking for a fever. At least if I'm sick, these strange sensations have purpose.

Raven peeks around the corner, carrying a tray of something delicious. She stops short when she notices me. After stashing the treats away, she moves toward me. "You okay? Looks like you've seen a ghost, D."

I blink rapidly and glance away. "Not yet."

"What's that supposed to mean?"

I cover my face and moan. "Nothing. Marlene got to me."

Raven gapes at me. "No way. What did she say?"

"She's leading me to believe I'll remember one of the guys working on Roosters' remodel. Kind of made me think of . . ." I let my words trail off.

My friend catches the drift. "Shit. Could it be him?"

I sniff, taking comfort in the sugary scent wafting over. "No, he's gone. It's not him. Just got me in a weird mood." I have to believe that. The alternative is not an option I'm able to consider.

Raven looks at me like she wants to say more, but she doesn't. I'm thankful for that. She wraps her arm around me, and I lean into the kind embrace. She reaches back and plucks some gooey goodness from the cooling rack. Raven passes me a cookie and I eagerly take a bite. Chocolate and peanut butter burst on my tongue.

I hum happily at my favorite flavor. "Damn, this hits the spot."

"There's plenty more where that came from."

"Knew I kept you around for a reason."

Raven smirks. "A cookie a day keeps the bad boys away."

I quirk a brow at her. "Didn't seem to work with Trey."

A flush races up her neck. "He's an exception." Then she adds, "To *every* rule."

I laugh and reach for another, hoping she's right.

# THREE

## WATCH

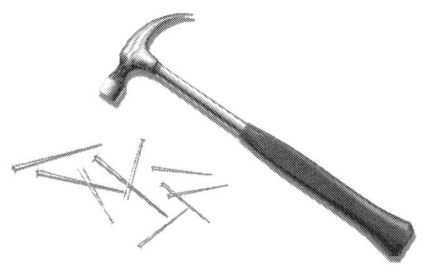

## ZEKE

I SCAN THE COBBLED SIDEWALK, checking for curious glances or prying eyes, but find none. People don't seem to care—or notice—that I've been sitting on this bench for almost an hour. I adjust the ball cap on my head, shielding my eyes from view. I'm staring into Jitters like my pathetic life depends on it, but no one else needs to know that. The popular coffee shop is a new addition since I've been gone. It's one of many things that's changed around Garden Grove.

Pride swells in my chest as I watch Delilah flit around the small tables. My original plan was to keep a safe distance, but it only took a few days before I was wandering down Main Street. When I discovered who owned this place, there was no staying away. And each time I get a bit bolder. Being close to her again gives me a small sense of peace I haven't felt in far too long. She always had that effect on me.

Leaving Delilah was a fateful mistake, but there's no point in dwelling over shit I can't change. Watching her now, in this element she was meant for, my decision is cemented all over again. Had I stayed, or come back for her, she wouldn't have this. I have no future, and Delilah's has always been bright. My failures are blinking in front of me like that damn neon welcome sign. I don't belong here, with her. She's better off without me—that much is clear. If only my life wasn't completely worthless without her. But that's not important. I'll continue trudging on in silence, taking quick glimpses when they're offered. This isn't how I imagined things would turn out between us, but it could always be worse.

My muscles seize when Delilah shifts closer to the window. I lower my face, hiding under the hat's curved brim like a chicken shit. Somehow, she's more beautiful than I remember. There's a rosy flush lighting up her flawless face, making those stunning features glow. Delilah's blonde hair is piled in a messy bun with wispy tendrils falling loose. If I tucked the strands behind her ear, maybe she'd lean into my touch. A pink apron covers what I know to be subtle curves and smooth skin. She's the vision of chaotic perfection.

When she shifts slightly, I catch sight of the ink across her shoulder. Each time I see those colorful lines, the boulder in my gut doubles in size. My eyes sting and I have to look away for a moment. We'd always planned to get tattoos together. This is one more thing I've missed out on experiencing with her. I glare at the setting sun as a string of curses fall from my lips.

Dammit, Delilah has become a totally different person with a brand-new life. I have no place in this version and that solid fact makes me nauseous. I surrendered all these years with her, but for what gain? I'm sitting out here with nothing to show for my absence. She's in there, close enough to touch, but might as well be miles away. Each second she moves further, and without pause.

Delilah doesn't seem to notice I'm around, but her distracted gaze could convince me otherwise. Maybe she senses me somehow, feels the weight of my leering stare. We always had a surreal connection. I consider this while getting caught in her green eyes. If she glanced a little to her left . . .

Delilah quickly twists away, and the moment vanishes in a puff of coffee-scented smoke. I look around again, paranoid and on edge, but this situation calls for that. If Delilah knew I was out here, peeping through the decorated glass, she'd slap me. Or scream in my face. Maybe she'd ignore me all together. The last option stops me short, and I squeeze my eyes shut. I can take her anger and sadness, but not this silence.

It's been too long since I've heard her voice.

I tap my phone, checking the time. She'll be closing up soon, which means I've got to get lost. With defeat heavy on my shoulders, I stand from my perch and stretch the ache away. Lewis and a few guys are meeting at Dagos, a local favorite down the road. I head that way to join them for happy hour. I usually prefer being alone, but this afternoon has been rough. I'm hoping that surrounding myself with others will give me a much needed distraction.

My shoes scuff over the bumpy concrete but come to an abrupt halt before reaching the bar. I almost dive into the alley when Marlene and Betty step out of a parked sedan. I remember them all too well and would bet a lot of money they're still running the rumor mill. Being a conversation topic during their tea time isn't appealing. Plus, if they catch sight of me, it will be a matter of moments before the entire town knows I'm here. After turning toward the building, I dart behind a group of teens gathering for a picture. Then I manage to slink inside undetected.

That was a fucking close one.

Lewis waves from a table in the far corner and I absorb the familiar space. This joint hasn't changed much by the looks of it. The floor is still littered with peanut shells and random memorabilia covers the walls. It smells like fried food, stale beer, and drunken nights. This is exactly what I need.

I shuffle over to the guys and take a seat on the end. I bob my chin to Brody and Kayne across from me.

"What's wrong, man? You look a little shaken up," Lewis says with a slap to my back.

I shrug him off. "This damn town is full of reminders."

He gives me a weird look. "Is that bad? I figured you'd have fun with old friends."

A low grunt tickles my throat. "Not even close."

"Doesn't your dad have a house here?"

"Not anymore." I scowl at the cup of water in my hand. "He ran off like a little bitch."

"Was this before you left?"

For whatever reason, I find myself answering honestly. "No, after. The neighbor called my aunt, who I happened to be staying with at the time. She came out and dealt with the place. Guess my dad let the bills go and there were piles stacked on the table."

"You didn't help?" His question feels like an accusation whipping into my flesh.

I hunch lower in the seat and shame sticks to my skin. "Nah, I was busy." But the truth is I'm a worthless sack of lying shit. I didn't want to risk running into Delilah. Considering her parents lived next door to my father, that outcome was more than extremely likely.

Lewis looks like he wants to rip into me further, but we're interrupted.

A perky voice calls, "Hey, stranger. What can I get you to drink?"

I turn to look at the server and the air stalls in my lungs. Shit.

"Holy balls! Zeke?" Addison's shriek travels across the room.

A rumble builds in my chest. "No need to alert the neighborhood."

"Wow, you're not a stranger at all. Well, maybe you are now. Where the hell have you been?" Disappointment paints her tone.

"Away," is all I offer with a shrug.

Her forehead pinches. "That's all I get?"

I mess with my hat, avoiding her searching gaze. Addison fidgets in front of me, shifting her stance and looking uncomfortable. Her awkward actions cause a fresh wave of guilt to hammer into me. I'm making her feel this way.

"You two know each other?" Lewis asks, pointing between us.

I welcome the interruption and scrub a hand across my stubbled jaw. "Ah, yeah. Addison and I went to school together."

She coughs. "There's far more to it than that."

I drag in a deep breath. "She's also best friends with . . . someone I used to date."

She smirks, a deep dimple denting her freckled cheek. "Someone? Really, Zeke? You're gonna downplay her that way? Can't even say her name?" Her questions blast out like rapid fire.

I narrow my eyes, unease slithering around me. "That's ancient history," I say with finality.

But Addison isn't done. She shifts closer, staring down her nose at me. "Have you seen her?" I shake my head and she adds, "D is gonna flip out."

I grab her wrist, stilling all movement. "That's why we're not telling her."

"As if," she huffs. "There's no keeping *you* a secret."

I glare at the ceiling, regretting my genius decision of venturing out tonight. "Guess we'll wait and see," I mutter.

Addison points at me. "You better talk to her, Zeke. Think about how your abandonment affected her."

"I didn't—"

"But you did. That's how D feels. I know there are reasons you left, but that doesn't matter. You didn't come back and left all of us behind," she grumbles.

"Enough of the guilt trip, Addy. I'll go somewhere else if this is how you treat customers," I complain.

She doesn't need to rake me over the coals. I take care of that all on my own. The reminders of how badly I've fucked up never cease, playing on repeat. I'll never escape that shit, but I have the power of walking out of this place.

"Get over yourself," Addison says.

"Why don't you pretend I'm not here? That'd be best for everyone."

"Unlikely, but whatever. We are so discussing this after my shift. You better stick around." She flicks my bicep.

We most definitely aren't, but I don't say that. Instead I mumble, "Shouldn't you be working now? How 'bout a beer?"

Addison pops out her hip. "Never knew you to be a bossy asshole, Zeke. It doesn't suit you."

"Sorry to disappoint. Good thing it doesn't really matter what you think," I say.

She shakes out her hand. "Oooh, burn. What the eff happened to you?"

"Too fucking much," I respond.

"Clearly. You've got some explaining to do," Addison says.

"Not the time. Probably never will be." I wave her demand away. She needs to get the fuck out of my space and take the past with her.

Addison darts away in a flurry of red hair and expletives. Lewis chuckles beside me. "Damn, she's feisty. Guess she fits the redhead stereotype."

"Don't start," I snap.

"Always shutting me down. Whatever, man. Did you talk to Devon today?"

I nod, grateful for the subject change. "The demolition is done. We've gotta start clearing the junk out. He wants us out there early tomorrow. All hands on deck."

"Suppose the easy shifts were bound to run out. Damn."

I snort. "Yeah, no more fucking off early. At least until the foundation is poured. Get ready for heavy lifting."

"I know excavating is scheduled for next week so we better hustle. Then the concrete trucks move in," he shares and I nod along.

Addison slams a few mugs on the table, the beer sloshing out. "I'll add them to your tab," she spits before dashing away again.

Lewis leaps away from the flying liquid. "Someone's holding a grudge."

"Tab? What the fuck?" I mutter quietly at the same time.

He laughs. "Forgot to pay up last time?"

"Wasn't old enough to drink. Doubtful I ran up a bill for pizza and soda," I gripe.

There's no further grumbling about Addison's mess. We gladly turn our focus to the frosty brews and take healthy gulps. I relax a fraction when the cool liquid hits my lips.

Lewis drags a palm over his buzzed hair. "At least we've got our weekends free. I'm a big fan of Garden Grove already. The women are sexy as sin. I can't wait to explore some more." He wags his brows and I have the urge to punch his throat.

"Don't be a douche," I mutter.

"You're just jealous."

A disbelieving laugh bursts from me. "Of what?"

Lewis motions down his torso. "All this."

"Hardly, dude. Keep dreaming."

His comeback doesn't register because all the air is suddenly sucked out of the room. I can't breathe or move or . . . fucking think. Everything I am is lost to the blonde beauty who just stepped into Dagos. I have tunnel vision, and Delilah is the spotlight.

*Christ, can this situation get any worse?*

He follows my line of sight. "Another girl you know?"

"Used to."

"Ah, the plot thickens. Is she the someone you referred to earlier?"

"You don't know shit."

"But your clues leave little to the imagination." Lewis chuckles and I hate him for it.

As I tear my gaze away from Delilah, frustration cinches my chest. But he's right. Chills race up my arms and I shiver despite the balmy temperature. Delilah is bound to see me hunkered down over here. Thankfully this part of the table is cloaked in shadows so my presence has a chance of remaining hidden.

I watch her make a beeline for the bar, dragging some random chick behind her. I squint to get a better look. Pretty sure I saw her working with Delilah at Jitters earlier, but she's not someone who grew up with us. When Addison skips up to them, my heart stutters to a stop. Fuck, she's bound to point me out.

Lewis juts his chin toward Delilah, my staring obvious. "She's hot as fuck," he whistles. I jab him in the ribs and he almost falls off the chair.

"Shut the fuck up," I growl.

"You're grumpier than usual. Maybe she can help with that. You should say hello. Clearly you've missed her."

I grunt. "Nah. Wouldn't end well."

Lewis gives me a blank look, like I'm not making sense.

"What?" I ask.

"You're giving me crumbs of something big. Care to share more?"

"You wanna sit around and gossip like a bunch a chicks?" I question, trying to throw him off track.

"I think you do," he prods.

"No. Not even a little bit."

He sighs and grips my shoulder. "You're always locked up so fucking tight. It won't hurt to lean on someone, you know? I've got two ears and can keep my mouth shut. Right now, you've got that defeated and broken thing going. Wanna talk about it?"

"No," I repeat. "There's nothing to tell. It's all a dead end." A spasm cramps my chest but I ignore it. Best to leave all that shit behind me where it belongs. I look away from Delilah's gorgeous face and focus on my beer, watching the condensation drip down. After a few more minutes of tense silence, I decide to break it. "How long do you think this job will take?"

Lewis has been part of Devon's crew for the longest, going on seven years. If anyone can predict this type of project, it's him.

He shrugs and spins his mug around. "Meh, at least five months? Maybe more. I swear these small-town gigs always take twice as long. When the owners decided to tear down the entire building, that tacked on some serious weeks. Starting from scratch takes time, but it's easier in a lot of ways. Why some wanna hold onto debilitating remains is beyond me."

"Sometimes it's hard to let go," I mumble almost silently.

"Huh?"

I jerk my gaze up, not realizing I'd spoken aloud. I scratch the back of my neck, trying to get rid of the heat rising there. "If the roots and foundation are still solid, why ruin it? There's beauty in the original."

Lewis doubles over and busts out laughing. "Wow, that's some sappy shit. Never thought I'd hear you getting sentimental over concrete."

I shake my head. He doesn't get it. "It's far more complicated than that."

# FOUR

## STRANGE

## DELILAH

THE BUBBLING WATER FEELS HEAVENLY on my feet, and I recline lower in the massage chair. I needed this—big time. I'm burning the soles off my shoes with Jitters being extra busy lately. But let's be honest, no one needs an excuse to get a pedicure.

I moan when Ruby, the nail technician, starts rubbing my sore arches. "Oh, Lord. That feels so good. Ah, yeah, right there. Please don't stop. Like, never ever."

Raven giggles next to me. "You're feeding every male fantasy right now. I should record you and play it for Mister Large Dark Roast next time he drops by."

I shoot her a glare, my relaxing cloud of bliss evaporating instantly. "Don't you dare, Rave. That dude is duller than his coffee order."

"But he likes you. Hearing you groan would definitely give him a rise," she laughs.

I wrinkle my nose. "Ew, no. I'm so not interested."

"Come on, D. He practically drools all over the counter

whenever you're nearby."

"That's a gross visual. You're ruining this experience for me," I say with an exaggerated frown. My attention refocuses on the goddess working me over. "Rubes is giving me the royal treatment with all the perks. You're getting a seriously big tip," I tell her with a lazy smile.

Ruby grins back. "You're hilarious. Moan away. It makes the day more interesting. I don't mind the commentary at all." She digs into my heels and tingles shoot up my calf. I lower my eyelids and get sucked back into paradise. Damn, this woman knows how to treat a lady.

Raven flicks me and says, "Hey."

"Ouch. What the heck?" I ask.

"We're having a conversation."

I make a noncommittal noise. "Oh, really?"

"Yes, really. You're not into the dark roast guy. But how about the hottie with the delicious arm-porn from Boomers?"

"Meh, he's all right. Maybe I'll give him a call."

"What's your deal lately?" She raises a questioning brow.

I motion toward my pampered toes. "Pretty sure it's obvious."

She rolls her blue eyes. "Not in this exact moment. In general. You seem off. Especially when it comes to guys."

I cringe when she strikes a serious truth. Guess I haven't been that sneaky with hiding my feelings. "Uh, I have no idea. It's just been seriously busy at work. Who has time for guys right now?" I hedge.

Raven points at herself. "Yours truly."

"That's different. You started dating before the summer's craziness really started."

She gives me a look that tells me I'm busted. "Don't lie to me, D. What's really going on?"

I sigh with purpose. "I dunno. I'm in a funk or something. I'm not feeling anyone lately. Like, at all. Maybe it's a sign I need to focus on myself." I pick at my cuticles.

Raven hums. "Huh, well then. That's understandable. More girl time for us."

I snort. "Yeah, when Trey isn't dragging you away. Lucky bi-atch getting it on the regular. Speaking of, are you two meeting up after this?"

She squints at me, ignoring my attempt to deflect the attention. "Did we not just discuss two very eligible men willing to give you plenty?"

"I don't want them, though. There's gotta be passion and desire. Doesn't help that I feel like a limp noodle," I complain.

"Talk about a bad visual." She crooks her finger to symbolize certain male genitalia.

It's my turn to flick her arm. "Perv. Don't worry, I'll get my groove back. Eventually."

"Seems to be more to it than just that," Raven mutters absently.

I don't comment on her observation, choosing to enjoy the rest of Ruby's pampering. When my toenails are painted a perfect glittery pink, she helps me out of the chair. I waddle to the dryer and plop down. I'm about to open a magazine when Raven sits down beside me.

"You're not getting away from me that easily."

"Clearly," I mumble.

"So? What's got your lady bits in a twist?"

"Ugh, I thought we were dropping this."

She winks at me. "Wishful thinking."

"Isn't it my job to be the bossy one?"

"Oh, you are. But not right now. Consider this a little role reversal. It's always helpful when you push me to realize the truth. I want to return the favor," she presses.

I pick at a glob of glue on the counter ledge. "I'd hardly say this is the place to divulge secrets."

Raven makes it a point of peering around the empty salon.

"Nice try, but you're avoiding. There's something bothering you and I'm here to be supportive. Spill it."

I scratch my scalp while the knot inside my stomach tightens. "I'm perfectly capable of handling my own needs, thank you very much." I give her a quick side-eye. "But most recently? With you happily humping Trey and Addy making kissy faces at Shane, I feel a bit left out. Mostly because all the romance clogging the air makes me think about . . ." I let my implication hang between us.

Raven gapes at me. "Zeke?"

I pop my lips while a lead weight drops on me. "Wasn't going to say his name, but yes."

"Does this have anything to with the news Marlene shared the other day? Do you think he's back in town?"

I make a seesaw motion. "Sort of? Her suggestion definitely brought him to mind. But he's already been swirling around in there for years. She was probably referring to one of her crotchety grandsons. That woman is desperate to marry them off." I glance at her from the corner of my eye. "This is going to sound weird, but no judgement?"

She nods and motions for me to keep going.

"It's like I can sense him nearby within the last few weeks. I sound crazy, but it's always been that way with Zeke. I've determined the summer heat and sexual drought are playing tricks on me," I quip.

Raven squeezes my arm. "Sounds like you're missing him more than usual."

"You have no idea how much I hate this. He makes me feel weak and stupid."

"But you're not. You're a strong warrior. You know that."

"Do I? Honestly, I'm not so mighty when it comes to him."

"You don't have to constantly put on a brave face. It's okay to be vulnerable, D. Especially when it comes to this guy. He made a huge impact on your life," she soothes.

I shoot her a sassy smirk. "You're being awfully wise."

Raven makes an agreeable sound. "This is a safe space. Blab away."

Emotion stings my eyes and I hate that Zeke has this power over me. "I shouldn't feel this way anymore. It's been over five years, Rave. I probably never cross his mind." I sniff, getting a heavy dose of polish remover.

She bumps me lightly. "Yeah, right. No one could ever get over you."

"You have to say shit like that in these situations."

"Not true. I could make up something far sweeter. Such as you're brilliant, selfless, gorgeous, crazy successful, yadda yadda, on and on."

I grimace. "That sounds like a dating site profile."

Her baby blues sparkle with interest. "That's an entertaining idea."

"No, thanks. I've got enough trouble in the men department."

She holds up a finger. "Right. Sorry. I got distracted. Why wouldn't Zeke be constantly thinking of you? You told me a bit of your history together. Maybe it would offer some sort of relief to purge more. Since he's already on your mind?" She looks at me expectantly, urging me in her subtle way.

I puff up my cheeks, then release the pent-up air slowly. That's how my entire body feels—trapped and suspended in this stagnant spot. All because he's got an unrelenting grip on my heart. "We weren't ever going to bring him up again, remember?" I tease.

Raven lifts a shoulder. "Meh, rules don't apply to us. Tell me whatever you want."

I bite the inside of my cheek, deciding what else to share. Talking about Zeke is like stabbing at a wound that refuses to heal. Might as well scrub the surface and hope the damage finally scabs over.

"Zeke was different for me from the beginning," I whisper.

"He moved into the house next to mine, so obviously destiny was involved. I was certain the stars aligned and all the elements pointed to us living happily ever after. All after five seconds." With a finger at my temple, I imitate having a screw loose.

"I was sunk from the moment he stepped out of the U-Haul. I blame his eyes. They're a special shade of blue. Those bad boys sucked me in like Lake Superior." I point at hers for emphasis. "With his dark hair, he's got that attractive contrast going on. Plus, he leveled me with a cocky smirk. That kid knew he was hot. I was a bee stuck in honey and couldn't race out there fast enough to introduce myself." I laugh, but the sound is flat. "Lost cause right here. Or hopeless. Either way we managed to hit it off. Over five years, tween innocence morphed into all-encompassing love. We were rarely apart and barely argued. At least until he left," I force out past the lump in my throat.

I shrug weakly. "I don't fault him for going. His dad was abusive and a mean drunk. Zeke became his personal punching bag after a night at the bar. He needed out of that shitastic situation before things went beyond repair. I'm glad he survived that and moved on," I tell her honestly. "But I gave him everything and always thought we'd be together. Our future dreams were each other. So, the part I haven't gotten over is his broken promise. That's what has me trapped in the past."

My chest is tight and I rub at the ache. "Zeke told me he'd come back for me. He was supposed to call, but that didn't happen either. Turns out the lying asshole couldn't be fucking bothered to pick up the phone." A sob hiccups out of me and I cover my mouth. Every cell in my body is screaming, but there's no escape. I squeeze my eyes shut against the onslaught of memories. His striking blue gaze attempts to penetrate my thoughts, but I shove him away.

I snap out of it when Raven rubs my back. "Hey, let's drop it. I didn't mean to push so hard. I had no idea—"

"It's fine," I cut in. "I should talk about him. Maybe I can finally get rid of this lingering crap shackled around my ankles. Like desensitizing? Is that a thing?"

"Uh, maybe? Sounds like a fancy term a therapist would use. Have you ever tried finding Zeke on social media?" Raven suggests.

I scrub at my stinging face. "That's a good joke. He was always very private about his life. There's no way he'd be caught having an online account." She gives me a blank stare and I roll my eyes. "Yeah, I double checked."

"Maybe we could make a voodoo doll and expel the negative energy."

A genuine laugh bubbles out of me. "Oh, yes. Let's do that for sure." I twist my lips while looking at her. "Thanks for being here. In case I don't tell you enough."

Raven blows me a kiss. "There's nowhere else I'd rather be. Love you, sista-friend."

"Love you more, bestie."

Quiet contentment settles around us. The barely-there buzz from the dryer's fluorescent bulbs stops, reminding me to start the timer for another round. I tap Raven's machine while I'm at it. When I look over, her bright blues sparkle mischievously.

"What are we doing after this?" she asks.

"By the looks of it, you've already got an idea," I say with suspicion in my voice.

"Are you up for a little adventure?"

"Maybe, but that depends. You're kind of freaking me out."

She rubs her hands together. "What if Zeke is actually at Roosters? Can you imagine? Let's wander down there, just for fun. If he does happen to be around, you can give him a piece of your mind."

I'm already shaking my head before she finishes. "Not happening."

"Why not?" she whines. "The unknown is bothering you. I can tell."

"Which is fine. I can manage. If by some small chance he's working on the rebuild, that jerk-face can come to me." I cross my arms defiantly.

Raven laughs. "That's true. But he doesn't need to know we're spying."

For a moment, I'm stunned silent by the potential of seeing him again. My chest is heavy and it's difficult to get a decent breath. That reaction alone tells me I need to stay the eff away.

"I think shopping is a safer choice," I mumble.

She pouts for only a second. Then, she suddenly bounces in her seat. "Oooh, for new panties? That always makes me feel better."

I shrug. "Sure. I can get hip to that."

She taps her chin. "What can I surprise Trey with most?"

"A sex swing?" I joke.

She blushes. "We, ah, already tried that."

I giggle loudly. "Why am I not surprised? You're such a kinky hussy."

"Only for him," she states proudly.

"I'm happy for you guys," I tell her honestly. They've got that special sauce that lasts forever.

Raven smiles. "Thanks, babe. Next on the love agenda is finding your Mister Right."

"Yeah, good luck with that," I reply dryly.

That's a lost cause because I've already found him. Too bad he didn't want the title.

# FIVE

## AGAIN

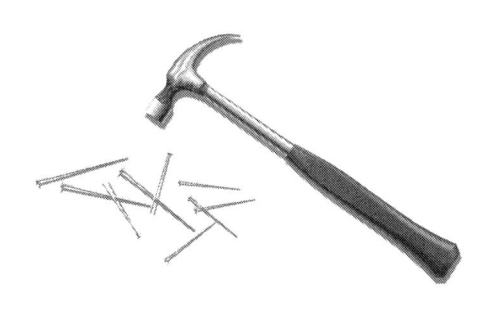

### ZEKE

I COLLAPSE ONTO THE LUMPY sofa with an exaggerated groan. The workload has been brutal this week. Cleaning up after a bulldozer and wrecking ball is no fucking joke. I wince as a roaring ache rolls through every part of me. Even my damn teeth are sore. I couldn't lift another chunk of concrete if my paycheck depended on it. Luckily Devon called it quits before I had to make that choice.

The clock on the stained wall reads a quarter to five. Might as well be midnight for how drained I'm feeling. I glance around the rundown cabin while pleading with my muscles to quit twitching. The couple that owns Roosters was kind enough to book a bunch of these so-called luxury rentals at The Mossy Den resort for the construction crew. Other than being walking distance to the jobsite and one of the town's nicest lakes, Grove Gulley, I've found no other perks. Guess all that matters is having a spot to sleep at night. Lord knows I've seen far worse conditions.

I slouch deeper into the worn cushions to rest my head. Just as I'm dozing off, someone kicks the couch. I peel an eyelid open to give my intruder a death glare.

"Coming out with us?" Lewis asks. He finishes buttoning his shirt before looking at me.

"What the hell do you think?" I manage to mutter. "I was barely able to stand in the shower."

He shrugs. "Good thing you washed the stank away. You reeked worse than this place. Now it'd do you some good to get out of this musty pit for a night."

"The answer's no, man."

"Fucking fun sponge."

"Damn straight. Now run along," I say with a wave. "There's plenty of beers that need drinking and lonely women wanting company. Good luck with all that."

Lewis makes a frustrated sound. "What the fuck are you gonna do? Sit around and mope? I know you're too tired to beat on the punching bag."

"Fuck off," I jab, but there's no heat behind it. I have no strength to argue. And he's right.

The good thing about busting ass on this restoration is not feeling the need to wreck myself in the gym. I can barely stay awake past nine o'clock as it is. I clear my throat and say, "I was about to take a nap and you're ruining it. Why do you always gotta be so loud?"

He chuckles. "Quit bitchin'. Not like you gotta stay here. Don't you have buddies around to crash with? Why do you wanna be stuck in this shithole with us?"

An angry wave of guilt crashes over me. Delilah isn't the only one who's received a cold shoulder all these years. My best friends, guys I grew up with, haven't heard from me either. I'm not even sure they're still around. I reach for my neck and rub, trying to alleviate the strangling pressure that shame has on me.

"That would defeat the purpose," I choke.

His brow bounces up. "Of what?"

"Staying under the damn radar."

"You realize we'll be stationed in Garden Grove for close to six months, right?"

I stare at the peeling paint on the ceiling. "So I've been told."

"Well, that's a long damn time to keep hiding."

"Thanks for the unsolicited advice."

There's an awkward beat of silence before Lewis says, "Bet she'd forgive you."

His words have me jerking upright in a split second. "What was that?"

If he's aiming for a reaction, I'm giving him one. I can feel the heat rising in my blood, begging for a fight. Talking about Delilah is a sure way to piss me off. I shut down his questioning when we saw her at Dagos. Not sure why Lewis insists on pressing the issue.

I'm tossing down the gauntlet with a frosty glare. A challenge is thrashing between us, and I almost throw out a taunt to get him talking. But I wait for his comeback, daring him to take the bait.

I shouldn't blow up like this. The dank air stings my nostrils when I inhale slowly in an attempt to calm down. It's just that the fire inside of me is reflexive and unavoidable.

The temperature seems to skyrocket while our standoff drags on. Who's going to crack first? I guaran-fucking-tee it won't be me. When Lewis takes a step back and cracks a grin, a sliver of relief passes through me. That's his version of a surrender, and I accept it as always. It's not his fault I'm a fucking hothead. With hands buried deep in his pockets, Lewis's posture is loose and relaxed. I'm strung tighter than a hunter's bow.

"I sure know how to piss you off, huh?" he murmurs.

Before I can respond, Brody and Kayne emerge from their room. They look between us with wide eyes. The lingering tension must be visible because their lazy pace speeds up. Kayne moves closer and claps Lewis on the shoulder.

"Ready to go?" he asks, giving me a sideways glance.

"Yup," Lewis replies. "Just wrapping up my chat with Zeke."

Kayne looks at me with purpose this time. "You coming?"

I shake my head, choosing to stay quiet. I'm a grumpy asshole, but they put up with me.

He jerks his chin. "Have a good one."

Lewis hangs back, and I glance up at him. "We all right? Sorry for bringing up shit I shouldn't. I can't seem to help it," he says with a shrug.

I press along my throbbing temple. "Yeah, we're solid. Have fun tonight."

He nods. "Will do. Later."

I offer a half-assed wave, and then he's gone. When the door closes behind him, all remaining energy pours out of me. I'm wiped and more than ready to pass out. I sprawl out on the couch with every intention of putting this day to rest. The only problem is my brain won't shut off. I can't stop thinking of Delilah. With my eyes closed, she's all I see.

Blonde hair, green eyes, curves in all the right places.

Fuck, I'm getting hard just picturing her thighs opening for me again. Arousal replaces exhaustion when I reach under the waistband of my sweats. I give a few trial tugs, testing out the possibility. My bicep screams in agony but I ignore it. The relief of a release will be worth a bit more pain.

I fist my cock and start jerking. The heat that's flooding me now is pleasurable, and my motions speed up in response. This shouldn't take long at all. In my mind, Delilah takes control and strokes me with her silky palm. She bites her lip and grins coyly, like there's a secret between us. No one can know she's doing this for me. I grip harder and feel the raging pulse in my dick. The pressure builds in my groin, signaling a fast approaching climax. Blinding desire rips into me when I imagine Delilah tightening her grasp, those talented fingers forming a snug vice. But suddenly her smile morphs into a frown. She pierces me with anguish, with tears clumping her lashes. My euphoria and burning need evaporates instantly. There's no fucking way I'm getting off when she's crying, no matter how imaginary this is. Ice freezes my veins, and I yank my hand away with a frustrated grunt.

*What the hell was that?*

I lay panting in a half-dazed state while deciding my next move. Even my fantasies are fucked since returning to Garden Grove. A knot builds and squeezes inside my gut. I watch my chest rise and fall, knowing what needs to happen. I'm just too damn petrified of the result. She deserves answers at the very least. The need to speak with Delilah, at least once, has been growing inside my gut like a poisonous weed. To make matters worse, Addison's words have been haunting me since our little chat at Dagos.

The years away from this town haven't been kind. I've been kicked and beat down more times than I can remember. My own relatives turned their back on me. The cramp in my stomach intensifies while I recall their words. It's hard to keep a positive attitude when everyone thinks I'm a piece of trash. Just like my father. I'm no longer under his thumb, but the toxic shadow still clings. How could I not fall victim to their attacks?

I grab my wallet off the table and take out the faded picture. This is the worst form of torture. I brush my finger over the image, tracing Delilah's youthful features. Her lanky arm hangs around me as we smile for the camera. Braces decorate her crooked teeth, and I can almost hear the high pitch of her complaints. These were good fucking times. And I ruined them.

Delilah was the only one who could piece me back together. But that wasn't her job. I relied on her too much, which became abundantly clear when she was no longer around. Without her building me up, the doubt slithered in. My confidence crumbled faster than a cardboard box in the rain. I have zero worth. Why would she want a piece of shit like me? My own father couldn't love me. He could barely stand the sight of me after my mom died.

Feeling sorry for myself isn't going to solve shit, of course. If anything, this pity party makes the dread heavier. Maybe I should actually do something productive this time. The physical labor is supposed to dull me, calm the turmoil constantly thrumming beneath the surface. But it turns out today wasn't enough.

Before I can stop myself, a decision strikes like a match. There's no stopping the idea after it sparks and takes shape. I don't have control over much, but this is well within my reach. I can be strong and face this head-on. The moments of hiding in the shadows are over.

There's still time before Jitters closes. I can make it down there for a quick visit. She'll probably kick me out on sight, but that's a chance I'm willing to take. In the next beat, I find a clean shirt and my truck keys. All I can think about is getting to her. Just once, then I'll leave her alone. Permanently.

The drive to Jitters doesn't take long. The Mossy Den is on the opposite end of Main Street, but that isn't very far in this town. Pretty sure I could cruise up and down the entire drag in less than ten minutes. Regardless, I could find the way with my eyes closed. An invisible tether pulls taut and drags me toward her.

In what feels like the snap of my fingers, I'm standing in front of her cafe. The uncertainty piles on while my feet remain frozen to the sidewalk. This is a mistake. A prickle of awareness shoots across my scalp. She's just beyond the painted door. Am I selfish enough to drag her back down with me? Is the fallout worth a couple moments in her presence? The best choice would be to turn around and forget this stupid plan.

But I'm weak. I always have been when it comes to her.

With a determined breath, I yank open the door. A soft bell chimes, announcing my disruption. It might as well be a foghorn considering how everyone in the place is staring. But I don't pay any attention to them. My focus is locked solely on one beautiful blonde.

Delilah looks like she sees a ghost. Guess I kind of am one. She gapes and blinks slowly, no words escaping her pouty lips. In my peripheral, I notice another girl standing close to her. They wear matching expressions of shock, which has curiosity digging into me. This other blonde is slightly familiar, and I realize she's the one often around Delilah.

Her head swivels back and forth as she looks between us. Eventually she settles on me, pointing at my face.

"Are you *Zeke*?" she asks far too loudly.

The emphasis on my name makes it sound like Delilah has mentioned me a time or two. My chest puffs up a bit at that, but only slightly. I don't answer her, choosing to study my girl instead. At the chick's question, Delilah snaps out of it. Her mouth opens and closes without a sound. She swallows audibly but still doesn't speak. I suppose it's now or never.

While striding to the register, my gaze never wavers from her bottomless sea of green. I lean forward until I'm close enough to whisper. *"Hey, Trip."*

# SIX

## HAUNT

## DELILAH

ZEKE STROLLS IN LIKE HE owns the place. He doesn't—I do. But in this moment, I'm not aware of that fact. Regardless, my ears whoosh uselessly, blocking out my surroundings. All I hear is my heartbeat, which pounds to the steady rhythm of his footfalls as they carry him toward me. One measured step at a time. *Shit.*

My first instinct is to hug him. Then punch him. But I do neither. I stand frozen like a statue, unsure of what the hell is happening. Zeke is here? In front of me? We aren't alone, but might as well be. I'm pretty sure Raven says something, but who knows what. I'm developing an extreme case of tunnel vision with Zeke as the target. The very real threat of tears sting my eyes, and I blink the unwanted emotion away.

The last five years vanish. I'm seventeen again. Jesus, the past is materializing in front of me in a very attractive package. It would be criminal if I didn't check him out, in a very lazy fashion.

Zeke has always been tall, but he seems larger and even broader as he stomps into my shop like a giant force. He's selling masculinity like a Times Square billboard. The defined muscles in his shoulders and arms strain the grey shirt he's wearing. His dark hair is longer than I remember but swept away from his chiseled face. The defined jaw I'm all too familiar with is covered in thick stubble. When my perusal reaches his startling blue eyes, it's game fucking over. I wobble on shaky legs and reach for balance on the counter.

After the initial slam of shock wears off, I have to force my feet to remain in place. Once again, the deeply ingrained need to wrap my arms around him flares to life. My body is naturally drawn to Zeke, and I've never hated it before this moment. He no longer deserves that unconditional response. With that thought barreling forward, I strengthen my resolve to remain cool and detached. Damn him for making me this way.

When he's close enough to touch, Zeke stops and leans in. "Hey, Trip."

My belly swoops at the nickname I haven't heard since he left. The reminder of his absence immediately replaces the flutters with stones.

"Hello, Zeke," I say between clenched teeth.

I don't need to look at Raven to know she's putting the pieces together. Her gasp says it all. She fumbles with some plates before murmuring, "Holy shit, D."

"You can say that again," I mutter in return.

Zeke remains silent in front of us, but his cool blue stare swirls with meaning. I take a deep breath to gather my wits but instantly regret doing so. His familiar scent goes straight to my head. Irish Spring soap floats above the always-present rich coffee aroma, somehow overpowering the bold flavor. Apparently not everything has changed. All I want to do is drink him in. But I won't.

"I think the oven just dinged," Raven murmurs from the side of her mouth. That's her telltale excuse. She slinks behind me as if we can't see her go.

I turn my focus back on the liar in front of me.

"What are you doing here?" The lash of my voice echoes between us. I almost cringe, but decide he deserves my hostility.

He shrugs his impossibly wide shoulders. "Got a job in town. Figured it was time for me to swing by."

His nonchalant approach has my blood boiling. "Are you fucking serious right now?"

Zeke squints at me like I'm a puzzle he needs to solve. "You look good, Trip. Even better than in my imagination."

"Are you stoned? You realize we haven't spoken in over five years," I grind out through clenched teeth.

"I'm aware, Delilah. No need to point out the obvious."

I narrow my eyes into pissed-off slits. "You left and never came back," I growl low but fierce.

He tilts his head and appraises me coolly. "Didn't you hear what I just said?"

The gears in my brain are misfiring while I try to come up with a solid retort. He's totally screwing with me. "I can't handle . . . whatever this is. You're acting like a totally different person."

"Is that a compliment?"

"What?" I sputter. I comb through my hair, yanking at the roots. I must be dreaming.

"I'm trying to make amends, you know? Let bygones be bygones and all that."

Zeke's change of direction causes my head to spin, but I don't let it show. "This is where you're choosing to do this?" I hiss quietly.

"Do what?"

"Don't play dumb. What the fuck are you here for?" Betrayal burns across my skin.

"Coffee," he says simply, and I want to scream at him.

"You don't even like coffee," I say.

"I'm allowed to change my mind. The flavor has grown on me."

It feels like steam is spouting from my ears. "I have a very fucking personal experience with you and those revolving tastes. Here one day, gone the next. Sound familiar?"

For a second, Zeke almost looks sheepish while his gaze drops to the floor. "There's nothing to be mad about, D. You shouldn't give a shit about me anymore, not after what I did."

I pop out my hip, taking a disinterested stance. "Where did you get the idea I care?"

"You're joking? Someone unaffected doesn't act this way," he says with a gesture toward me.

"You think this is angry?" I spit and jab a finger to my chest. "This is my place of business, Zeke. I can't react how I want, and have the right to do so too. All I want is to throttle you, but that wouldn't go over well with my customers." I sweep an arm out to the occupied tables. Marlene is going to catch wind of this altercation in five seconds.

"Let's go out back." He hitches a thumb over his shoulder. Why is he acting so unaffected? Does seeing me again mean nothing? I imagine my fingers wrapping around his throat and squeezing. What a fucking ass.

I try to keep my voice even when telling him, "You don't deserve a conversation. In fact, you don't deserve shit."

My words hit the mark. Zeke visibly deflates, and the light in his eyes flickers off. He morphs before my eyes, exposing the wounded version I'm sadly familiar with. Shit, fuck, dammit. The expletives take turns tumbling all about in my brain. His pain was always mine, and right now it hurts like a bitch.

"Sorry," I mumble. "That was below the line. You're just really . . ." I search for the right word.

Zeke crosses his arms and fills in the gap. "Worthless?"

I crinkle my forehead. "Um, no. Not at all. I'd never describe you that way. Infuriating is the word I'd choose. I mean, you just waltzed in without warning." I study his features closely. His eyes are haunted, and I swear there're ghosts swirling in those blue depths. I know about the scars marking his skin, but it seems like the damage has penetrated deeper. "Are you okay? I mean, in general?"

"You're asking me?" His laugh is hollow. "You were right before. I definitely don't deserve your concern." Zeke's despondent tone causes worry to shiver up my spine.

Out of the corner of my eye, I notice the final few customers are leaving. I'm thankful there won't be further witness to our fight. My full attention locks on Zeke once they're out the door.

"Why are you being like this?" I ask softly.

His voice is even more flat when he says, "Not sure what you mean. This is me."

"You're acting so detached and strange. This isn't like you."

"Well, you don't know me anymore."

That response brings fury and betrayal roaring to the surface again. "And whose fault is that, Zeke?" I grab a nearby mug with the intention of throwing it at his head. He's giving me worse mood swings than Aunt Flo.

"We both know the answer. Let's not play guessing games."

"You're ridiculous. I don't understand you at all," I say.

"A lot happens in five years. You're not the only one who's changed." He gestures around the store.

"What is that supposed to mean? Are you upset about my career choice?"

"Nah, that isn't it."

"What then? Let's stop dancing around. You came here for a reason," I point out.

A flush races up his neck, painting the stubbled skin an angry red. "All of this is proof you never needed me. Not like I fucking depend on you."

I jerk my head back. "Oh my God. Are you acting this way on purpose? *You're* the one who never came back," I accuse.

"Didn't have many options. But that doesn't stop me from wishing things turned out differently. Guess I was expecting something else from you."

It feels like daggers are stabbing into my broken heart. I rub at the ache in my chest. "Wow, you're being callous. What did you expect? Should I be wallowing in misery and crying myself to sleep?"

Zeke rakes through his hair. I catch the tension in his shaking arm, which almost has me reaching for him. Then he ruins it. "I'm glad you've moved on. This makes me realize I made the right choice by staying away. It's good to see you didn't care one way or another."

The anger crackles in my belly, building off his animosity. "That's bullshit. You don't know what I'm feeling or thinking. You fucked off and forgot about me."

"You think that's what happened? You have no idea."

"Care to enlighten me? Please do because otherwise that seems to be the case. And you're not telling me anything. For all I know, you've been busy—"

"Stop talking," he interrupts.

"Excuse me?" There's no way he's bossing me around in my shop.

"You heard me, Trip. You've got no right to assume shit."

I gawk at him. "I have no right? What's gotten into you? I didn't start this. You came in here for who knows what reason. Probably to rub your disappearing act in my face." My bitchy defense is taking over. I have him to thank for that, and he's only making it worse.

Zeke sneers at me and I hardly recognize him at all. "Ah, yeah. Give me that hate. Let me hear all about it. Judge me for taking off and breaking my promises." His brow lowers, giving him a menacing appearance.

"I'm not—"

"You most certainly are. Thinking I didn't wanna come back here. That I left you for greener fucking pasture. You're clueless."

"And you're a liar and a thief."

"I haven't stolen shit," he fires in return. His massive body is practically vibrating, making him even more intimidating, but I'm not afraid of him.

I glare and take a shaky breath. "You're right. I took it all back when you left me."

His chin tilts down as he stares at me. "Fuck, Trip. You think I wanted to stay gone? Nah. Every dark night and lonely day I thought of you. I'm caged by the past. You're soaring into the future. Be thankful I didn't come back."

"Yet you're standing in front of me now."

"Didn't seem like a choice." His rough timbre reaches a forgotten spot inside me. Zeke awakens that barren place with a gentle nudge, and there's so much behind the simple gesture. I watch his lips move, forming words that don't register. All I hear are teasing kisses to my neck. A delicate trail of velvet skin heading toward my—

I jolt in place, blinking the vision away. He's still talking and doesn't seem to notice my little lapse in sanity.

"I'm proud of you, D. I'd never be anything but supportive," Zeke says quietly.

This distance between us stings. I want to close the gap, wrap around him like an ivy vine, and never let go. Damn, I'm pathetic. I rest a sweaty palm to my forehead and consider the options. Arguing with Zeke is going nowhere.

"What are we doing? This isn't us," I choke over the lump in my throat.

Zeke offers a sad smile. "There hasn't been an us in a long while." He lowers his tumultuous blue gaze, and I feel the loss immediately. But the lack of connection makes it easier to survive this war.

"So, what? You came looking for a fight? Does that make you feel better about leaving? Maybe if you can shove some of the blame onto my shitty attitude, the wreckage won't be all yours?"

"Causing more damage was not my intention, believe it or not. Seeing you, at least one more time, wasn't an option. This was something I had to do. For closure or some semblance of peace. Maybe to torture myself a bit more than usual," he mutters bitterly. After a defeated sigh, Zeke rambles on and cuts me deeper. "I'm a broken piece of shit, D. You don't need me dragging you down. I would've ruined you like I've destroyed myself."

This feels like goodbye all over again, and I fucking hate him for it. Regardless, all traces of rage melt away while a heavy dose of grief pours in. The weight of his desolate stare is too much, so I look away. I want to let my legs give out and collapse on the tile floor. I want to sob at the strangers we've become. This isn't how it should be between us. I run a trembling finger under my stinging eyes.

My tongue feels swollen when I say, "But you were mine. My everything. You only brought me happiness. I loved you so much."

My words have little impact. It's clear he's done with this conversation.

"That seems like forever ago," he responds quietly.

The silver chain around my neck burns. Why I chose to wear this particular one today is beyond me. But I hadn't thought twice before putting it on earlier. Maybe there was a reason. Mysterious ways and all that. I fidget with the ring tucked safely under my shirt, hidden from sight. I can only imagine Zeke's reaction if he noticed my choice of jewelry.

When he coughs, I raise my eyes to meet his. Those intimately familiar lips are pulled into a frown, and his light eyes have lost any trace of sparkle. "I'm so fucking sorry, Trip."

My breath wheezes out on a shuddering exhale. "I'm not that girl anymore."

"Please don't . . ."

I shoot him a look, daring him to continue. "What?"

He shakes his head. "You're right. I don't deserve to ask anything of you."

I sniff loudly. "It isn't that. I just don't need the reminder, all right?"

He agrees with a nod and a somewhat comforting silence blankets around us. I should probably kick him out and go take shots of something strong at Dagos. That would be the smart decision. But he smells good, and I've missed him too fucking much. I give myself permission to enjoy however little time is left until he leaves.

Zeke places a palm flat on the glass top between us. I have to fight every urge within me to keep from touching him. To distract myself, I study the map of scars crisscrossing over his tan skin. Most of the lines are faded and old, but some are new and still healing.

"What are those from?" I ask and point to the fresh wounds.

He looks down and shrugs. "Work mostly. Construction is rough on the hands."

That reminds me. "So, Roosters?"

He nods. "Yup, I'll be around town for a bit."

I tilt my head to the side. "Huh. Marlene must have been talking about you after all."

Zeke's shoulders visibly flex. "She's never good news. Have you started believing her nonsense?"

A giggle bursts through my pursed lips. "Lord, no. That crazy biddy mentioned someone I know was working on the bar's rebuild. She didn't say anything too specific, but I thought of you." I immediately want to smack myself for admitting that.

He rocks back on his heels as if my response startles him.

"Really?"

"Don't read into it. There are only so many possibilities she'd know about. You were a relatively safe bet."

"Gotcha," he says.

Zeke looks around and I get the feeling he might be itching to leave. The thought makes my pulse gallop, but I keep a straight face. I'm mentally preparing for his departure when he surprises me.

"Listen, this isn't how I expected our conversation to—"

It's my turn to cut him off. "Because plans always work out so well?"

He scratches the back of his neck. "Something like that. I'll be in Garden Grove until the building is done, so you might see me around. Just a heads-up."

And just like that, I slam the door on forgiving and forgetting. "Thanks for the warning."

"Maybe I can stop by for coffee sometime?"

I motion around the empty space. "It's a free country. We don't make it a habit of turning away customers."

His brow wrinkles. "Okay? I'm not sure my point was clear. I was expecting a different reaction."

"Well, I stopped waiting for you years ago. If I see you, I see you."

"All right," he says and knocks on the counter. "On that note, I better get going. Take care, Delilah."

I almost cringe at his use of my real name, but that's stupid. I give him a small wave in return. After a final glance, with my green eyes burning into his blues, Zeke walks away.

While I'm watching him leave, Raven slides up next to me. I nearly jump ten feet in the air. "Jesus, Rave. You scared the crap out of me," I say with a palm to my racing heart.

She shrugs. "You were too busy drooling over Zeke's ass."

Apparently I'm not hiding my reaction very well. She's

speaking the truth.

"I've been Zeed," I mutter. "All over again."

Raven's face lights up with a huge smile. "That's adorable. You're making him a verb. I'm going to put that on a shirt. Then you can wear it whenever he's around."

"Whatever. This is not a good thing," I mumble.

"We'll see about that. Seriously, I thought he'd never leave, though," she complains. "We closed almost thirty minutes ago. I can only keep busy cleaning the kitchen for so long, D."

I laugh. "You could have gone upstairs."

"And miss the juicy details? As if. So, how did you two leave it?" Raven claps her hands excitedly.

"Eh, sorry to disappoint. Not very well. I might see him around," I say on a long sigh.

She scratches her cheek. "What's that mean?"

"It means Zeke is in town for an extended period time."

"And you're going to hang out with him?"

I shake my head. "I don't think that's a good idea."

Raven pouts. "Or it could be the most brilliant one ever."

"There's too much between us. It's better to leave our story closed."

"What if he doesn't agree? Not everyone enjoys a cliffhanger ending."

I look in the direction Zeke disappeared and sag against the wall. "Yeah, the unknown is what terrifies me most."

# SEVEN

## REGRETS

### ZEKE

PEOPLE ON THE SIDEWALK TURN to gawk as my truck rumbles along Main Street. Maybe their stare is due to the blaring noise from the broken muffler. But I'm betting they're looking at the man driving. I deserve the disdain reflecting back at me, yet accepting the blame doesn't make it any better. I swallow the bitter acid coating my mouth and push harder on the accelerator.

I'm stuck in a town where everyone used to know my name. After fleeing the way I did, the glares and gossip are expected. I've been feeling like a sitting duck, waiting for people to discover me. The decision to stop sulking and face reality hit me hard this morning. After my less than friendly chat with Delilah last night, I'm feeling the pressure to right the wrongs.

Five years ago, I made the worst fucking choice. Returning to Garden Grove has made that abundantly clear. Not that I needed the reminder. The constant bile bubbling up my throat is plenty to keep me humbly aware of my mistakes. But I'm done being foolish. There's no moving on from Delilah Sage, not that I'd even bother trying. It's pointless. What's between us will never go away.

I don't deserve her forgiveness. She definitely doesn't owe me a chance at winning her back. That isn't going to stop me. After walking into Jitters yesterday, my path was set in stone. Being near her again gave me a glimmer of hope in an otherwise bottomless pit of doom. Those fiery green eyes threatened to sear the flesh from my bones. I found so much pleasure in the burn. I've been so cold and isolated without her. I hope Delilah is ready because I'm coming for her.

But not today.

There's someone else I need to see first. I pull into the full parking lot and wedge my truck into a cramped space in the far corner. I lower the brim of my hat while checking out the swarm of activity surrounding Green Thumb. Seems like business is better than ever for the plant and garden nursery. As I walk toward the bustling entrance, my focus is set on finding Ryan. Other than Delilah, he was my closest friend so this visit is long overdue.

Considering his parents own the joint, I figured this would be a logical place to start my search. After wandering around the building for a bit, I find Ryan stacking bags of mulch in the greenhouse. Excuses stumble through my mind as I shuffle over the gravel ground. I'm not sure how he'll react but expecting the worst is my default setting.

"Hey, Ryan," I call across the space between us.

When he throws a glance in my direction, his long stride comes to an abrupt halt. "Holy shit," he drags the curse out. Ryan tosses the bags he's carrying and turns toward me, eyes blown wide while he scans me up and down. "Zeke fucking Kruegan in the flesh. Alive and well. Wasn't sure I'd see the day. Figured you fucked off and forgot all about us."

I hang my head while shame rains down on me. "Yeah, I deserve the heat. Bring it on."

He makes a noise in his throat. "Nah, that isn't my style." Ryan shocks the hell out of me by rushing forward and slinging an arm around my shoulders for a quick chest-bump. With a pound to my back, he murmurs, "Good to see you, Krue."

The old nickname makes me smile slightly. That's what the guys called me in school, but I haven't heard it since. With his warm welcome, the weight of this situation doesn't feel so heavy. He's reminding me of brighter days, and I'm thankful. I definitely wasn't anticipating an open-arms greeting, and my chest cinches tight.

I swallow the emotion down. "Fuck, I needed to hear that."

Ryan pulls away, and a frown replaces his grin. "What's wrong?"

"It's been a tough adjustment being back," I admit.

He nods. "I get that. Looks like you're hauling a lot of troubling weight around. More than before." I'm not surprised by his observation. Ryan has always been the perceptive type.

"Eh, I'm surviving. But I have bad days like anyone else," I share honestly.

He scratches his temple. "So, where have you been?"

The knot in my stomach doubles in size. It's never easy talking about this shit. "A lot of places. Never outta state, though. I bounced around between family members for a bit. My aunt took me in. She helped me connect with my mom's brother, who I'd never met. He was all right but couldn't seem to look at me without thinking of his dead sister." I cringe at the truth, but shrug it off. "I stayed with a cousin after that. Once she kicked me out, I moved from one sketchy spot to the next. Nothing permanent, and I couldn't find a decent job to save any money. Not gonna lie, I struggled for a few years, there."

Ryan blows out a heavy breath. "But you figured something out?"

I work my jaw back and forth. "Devon found me when I was at a real low point. He owns a construction company and was looking for reliable help. I needed a job and jumped at the chance. He changed the game for me. I wasn't sure what to expect, but he's a great boss and the crew is pretty cool. He keeps me busy. There's less downtime to let my mind wander.

"And here you are," he fills in.

"Yup, which was a fucking reality check. Never thought we'd land a gig in Garden Grove. Guess I couldn't escape forever."

Hurt flares in his narrowed eyes. "Was that the plan? You weren't gonna come back for her?"

I flinch at his accusing tone. "It's not like that. You think I meant to leave her behind? Nah, I wanted to go off and build a life for us. Be a man she could be proud of. But my ambitions and confidence were far too high. I made Delilah a promise but couldn't keep it. Turns out I had no right to offer her a future. I'm a loser, and ashamed more than anything. Why would I be rushing back here to show off my failures?"

He raises a brow and juts his chin forward. "Maybe because your girl was waiting for you?" Ryan says it like a question but the meaning is clear.

My neck gets hot under his pressing stare. Suddenly I'm feeling forced into the corner, with rage thrashing in my chest. Regret crashes over me when the burn boils my blood. Coming here was a mistake. All of my muscles strain while I search for the nearest exit.

"Don't even," he chides. My glare clashes with his.

"We grew up together, dude. I can still read you like a picture book. Stick this out and fight for what you want."

I want to lash out, spew the pain and venom gathering on my tongue. Ryan is getting to me, digging into the recesses of shit I keep hidden. But he knows me, and everything that's buried inside. This is different than Lewis picking at me. My old friend isn't shoving harder to be a jerk. He only wants to shake me awake. Too bad I'm not ready to crawl out of hibernation.

A boulder drops in my gut and I kick at the gravel. I walked into this fucking pit of darkness on my own. Seems there's light just beyond the horizon. If only I could reach out . . .

Ryan prods further. "What's storming off going to accomplish? You can't disappear whenever the road gets rough."

"Not sure what you mean. I'm fine," I grumble and avoid his stare.

"Didn't take you for a pansy. Don't let Delilah know you've gone soft." My head snaps up at his mention of her. Ryan notices my interest and adds, "Ah, she's still a person of interest."

"Fuck that. Are you trying to get punched out at work?" My fists tremble from the unyielding tension propelling through me.

His palm muffles a bark of disbelieving laughter. "You're not a douche, so don't act like one."

"And I thought this would be a pleasant conversation," I reply with sarcasm coating my tone.

"That's why expectations get dropped at the door. So, have you seen her yet? I'd sure as shit hope you'd go there before coming to visit me."

I grunt at his assumption. "I don't remember you being such a dick," I mumble. "But for your information, I went to Jitters last night."

Ryan's grin returns. "And?"

"I talked to Delilah."

"Stop being evasive, Krue. What happened?" Ryan widens his stance, like he's bracing for something.

I squint into the distance. "I'm fucked. She's rightfully pissed and shut down, wants nothing to do with me."

"Sure," he says, "but she still loves you."

"Fucking doubt it." My nostrils flare with a forced exhale while I work up some courage. "Do you, uh, know if D's dating anyone?"

Ryan chuckles and rocks forward. "Digging for dirt? Bet

Marlene would be more than willing to share."

"Dude, I didn't come here for a lecture—"

"I'm fucking with you," he interrupts. "She's not seeing anyone, at least not seriously. She runs around with Addy, Trey, and that new chick. I think her name is Raven. She works with Delilah at Jitters."

My processing grinds to a halt and I gawk at this revelation. "Did you say Trey? As in Sollens?"

"Yup. Hilarious, right?"

Everything inside of my body locks up. "That asshole has always been a real tool to Delilah. What the fuck is she doing hanging out with him?"

Ryan doesn't seem to catch my distress. "Well, it's hard to avoid your best friend's boyfriend."

"Addison is dating him?" I sputter.

He tosses his head back and belts out another laugh. "You nuts? Hell no. That Raven girl is all his. Trey locked that shit down."

"Huh," I say. "I wonder what Delilah thinks of that."

"Maybe you should ask her."

"Thanks for the advice, smart ass."

"I'll be here all day," he replies with a smirk.

"Yeah, not sure she would appreciate seeing me again."

Ryan waves my concern away. "No way. You two are the real deal." I lift a questioning brow and he continues. "That woman loves you. Everyone can see it. You can fix the cracks. Aren't you a carpenter now?"

"I need more than a coat of paint and spackle to repair this disaster."

"Won't know if you don't try."

He's got me there. "We'll see," I mutter and take in his easy expression. "Speaking of great loves, have you talked to Emery?" Ryan always had a thing for Delilah's younger sister. Not sure he still does.

The red flush racing up his neck gives him away. He rubs at the blushing skin and says, "Nah. She graduated and took off for college. I haven't seen her in a few years."

I frown at that. "She doesn't come back for holidays?"

Ryan's posture deflates like he's losing steam. "Probably, but I lost my connection to her family when you fucked off."

"Shit, I'm sorry." Another cold blast of guilt slams into me. I adjust my hat, wiping my brow in the process. Ryan mimics my movements, messing with the Green Thumb cap he's wearing. We allow silence to envelope us for a few beats.

Ryan clears his throat. "Don't apologize for that. I'm the one who never pulled the trigger. She never knew how I felt. Not sure it would have mattered either way."

"Fucking chicks, man. Can't survive without 'em, right?"

He gives a frustrated groan. "At least Delilah was yours."

I have to bite my tongue from correcting him, but he's right. She *was* mine, as in past tense. I crack my knuckles to release some agitation. The nasty habit is better than biting my friend's head off. After an inhale, I'm able to respond. "But I lost her."

"You know her, man. She'll come around. Delilah has been wrapped around your pinkie since she was twelve. Pull out all the stops and win her back," Ryan insists.

"She deserves far better than me," I argue.

"Says who? Why don't you let her be the judge of that? Don't close the case before going to trial, Krue."

"You sound like a damn episode of Law and Order."

"Hey, whatever gets you believing."

His kindness and genuine encouragement are a healing balm to my battered esteem. Yet it doesn't close the gaping chasm between what Delilah needs and what I can offer. I'll never be good enough.

Ryan seems to sense my hesitation. "I'm not saying you gotta get down on one knee tomorrow. But you're in town for a bit so take advantage of the situation."

I hesitate. Then, I ask, "Got any suggestions?"

He jerks away. "Uh, sure. We can talk through some stuff."

"Thanks, man. I don't deserve—"

Ryan interrupts, "Knock it off. We're friends. That hasn't changed."

"Sorry I've been an asshole."

"I understand. It's not easy to admit defeat," he says.

He's returning a piece I've been missing. Maybe things can actually work out. I glance around the busy greenhouse. "When's your shift done?"

He checks his phone. "I can leave after three. Perfect for happy hour."

"Wanna meet at Chasers?"

"That dive?" He laughs. "Too chicken for Dagos or Boomers?"

I sigh loudly, letting my frustration show. "You up for a drink or not?"

Ryan fist pumps. "Hell yeah. I'll see you there. Delilah won't be able to resist the epic plan we create."

"Right, right," I mumble. "Thanks again." After a quick salute, I walk away.

"Hey, Krue," he calls out before I get too far.

I turn around. "Yeah?"

"Thanks for stopping by."

"I appreciate you not punching me in the face," I return.

Ryan shakes his head, hiding a grin. "I'm damn glad you're back. This town sucks without you."

I smile, and the expression is real. "Me too," I say quietly.

And for the first time since arriving in Garden Grove, I actually mean it.

# EIGHT

## FARCE

## DELILAH

TIME HAS NEVER TICKED BY so slowly. Three measly days have dragged on since Zeke stomped into Jitters out of thin air. Last week he was nothing but a fading memory. Now he's rammed into the forefront of my brain, and there's no reprieve. He shocked the hell out of me with his overbearing presence and grouchy attitude. He's got some nerve barking demands and making crude accusations.

A humorless laugh huffs out of me.

That's a bold lie—he was fairly pleasant. But it makes me feel better to pretend Zeke was horrible when our exchange replays in my mind. Considering I've been stewing nonstop over his unwanted intrusion, there's been a lot of nonsense revisions. Imagining him as a massive ogre, ripping shit up left and right, isn't hurting anyone. It's the solid defense I need against crumbling and running straight to Roosters.

Why did Zeke come back? My life was fine. Now he's ruining it all over again. I wish he'd stay away, at least from me.

I immediately retract that thought. My stomach cramps painfully at the idea of him gone again. Having him nearby in whatever capacity is better than not at all. It seems no matter how mad or betrayed I feel, that man will always be in my heart. He's here, so close, that the possibility of reconciliation has been planted and is sprouting to life. I smack my forehead for that one.

*What is wrong with me?*

"Uh, D? You okay?" Raven asks.

I snap out of my stupor and paste on a huge smile for her benefit. "Yeah. Why?"

She points to my plate. "You're turning that salad into pulp."

I glance down and realize she's right. My dinner is now a pulverized lump of spinach. *Shit.* I worry my bottom lip and think of an excuse. This Zeke business is clogging all avenues.

Raven pokes my arm. "What's wrong?"

I blow stray hairs off my face. "I think we both know."

She gives me a sad smile, sympathy shining in her blue eyes. "Boy trouble," she mutters.

"Ugh, but why? I'm so freaking pissed. He doesn't have the right to do this," I say.

She pushes my cocktail closer. "You're right. He's an ass. Men suck," Raven says with a shake of her fist. I hear Trey grunt beside her, but he doesn't comment further. I grin at that, thinking of how far that dingbat has come. Maybe not all hope is lost . . .

"Not always," I murmur. "But in this moment, I agree one-hundred percent. Zeke warped my effing heart strings. I can feel him all around me. Everywhere I look he's there, buried under my skin. I can't wash him off, even after years of trying. Who's going to fix the mess in here?" I gesture between my head and chest. "It's a total disaster. I don't understand why he chose to come back after all this time."

"Isn't he working on a construction crew?"

I shoot her a scathing look." I didn't mean literally. Yes, he's supposedly rebuilding Roosters. Apparently there were no jobs for him in any other cities."

Raven raises a brow. "Uh, okay? I feel like he sticks with the group. Isn't that how it works?"

I wave off her logic. "Whatever. He could have sat this round out."

"You're being silly. That doesn't even make sense."

I smack my palm on the table. "Lordy, are you hearing this stupid crap? Why is this happening? I'm already going crazy and he's only been around a few weeks."

She scoots her stool closer to mine. "What's bugging you the most? How he acted on Friday?"

I nod. "What I saw was a totally new version of Zeke. I didn't know how to handle him like that. He was trying to repel and dissuade me, and I still felt compelled to move closer. It makes me insanely curious and extremely sad at the same time. What the hell happened to him, you know?" I whisper softly.

My need to know was a living thing, growing and festering inside me. Against my better judgement, I needed to find that answer by any means necessary. Zeke's face was pained, hinting at a struggle. I was desperate to catch a glimpse of his trademark grin, but the expression never appeared. My chest grows tight when I recall his flat reactions. It was as if the light had been snuffed from him.

I clear the lump from my throat. "I'm furious at him, Rave. But my heart breaks too. It's really difficult to watch someone suffer, especially when I loved him."

Her features pinch tight. "Do you need to get away?" She leans closer and whispers, "I know of a great beach town that's awesome for clearing your head."

I wrinkle my nose. "Yeah, you biatch. I'm well aware of your solo vacay spot. Thanks a lot for the recommendation."

She winks. "Let me know if you need directions."

I stir my drink and consider taking a timeout from this Zeke fiasco. "That's an appealing idea, Rave. My body is begging for a cleanse from all this stress. But I can't run off during our busiest season. Garden Daze is a few weeks away. Maybe in the fall when things slow down."

Raven rubs her temples. "Oh, man. That's a good point. And how is this event different than Garden Graze?"

"Oh, my sweet rookie. You'll get the hang of all our silly summer shenanigans. The Graze is all food based. The Daze is so much more. There's a parade, scavenger hunt, and town-wide deals. All of the shops and businesses get involved. I'm talking sales and specials galore. Be prepared to buy all the treasures. Bring lots of cash," I suggest.

She blows out a lungful of air. "Well, I've gotta plan new cupcakes and start master-baking my ass off."

I laugh. "The Dirty Mechanic and Filthy Princess go over real well. Not sure you need to add more into the mix."

Trey leans over to join the conversation. "Did someone say Dirty Mechanic? You making some, Princess?"

She rolls her eyes. "Maybe. But I like presenting different recipes for these events. Let's not talk about that right now." Raven nudges him away and shifts into my personal space. "So, what should we do about the ex-factor?"

"We?" I ask and tilt my head.

"Oh, yeah. I'm so in on this mission. Do you think he'll drop by again? We can make a secret code name. Oh, like Zeed! I'll call it out and you'll go hide in the kitchen."

I squint at her. "Won't that be kind of obvious? And I'm not sure there's enough time to make a getaway after he walks in the door."

Raven taps her chin. "Maybe, but that's not really the point. Imagine his reaction when you tuck and roll toward the back. That will be hilarious."

I giggle because she's right, it would be a funny sight to see. "Eh, I appreciate the effort. But I'm not hiding from him. If Zeke decides to come in, I'll face him. Until then, I'm trying to ignore the fact he's in Garden Grove. It's proving to be very difficult. Having him around such close quarters makes the potential of bumping into him that much higher. I'm boarding on the edge of paranoid with the possibility of him stopping by unannounced," I say.

"Why don't you go to him? His schedule is probably fairly consistent. That would give you the control of this situation."

I shake my head wildly. "Not happening. The love-sick teenager who'd follow him all around town is gone. Zeke abandoned me, Rave. I can't take reckless chances where he's concerned. Since he's here for several months, I'd maybe consider the very slight chance of us being friends. But he's got to seek me out. There's no way I'm going after him. He owes me that much," I say with conviction. "And it's clear Zeke knows where to find me."

Raven relaxes deeper into her chair while assessing me. "Ah, I see what's happening. You want him around but can't admit it. I did the same thing with this one." She hitches her thumb at Trey.

I scoff loudly and slash the air. "Absolutely not."

"Want me to kick his ass for you?" Trey interrupts with impeccable timing.

I raise a skeptical brow. "Defending my honor? How surprising."

"You're my concern by association," he says with a motion between Raven and me.

Raven frowns at him. "Didn't anyone teach you that eavesdropping is rude?"

Trey presses a loud smooch to her cheek, and she melts into him like warm butter. "Gotta take care of you, Princess," I hear him murmur.

*So effing romantic.*

My skin gets itchy with the desire to flee. I need to steer this conversation far away from my feelings for Zeke. In a split-second decision, I ask, "How's that sex swing working out?"

Trey gives Raven an accusing glance. "You told D about that?"

My friend shrugs and avoids his heated stare. "She asked."

"I most certainly did not," I reply quickly.

This is exactly the distraction I need. These two are highly entertaining when they discuss certain topics. They're still arguing about erotic furniture when Addison sweeps over in a graceful flurry.

"Hey, D. How's your . . ." Her words die off when she gets a look at my minced meal. "Um, was the salad bad?"

"Nope. I was using it as a punching bag of sorts," I explain.

Addy sets her empty tray on our high-top table and fixes her ponytail. "Picturing someone's face in the lettuce?"

I send her a look, explaining everything without a word. She knows all about Zeke's return to Garden Grove. Addy served him here, at Dagos, last week. Apparently they exchanged a few words that weren't super friendly. I'm not the only lucky one to get his frosty attitude.

She pops out her hip. "Want me to bring you a Ball Crusher?"

The mention of our favorite male-hating shot makes me grin.

"Make it a double, okay?"

"You've got it girl," she responds.

Trey jerks his chin at Addy. "Talk to Shane lately?"

She glares into the distance. "No."

Trey's co-worker has the serious hots for my friend but is a total chicken shit. Addy has made her feelings extremely obvious so Shane is either blind or even more introverted than we think. Either way, her patience for him is running pretty damn thin.

"He hasn't texted you?" Trey sounds surprised.

"I didn't stutter, jerkface. He hasn't returned my messages," she spits.

He winces at her snappy tone. "Don't kill the messenger, Addy. Jeez."

"Sorry," she grumbles. "I'm sensitive."

"You on the rag or something?" Trey presses.

I choke on a snort, and Raven coughs into her fist. Addy hardly blinks, frustration flushing her face.

"It's a touchy subject, idiot. Get an effing clue," she says through clenched teeth.

Raven smacks Trey in the chest. "Yeah, shut up, Dirty. That's something you never ask a girl." She keeps shushing him while mouthing an apology to Addison, who brushes the concern away.

I rub Addy's hunched shoulder. "Prime example of why we need all the booze. It's one of those days. We're due for a night of female bonding. Let's go out and forget our troubles. Pretty sure Boomers rooftop is calling our name." I cup a hand around my ear and pretend to listen.

Her green eyes brighten. "Oooooh, yay. That gives me something to look forward to. Forget Shane and his mixed signals. Let's go out and have fun. My shift is done at nine so I can meet you there."

I glance over at Trey and Raven just as they start making out. "Pretty sure these two are heading home any minute. I'll hang here and wait for you. I can drown some sorrows over a few Ball Crushers."

Addy's strawberry-red hair shines in the overhead lights when she bounces in place. "Yes! And I'll sneak a few on the sly. Greyson won't care since it's pretty slow. My tables are all closing out."

"Good thing you've got a nice boss," I say with a raised brow.

She smiles. "If you can match my salary, I'll be sporting a pink apron from Jitters like that." Addy snaps for emphasis.

I cross my arms in mock offense. "Yeah, I can't afford you."

"High quality labor is expensive." She points to herself.

I lean back and laugh. Addy is already doing a great job taking my mind off Zeke. My spirits are lifting like the hem of Raven's shirt. Yeah, they need to get a room. I roll my eyes and return Addy's cheeky grin.

"Well, run along then," I say and wiggle my fingers in her direction. "Better put all those mad skills to use. Show me how good you whip up a drink."

"Biatch, you better be ready for a stiff one."

My mind plunges to the gutter. "I wouldn't have it any other way."

# NINE

## CHANCES

### ZEKE

ANOTHER SATURDAY HAS ARRIVED, MUCH to my dismay. The crack of dawn signals forty-eight hours of no work, and an abundance of free time I don't need. What are weekends good for when I'm always alone? The seconds tick by, mocking the seclusion I'm trapped in. Of course there's no one to blame for that but me and my warped mindset.

In the dark and loneliness of night, I can pretend. The whispering deceit is easy to believe. My life is the one I want. I'm proud of the man in the mirror. My future is full of possibility. And the biggest lie of all? Delilah is still mine. But it's broad daylight and the truth is undeniable, visible like a bottomless crater shoved between us. My hands are rougher. My heart is harder. My soul is jaded beyond belief. But nothing can stop those dreams of softer moments and happier times. Maybe they're not lost forever.

I stare at the dark ceiling, listening to my roommates stumble around in the kitchen. They're going fishing, but I have other plans. By some miracle I've managed to give Delilah space, but waiting a week to see her again has been torture. I only possess so much control, and her pull is strong. I had to force myself to stay away in the first place. That all ends today.

Thirty minutes later, I'm on the road with Jitters as my destination. My truck lurches to a stop along the curb after I slam the brakes too hard. The nerves are rattling my limbs and making me clumsy as fuck. Dammit, I need to pull my shit together. I run a shaky palm over my balmy forehead while taking a deep breath. What's the worst that's going to happen? Delilah didn't kick me out last time. I was expecting a larger explosion from her, but she kept shit locked down. I was boiling inside while she remained relatively unfazed. Why wasn't she more rattled? I shove those useless thoughts away. Her reaction then doesn't matter now.

Somehow the stakes seem higher today, like there's more on the line. I'm allowing hope and possibility to get involved, which is a risky game to play. This time I'm not going to forfeit. Ryan stoked my confidence to the point where I'm prepared to approach Delilah and asking for a chance. I'm expecting her to shoot me down at first, but who knows—maybe she gives eventually. I've got our memories and secrets on my side. I know her favorite places to visit. The dessert that makes her moan. There's a hidden spot behind Delilah's ear that turns her into a puddle. I have a collection of inside jokes at the ready. I'm prepared to be relentless.

The little bell above the door jingles when I step inside. My stomach rumbles when I catch a whiff of something sweet baking. Mixed with the punchy aroma of flavored coffee, this place is a jolt of energy. There aren't other customers scattered about this early in the morning, and that works in my favor.

Delilah smirks at me from behind the counter, as if this is a planned visit. Her blonde hair swishes to the side when she bends to rest an elbow on the glass. I suck in sharply and avert my eyes from her cleavage that's boldly on display. Maybe she's been expecting me. I've been biding my time, going crazy with want, and she's been anticipating how long it would take for me to break.

Delilah's emerald gaze sparkles. "Well, hello there. Back so soon?"

"Hard to stay away," I tell her honestly.

She glances at the clock. "Guess you've got a lot of making up to do for the last five years."

The dig goes straight to my gut, a knife piercing deep. I try to keep a straight face but grimace regardless. "Gotta start somewhere," I mutter.

Over Delilah's shoulder, I see that other blonde chick wildly waving her arms. She's making bird-like squawking noises that sound like . . . *zeed?*

I jerk my chin toward her, but address Delilah. "What's her deal?"

"Oh, Raven?" She glances at her and laughs. "She's, um, exercising." Delilah mouths something at her, but I can't hear it.

In response, Raven says, "Tuck and roll! It's not too late."

I scrub a hand over my mouth, trying not to laugh. "Uhh, is now a bad time?"

Delilah's eyes are alight with humor when she faces me again. The happiness shines brightly around her, and I soak in the sensation. I feel an easy smile lift my lips. When she realizes I'm gawking, her expression loses some mirth.

"What's up, Zeke?"

There's no point in stalling. "Can we talk?"

"Sorry, buddy. No can do. I'm busy working."

I peer around the empty cafe. "But there's no one else here."

"That doesn't matter. I have to do inventory and mentally prepare for the weekend rush. There's no time to scamper off with you," she says.

"I'm asking for a few minutes, not an eternity."

Delilah scoffs. "Trust me, I know. Your absence has made that perfectly clear."

I grip the counter until my knuckles are white. "All right, fine. I'll stick around until you sit and eat."

"Already did," she quips.

I exhale slowly, trying to cool the fire in my veins. "Fine, a coffee break."

She takes a long sip from her steaming mug. "That's loitering. Paying customers only."

There's a frigid breeze blowing off her, trying to freeze me out. Her icy attitude pairs well with the heat buzzing under my skin. I'm not backing down.

I nod at the display case. "What do you recommend?"

Delilah crosses her arms, appearing uninterested in my order. "Raven is a master baker. Everything is amazing."

I laugh at that. "Oh, really?"

She scowls. "Do you want something or not?" Her patience with me isn't improving.

"Choose for me."

Delilah taps her chin while searching the selection. She grabs a plate and scoops up a slice of cake. When she sets the decadent piece in front of me, it's my turn to frown. Coconut shavings litter the entire surface. There's only a few things I refuse to eat and that is one of them. Delilah is definitely aware of this.

Taking the safe route, I ask, "Don't you remember?"

She shrugs. "You wanted my opinion. The German chocolate is our best seller."

I rub my neck, hating that she's playing these games. I quickly glance at the shelves and point to a cupcake with yellow frosting, no coconut in sight. "What's this one?"

"Ah," Delilah says with a raised brow. "Interesting choice."

"Why's that?"

She doesn't answer, but snags one and drops it on a plate.

She tosses it on the counter unceremoniously, the crash echoing around us. I flinch from the noise, but recover easily enough.

Delilah looks over her shoulder before pointing at my breakfast. "This right here is a Broken Heart." Then with a closed fist, she smashes the delicate cupcake into a heap of ruin. "Look familiar? Suppose not since you weren't around for that part," she adds, digging the blade deeper into my stomach. My chest cracks in half and I'm bleeding out on her tiled floor. But that won't slow me down.

"I deserve that."

"Sure do." She throws me a spoon, narrowly missing my forehead.

"Shit, Trip. Watch it."

Furious flames spark to life, making her green eyes glow. Fuck, I'm in trouble.

"That's not my name. I'm not a stupid teenager anymore," she growls softly.

"Let me know you again."

"No."

I don't deserve an answer, but that doesn't hold me back. "Why not?"

"Because you left me, asshole," she spits through grinding teeth.

I clear my throat, desperate to get out of this sinking hole. It's obvious we're not moving forward this way. "Can I at least have another spoon?"

Her eyebrows pinch. "Why?"

"So you can share this with me. Let's clean up our broken mess together," I say with far too much hope in my voice.

Delilah blinks slowly while my words digest. The tension in her stance loosens with an audible sigh. A small fracture is splitting her frozen exterior, and I need to keep the thawing going. The paper in my pocket feels like hot lava, but uncertainty plagues me.

Before I make a move, she murmurs, "Maybe you should go."

"Do you really mean that?"

She gnaws on her bottom lip. "I don't know," comes out as a barely-there whisper.

Her hesitation—no matter how slight—gives me the green light I've been waiting for. I reach for the small square and place it on the smooth glass between us. Delilah glances at the paper and gasps, her head shaking back and forth. When she looks at me, all traces of frost and ice are long gone. All I see is the beautiful girl who's always been mine.

"Say it," I urge.

She swipes at her lashes. "Damn you, Zeke. That's not playing fair."

"Just humor me."

Delilah sniffs, and the small noise hits me straight in the solar plexus. The whisper of her refusal might as well be a deafening roar. I want a chance to explain, more promised moments in her warmth. More than ever I'm determined to win her forgiveness. Delilah might not give in easy, but there's plenty of time to try. The pain clouding her eyes in my fault and I want to wipe all doubt away.

I try again. "Come on, Trip. Knock, knock?"

Her nostrils flare with the surrender. "Who's there?"

Leaning toward her, I whisper, "Me."

Delilah edges closer like we're connected on a pulley. "Me who?"

"The man who never stopped loving you," I finish.

She sucks in sharply, but doesn't move away. "What do you want from me?"

"Everything."

Her breath puffs out, and I feel the exhale on my lips. "I'm not—"

"Hey, D?" The interruption comes from behind her. Talk

about bad timing.

Delilah jerk upright and combs through her long hair. She stares at me with wide eyes, as if just realizing the position we were in. She presses quaking fingers against her mouth.

"Did you hear me?" her friend asks while coming into view around the corner. Raven stops short when she sees me. "Oh, shit, you're still here." Her gaze darts between us. "I didn't mean to interrupt."

Delilah "What? No, you're not. We're just talking. That's all. Nothing more," she stammers.

Raven lifts a brow. "Uh, okay. Carry on."

"Wait!" Delilah shouts, and Raven freezes in place. "Did you need something?"

Her friend waves her off. "It's not important. Inventory stuff."

"Oh, right. I need to get going on that." She looks at me. "I have to do inventory."

I smile. "Yeah, that was your first excuse to get rid of me earlier."

She scratches her ear. "Um, yeah. As you can see, I actually have a job to do."

Raven snorts. "D, you can continue catching up with Zeke. I can handle things for a bit."

Delilah shoots her a glare. "I wouldn't want to add more work for you."

"Really? Because we're so busy at the moment. Plus, this would be worth it," she responds, her eyes sparkling with interest.

I watch Delilah silently communicate with Raven through hand gestures and nods. The oddball blonde gives me a thumbs-up before retreating into the hall.

"She seems like a good friend," I say once she's out of sight.

"Ugh, I guess. When she's not throwing me under the bus," Delilah mutters.

"I appreciate her support."

"Yeah, yeah. Okay, moving on. I've got stuff to do. This has been . . . nice," she says.

"You're not getting rid of me quite yet."

Delilah huffs. "No? What's it gonna take? I'm nearing the end of my rope, Zeke."

I laugh at her pinched expression. "I need a chance to explain. I'm not giving up, Trip."

"Me either," she replies. After several tense beats, she adds, "But maybe we can see each other later. After close. Will you be around?"

I don't pause. "Of course. Where?"

"Just be in front of Jitters at six."

Delilah is giving me the greatest gift. The grin lifting my lips is a tiny bit cocky, but I can't seem to help it. "I'll take whatever you're willing to give."

She holds up a palm. "I'm only agreeing to a conversation."

I wink. "We'll see about that."

# TEN

## EXPLAIN

## DELILAH

I SLAM THE REGISTER SHUT with a resounding bang, signaling quitting time. That also means Zeke will be meeting me soon. I chew on a nail while considering running upstairs to change.

"Whatcha doing?" Raven asks.

I startle and slap a palm to my racing heart. "Shit, you need some damn tap shoes. You've been scaring me a lot lately."

She smirks. "That's because you're always zoning out thinking about Zeke."

I don't bother denying it. "Do you have plans tonight?"

"Trey is picking me up. We're going to the movies. Wanna come? It could be a double date." Raven wiggles her hips.

I try to keep my expression neutral, not wanting to show how happy the idea makes me. But it's silly to be giddy over that. Zeke and I are . . . nothing. A lot needs to happen before I consider going on an actual date with him. It also occurs to me that Trey and Zeke did not get along in high school. That was mostly for my benefit, I realize, but still.

"I'm gonna pass for now," I say gently. "But you're sweet to offer, Rave. Maybe we can set something up eventually. I'll see what he has to say first."

She pouts. "You've never had a boyfriend. I really want it to work out with Zeke."

I refrain from rolling my eyes. If she only knew the truth. "Fingers crossed."

"And toes," she adds.

"Let's not be too optimistic."

"Don't be a downer. Let me enjoy the possibility."

"I'm beginning to think you care more than me," I laugh.

Raven scoffs. "As if. I caught you practically climbing over the counter earlier. And he was no better. You two will be bumping uglies by next weekend."

I toss my head back with a cackle. "Gosh, you're hilarious. I really needed that."

She bows. "Happy to oblige." Raven's phone dings, and she glances at the screen, smiling wide. "Trey is outside. Do you need anything before I go?"

"Nah, I'm packing up. Have fun."

"You to-oo," she sing-songs and skips toward the door.

When I reach for my purse, Zeke's bold writing snags my attention. I grab the paper while a swarm of butterflies attack my stomach. When he slid that joke in front of me, my false bravado folded like a house of cards. Countless memories slammed into me and I struggled to remain standing. That glimmer of the past made him impossible to resist. But Zeke has some explaining to do.

After shutting off all the lights and triple-checking the locks, there're no more excuses to stall. I walk slowly to the door and step outside, my legs wiggling like jelly. A slight breeze helps cool off the July heat, making the temperature rather pleasant. People are milling all about, enjoying Saturday evening on Main Street.

But all of those inconsequential details fade into the background. Zeke is leaning on a bench directly in front of the store so he's all I see. But it's far more than his location.

*Holy crap cakes, he's sinfully delicious.*

Men shouldn't be allowed to wear white tees and faded jeans when girls are mad at them. Whoever spilled the beans and told them this outfit is our kryptonite should be ashamed. How do I stand a chance? I'm still pissed as hell at him, but it's hard to remember why when he looks this good. I hold my head high and swallow the pool of saliva threatening to drool out. I can totally appear unaffected.

But then he talks.

"Damn, Trip. How is it possible you're more gorgeous than this morning?" Zeke murmurs, straightening off his perch. He's different today, more like the old Zeke. Even though he seems lighter, there's a lot of mystery in those brilliant blue eyes. His stride is effortless as he moves toward me. The spicy scent of his cologne makes my knees wobble.

Let it be noted I gave a valiant effort. I tried, ladies.

While licking my lips, I scold my racing heart. Two can play at this game. "Thanks, Bear. You're not looking so bad either."

Zeke stumbles over nothing. "Oh, no way. You haven't called me that since sophomore year."

"Doesn't mean I ever forgot."

"You still have the shirt?"

Of course I do, but admitting that seems weak in this moment. We begin a slow stroll along the sidewalk while I search for the best response. I go with a nonchalant, "Maybe."

He smirks, totally busting me. "Buried under all your silk panties."

I laugh at his bold assumption. "Try again. That faded piece of cotton has been demoted."

"I've missed this. Talking to you has always been fun and easy,"

Zeke tells me offhandedly.

"Couldn't have missed this too much. You've always known where to find me," I retort.

That shuts his playful side up real quick, and I'm a total bitch for making it happen. Zeke's smile wilts and takes the effortless flow of our conversation with it. I want to kick myself for shoving this awkward tension between us. But maybe that's for the best. I shouldn't feel so comfortable with him after everything that's occurred . . . or hasn't. But try as I might, there's no stopping it.

His defeated sigh might as well be a bass drum. "You're right. I fucked us all up."

I don't argue, just offer a limp shrug.

Zeke nods slowly. "I'm gonna make us right again, Trip."

"If you say so," I say, still feeling the fingers of guilt around my neck.

We're quiet for several feet before he asks, "Where are we going?"

"Dagos," I supply with finality. There's no choice in the matter. I need to be in a safe space for whatever Zeke is going to share with me.

"Ah, is that your place to be?"

"Sure is."

"I saw Addison working here." He opens the wooden door and gesturing for me to go in.

"She told me." Although I reamed her out for waiting until Zeke surprised me at Jitters.

"Makes sense. You two have always been close."

I make a noncommittal noise. "We all were."

Zeke slams to a stop, his hands fisted and trembling. "Fucking dammit, Delilah. I'm well aware how thoroughly I've fucked up. You don't need to drive the knife in any deeper than it already is."

Is that what I'm doing? Most likely, but my reaction is instinctual. I have a lot of pent-up frustration where this man is concerned.

When Zeke left and didn't come back, I went through all the phases of loss on repeat. I'm totally screwed up because of him.

There's no easy out of this fucking disaster. We might as well be treading water while moving further from shore. I rub my forehead and mutter, "I'll try to keep the stabs to a minimum. For what it's worth, I'm not intentionally trying to go above and beyond to be a super bitch."

He grunts, but the pressure radiating off him visibly loosens. "That sounds like a complicated way to say you're actually doing it on purpose."

I turn to face him and cross my arms. "What do you expect? I have every right to be upset, Zeke. You fucked me over in a seriously shitty way."

His gaze swings around the bar before he leads me to an empty booth in the back. I don't mind the privacy, but the sensation of being trapped skitters up my spine. I sit and scoot into the middle on one side while Zeke occupies the other. After taking several calming breaths, my pulse quiets slightly. He reaches a hand across the table but must change his mind halfway. Zeke's palm rests flat and empty, calling to me, but I'm not ready to answer.

"Hopefully I can make things better, Trip. Can we try moving forward rather than spin in circles? I'm not interested in making this even worse between us. I need to believe in the possibility of . . ." His solemn voice trails off.

"What?" I question after he remains silent. My pulse picks up again while I wait for his answer.

Zeke sucks on his bottom lip and stares deeply into my eyes. "Us."

I have to bite my tongue to stop from agreeing to whatever he's suggesting. How nice would it be to collapse into his arms and ride off into the sunset? I grip the wooden bench and stay frozen in place. It physically hurts to remain separated from him, but I have to protect myself. I've already fallen for him once, and that didn't end so well for me.

"That's asking for something I can't guarantee. Not at all," I say.

"Not yet, but maybe . . . eventually?" The strangled hope in his voice makes me wince.

I ignore Zeke's question, giving him one of my own. "Why didn't you come back for me?"

His expression shutters, exposing flickers of raw agony and the desperation swallows me. I can't watch him suffer, but Zeke quickly clears the pain off his features. "Shit, Trip. Going straight for the jugular, eh?" He rubs the center of his chest.

"I don't see any reason to waste more time," I reply.

"Good point," Zeke agrees.

Myla, my second favorite server at Dagos, chooses this moment to stop by and grab our order. She gives Zeke a curious glance but doesn't comment before striding away.

He roughly scrubs over his mouth. "I had big plans for us, D. I was going to pave the way and get everything set up. All I needed was an opportunity to prove myself. My aunt opened her home to me under certain conditions. So long as I was working and helping around the house, she'd let me stay. How hard would that be, right?" Zeke laughs, but there's zero humor laced in the defeated sound.

"As it turns out, most people aren't interested in handing out chances to a punk-ass kid. Even with my employment history, I could only get shitty shifts with minimum wage. I didn't stop trying and kept moving on, but the bosses were assholes. It seemed like there was a target on my back and they all had it out for me. Makes sense since I was a worthless nobody. Without trying, I burned bridges faster than I could build them."

He leans back and stares at the ceiling, blowing out a weighted breath before continuing. "I even tried making friends, thinking that could help. But I'm a joke, you know?" Zeke's laugh is despondent and hollow.

He yanks at his hair, which I'm realizing is a new habit. "Even a bunch of teenage shits couldn't put up with me. At the first opportunity, they framed me for some vandalizing shit. I don't even remember where it was. The squad car pulled into my aunt's driveway and two minutes later I was handcuffed in the backseat. She was fucking furious, mostly because I was an embarrassment and got the neighbors talking. My prints weren't found on anything and I wasn't in the security footage. They had zero proof against me, but that didn't matter. Such bullshit. If my aunt wasn't buddies with the sheriff, I would have been charged. Because of her, I got cleared pretty quick. But the damage was done and my lesson was learned. There wasn't hope for me overcoming my pitfalls. I was destined to be a loser. My aunt agreed and I wasn't welcome in her house after that," Zeke mutters.

He swallows roughly and toys with the cocktail napkin. "At that point, I was broke, jobless, and just kicked out of my aunt's place. She told me to crash at my uncle's place, a man I'd never met. I was so fucking upset about everything piling up and didn't think twice before storming out. I hopped on a bus out of town, but trouble followed me. It didn't take more than a month or two before getting booted from wherever I was working or living. There was a curse embedded under my skin, I fucking swear. No matter what happened, I wasn't good enough. Eventually I found a boxing gym and figured out how to take the pain away. I beat myself bloody most nights, just so I could sleep. It's all fucked up," Zeke grumbles.

Myla drops off our drinks without a word, which I appreciate more than she knows. Maybe the tension vibrating around us is visible to others. I quickly take a few sips of to ease the gritty dryness from my mouth. The vodka pour is strong and scorches a path directly to my veins. That should definitely help with taking the edge off. Zeke grabs his beer and takes a healthy gulp. I look at his hand and the array of scars crisscrossing there.

He looks familiar, like the Zeke I love. I mean, loved. Past tense, of course. Life has always been testing his limits, dumping more shit than sugar. His sweet soul cracked under the pressure. I want to hug him, but that seemed like a surefire way of tumbling down the rabbit hole.

"So, you were hurting yourself? On purpose?" My disbelief clangs loudly between us.

He nods. "More often than I want to admit. I was so fucking angry inside, all the damn time. My dwindling confidence wasn't helpful. Excessive exercise was an outlet. I'd push until there was nothing left to shove."

"But you're so gentle . . . and kind. I never thought you'd get that angry."

Zeke grunts. His blue eyes take on an icy sheen that force my stare away. "You're wrong."

I can't stop the shudder from wracking my limbs. "Guess all that time in the gym explains a lot. I mean, you're seriously huge."

His biceps and pecs seem to flex on command. "Working construction does a body good. Doesn't hurt that I beat myself up, in more ways than one."

"Why? How did things change so dramatically? You had plans for a happy future. Or so I thought." The last part comes out slightly warbled.

Zeke takes a swig of his bottle before answering. "You got the soft side of me. No one else did. Being away from you and Garden Grove snuffed that fluffy shit out. I was forced down over and again. How much can a person take without losing the good? The jagged, furious parts survived and conquered. Leaving wasn't the fantasy I built up in my mind," he admits with a weak shrug.

"But you escaped the abuse," I offer, trying to find light in all this.

"Yeah, but lost you in the process. Pretty sure I royally fucked up."

"I think you made the right choice. Above all, you got away from him."

Zeke's frosty glare sears into my soul. "Seriously?"

Frustration prickles my scalp. "What am I supposed to say? When you didn't come back, I lost all faith in love and commitment?"

"Is that true?" he mumbles.

The liquor warms my belly, spreading lava through me. "Does it matter?"

"Five years is a long time. Shit was bound to go sideways."

"That was your choice," I remind uselessly.

"But it was for a reason with decent intentions."

I lift a questioning brow. "Which are?"

"Then you could move on. Find someone better." With Zeke's words, the hole in my chest expands.

"I didn't want anyone else," I say softly and avoid his gaze.

"And now?"

I shrug, unwilling to let my secrets flow. "Undecided."

He pushes harder. "You got a man, Trip?"

A lie tingles at the tip of my tongue, and I bite down on the sensation. I've never been dishonest with him and not all things should change. I offer another shrug, giving him a wimpy non-answer.

Of course Zeke can't let it go. "No? Been waiting for me?"

The truth is a sharp blade cutting fatally deep. The hurt stings my eyes and outrage spills over from his audacity. "You'd like that, wouldn't you?"

Apparently boundaries don't exist in these moments as he

reaches for me. Zeke's thumb brushes down my cheek. "You're stunning, Trip. More beautiful than I deserve, or anyone else for that matter. Giving you up is my greatest regret. It pains me to know I might never have you again."

I bite my wobbling lip and blink quickly, silently cursing him. He hums while his touch settles on my chin, tugging up until our eyes connect.

"My strong girl," Zeke whispers.

"Who says you don't deserve me? Isn't that for me to decide?" I question.

He strokes up my jaw, and I lean into his touch. My skin crackles, begging for more, but Zeke pulls away. A whimper climbs up my throat and I choke on the sound. He looks away, as if this is suddenly too much. Bastard.

"You've always been blind when it comes to me," he starts and I scoff. "It's true. You have some misguided belief in me that shouldn't be there. I was saving you from a life of misery, Trip. I was so damn angry, all the fucking time. I didn't want to subject you to that. You're everything good and I'm the opposite. I have no fucking idea what you see in me."

I guzzle the remaining vodka in my glass, delaying my response. I've been aware of the scars littering his skin, but now there are shadows reflecting in his eyes. Zeke is wounded inside and out. His past refuses to let him go, keeping him chained to the horrible memories. He hasn't been able to move on with a better life.

Before he left, I could always drag him back to the surface. I like to believe my presence kept the pain from cutting too deep, but there's been no one to save him since. Zeke believes this is it for him, that he deserves nothing better. Who will prove otherwise?

He breaks the silence before I can say anything. "Fuck, what was I thinking?" he growls. "I'm such a fucking loser. You don't want anything to do with me. And I don't blame you." His voice is a hollow shell, echoing straight into me. Zeke truly believes he's unworthy and it breaks my heart all over again.

How can I possibly stay cool and distant? The answer is I don't. "None of that is true. Who's been poisoning your mind, Zeke?"

He shifts along the bench seat. "I've got that handled on my own."

"Am I still the antidote?" I mumble under my breath, afraid of the answer but needing to hear it.

There's a battle brewing inside of him. The two sides are waging a war I only catch glimpses of. I can't help but worry which one will come out victorious. The storm crashing in his blue depths rages on for another moment before calming. He clasps my hand, lacing our fingers together. I don't protest.

Zeke shifts closer until he's practically hovering over my side of the table. "You're the air I breathe, Trip. Survival isn't possible without you. Hell, I'm barely existing at this point. You're the only one who can bring me back to life."

I flutter my lashes and get lost in his voice. But I need to be honest with him. "I'm not ready to forgive you. There's still so much I don't know . . ."

Zeke jumps in as my sentence trails off. "I don't expect you to, at least not right away. But is there a chance for us? We can go slow. Maybe hang out as just . . . friends?" He stumbles over the final word and his lips form an adorable twist. I almost laugh but manage to trap the bubbling sound. I don't hide my grin, though.

"You think that's possible? I'm not sure we've ever been *just friends*. Even in middle school," I remind him.

"This is a fresh start. We'll see what happens?"

His question sparks a reminder in my brain. I chew on the inside of my cheek, gathering guts to bring up his status in Garden Grove. "What happens when you're done with Roosters? You move to the next city?"

Zeke nods. "Yeah, that's how it works. We're a traveling crew."

"Do you go far?"

"Trying to keep me close?"

"Putting words in my mouth," I say.

"You can admit it. My ego could use a boost." His lips lift, showing me hints of the Zeke I'm familiar with. Flutters attack my belly, making my smile grow wider.

"Ah, way to put me in a tough spot. How can I refuse without being an asshole?"

He shrugs. "You can't."

I sigh as a weight lifts off my chest. Our banter makes things better. I think long and hard before suggesting, "Maybe we can hang out now and then. I mean, while you're staying in town."

Zeke's face lifts at that. "Yeah?"

I laugh at his hopeful expression. "Just a time or two, Zeke. That's all I'm offering."

"But we're heading in the right direction."

"Didn't you say we'll take it slow?"

I realize we're still holding hands when he squeezes mine.

"Yeah. One step at a time."

I gulp when a huge chunk of defense crumbles to dust. Pretty sure I'm in the best type of trouble.

# ELEVEN

## FRIENDS

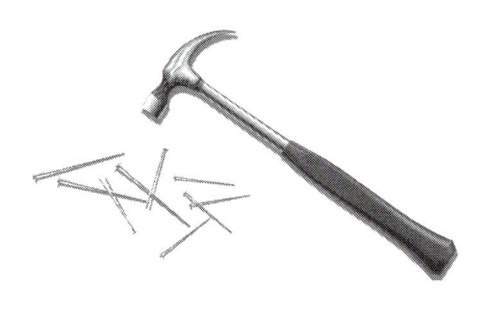

## ZEKE

I PULL OPEN THE DOOR to Boomers with uncertainty rattling in my chest. Delilah invited me to join her and some friends for dinner. Lord only knows what I'm walking into. Addison and Raven will most likely form a firing squad, shooting me with countless questions. I'm not at a point where this situation will be comfortable, but this wasn't an offer to refuse.

Delilah and I have been on shaky ground since our chat a few days ago. It's progress nonetheless. I feel unsteady in general since being around her again. She probably thinks I'm certifiable for bouncing between moods so quickly. Pretty sure I'm worse than a hormonal pregnant chick. Here's hoping the good parts rise above.

I glance around the crowded bar and catch Delilah waving from a high-top along the back wall. It's no surprise that Raven and Addison are with her, both wearing matching grins that speak of sneaky gossip. I almost laugh until my sight lands on Trey fucking Sollens. My muscles bunch in preparation for a fight, knowing he's not part of the welcome wagon. I cover the distance to the table with long strides, ready to get this over with.

Taking the empty seat next to Delilah is an easy choice. But that doesn't make a difference in who kicks off the conversion.

"Well, what the fuck do you know? Krue is around after all," Trey belts out from across the table.

I'm practically vibrating on the stool while trying to hold back. I curl my hands into fists to stop the shaking. "Not sure the folks in Canada heard. Could you announce it a bit louder?"

"Absolutely," he booms. "Everyone should get a heads-up."

"Don't start, Trey," Delilah scolds.

He snorts loudly. "I've got every right to give him shit. Or maybe I should thank him. I'm not the biggest asshole in Garden Grove anymore."

Raven elbows him. "Are you sure about that? Because the way you're acting makes me think otherwise."

When Trey looks at her, his expression softens. "You love me, Princess."

"That's debatable," she says with pinched lips.

"Need me to prove it?" he asks in a low tone that makes me feel like the rest of us are intruding.

"Not again," Delilah groans next to me.

I chuckle when she shields her eyes from them. "Are they always like this?"

"It's bordering on offensive. Pretty sure they've christened every establishment in this town."

"Wow, I'm almost impressed."

She wrinkles her nose. "Yeah. They're gross and way too happy."

I lean over to whisper in her ear, "Are you jealous?"

Before Delilah can respond, Addison pipes up. "How did I suddenly end up as the fifth wheel?" Trey sends her a questioning look, and Addison huffs. "No, I still haven't heard from him."

"Who?" I ask.

"I'll tell you later," Delilah says from the side of her mouth. "It's best not to bring him up."

I nod in false understanding, but drop the subject. I order a beer and onion rings when the server pops up. After she wanders off, I ask, "I could text Ryan. Maybe he could join us?"

Delilah's eyes sparkle with secrets. "I haven't seen much of him since Emmy went off to college."

"Uh, yeah. He mentioned something similar to me," I say while rubbing my temple.

"When did you see him? He hasn't come around Dagos as often lately," Addison muses.

I squint at the industrial ceiling. "The week before last. I should make a bigger effort to see him again. I'm not sure who he's spending time with."

Delilah taps her chin. "I bet he'd love to catch up with a certain bubbly blonde."

"Is she back for the summer?"

"Kind of. She comes and goes, hanging out with her new friends. Living the college life," she says with a wave.

Addison lifts her brow and gestures between all of us. "We should get the gang together for the reunion."

"Or something like that," I respond dryly.

I type out a quick message to Ryan, suggesting we hang out soon. During the slight lull in conversation, I study the bustling space around us. An enormous circular bar takes up the center, highlighting the purpose and drawing attention. There's an arcade area with pool tables and dart boards. The stage still runs along the right wall but the dance floor shines like new.

"This place has changed," I point out.

"Yeah," Delilah replies. "Boomers got a facelift a few years back. You should see their rooftop patio."

I whistle. "That's ritzy shit."

She laughs. "We have a lot of fun up there."

That's another reminder of what I've been missing. I mess with a stray coaster while lead fills my gut. "Bet it's great," I mutter.

She pokes my bicep. "Don't pout. You'll see it eventually."

"With you?"

"Maybe, if you play the right cards."

"I'll stack the deck."

Delilah shifts closer and whispers, "Cheaters never win." The flames in her green gaze sear into me. My roaring pulse might as well be blasting through the speakers because that's the only beat I hear.

I swallow audibly. "I'll only do right by you. I can promise that."

She crosses her arms. "We'll see."

I've got a lot to prove, but Delilah makes the effort more than worth it. I can fix my mistakes and be a better man for her. She's the only motivation I need. We hold one another captive as our eyes lock and hold. Her lids lower halfway, the hooded effect going straight to my dick. All the blood races south, forming a pool of lava and making my jeans uncomfortably tight. I want to yank Delilah into me so she can feel what's happening. Instead, I rock on my chair and awkwardly adjust positions.

Addison hoots and fans myself. "All right, guys. It's way too hot in here. Let's tone it down, yeah? There's children present."

I glance around, prepared to call her bluff. But she's right. I shouldn't be making these moves on Delilah, especially with an audience. Our trance is officially broken, and we settle back in our seats.

A long swig from my frosty mug cools the fire raging inside me. "We've discussed Emmy, but how're your parents?"

Delilah smiles after taking a drink from her glass. "They're so good. Both are still teaching at the elementary school. Not sure they'll ever retire." She shrugs. "I've told them to come work for me. My current baker is lazy and might need to be replaced."

Raven's face whips toward us so fast I'm surprised her head is still attached. "What!?" she cries in outrage.

Delilah giggles while pointing at her friend's shocked expression. "Sometimes I've gotta check if she can hear through the Trey fog."

Raven sticks her tongue out. "You're a shit."

"Love you, sista-friend," she says with an air kiss. She looks at me and adds, "All joking aside, my parents are great. They're happy to have me sticking around. Maybe Emmy will find a job nearby, but she's got plans to live in a big city. Guess we're not all Garden Grove lifers."

I wince for my buddy's sake. Looks like he's got an uphill battle on his hands. "Sometimes it takes breaking out and exploring to realize how great this town is. I've had my fair share of adventure, and let me tell you, nowhere else compares."

Delilah rests her cheek on a closed fist. "I suppose you'd know."

I hang my head. "Sure do."

Apparently, Addison is listening. "Where was your favorite spot?" she asks.

Through a scoff, I say, "None of the above. I've been a miserable shit since leaving and didn't enjoy much of anything. My aunt lives in a bad neighborhood outside of Millston. My uncle's house was uninviting as hell. Things got better when I started with Big Rock, but all the stops blend together after a while."

Addison's red hair swishes when she swivels on the stool. "Oh, yeah? Traveling construction sounds . . . entertaining. I bet it's somewhat fun to move around to new areas. Does the crew always live together?"

"Yup, the owners usually set up the accommodations for us. We've got several cabins at The Mossy Den."

Delilah gapes. "Really? I didn't know anyone was still paying to stay there overnight."

"Yeah, you guys should fix those up next. We rented one for prom but ended up sleeping outside. The cabin reeked of mildew," Addison shares on a shudder.

I exhale roughly. "That's nothing. I've had far worse than that place."

Addison nods. "Hopping around to different locations sounds nice, though. You never have to stick in one spot too long. And visiting all those cities? Good for the scrapbook," she giggles.

"Eh, it's overrated."

The two girls share a look. Delilah asks, "Then why are you doing it?"

I yank at the collar of my shirt, the temperature seeming to skyrocket. "What else am I going to do? It's good money, I've got a fair boss, and the hours keep me busy. Can't ask for more than that." Except staying here permanently, but it's far too soon to think like that.

Addison hums. "It doesn't seem like a forever-career. How long do most guys last?"

"Lewis has been with Devon the longest. He's lasted seven years so far."

"And you've been at it . . . ?" Her question trails off.

"Only a couple," I reply with a shrug.

She quirks a brow. "That's a decent amount of time. You might be ready for a change soon."

Delilah makes a strangled noise. "Addy, jeez. Pretty sure Zeke doesn't need you pressuring him to switch jobs."

I turn to her. "Trying to get rid of me already?" A sexy blush lights up her face and my chest expands with pride. At least I have the ability to fluster her.

She tucks hair behind her ear. "Uh, no. Well, I dunno. Just don't do anything crazy on my behalf."

"Relax, Trip. We just started talking again. I'm not ready to make any life-altering decisions based off a few conversations." Except if she was on board, I totally would.

Delilah nods and looks away. "Okay, that's good."

*Is it?* Doesn't feel that way, but I let the topic drop. I take a sip of beer, trying to relax, while checking out the room. Everyone is busy talking at their tables, enjoying a night out. There's no curious looks or questioning glances. It seems no one notices or really cares. My nerves aren't going haywire sitting in this crowded bar, surrounded by many I used to know. Maybe I can blend in without an issue. Wouldn't that be nice? I could regain some semblance of normal. It beats being alone all the damn time.

"I'm glad you showed up," Delilah says.

I shake off the reverie and get back in the moment. "Afraid I wouldn't?"

"I'm not sure what to expect. We obviously know each other, but there's new gaps. You're really different in many ways. I don't know how to act around you. Maybe that will level out eventually," she tells me.

"Uh." I stumble over my thoughts. "Am I making you uncomfortable?" I glance down at the respectable space between us and wish it didn't exist. *Should I leave?*

She vehemently shakes her head. "No, not at all. That's not it." Delilah studies me quietly, the seconds ticking by like a countdown to detonation. "It's more about getting used to being around you again."

"But this has been okay?" I clarify, and she nods.

Before I can push farther, Addison asks, "Wanna go to the bathroom, D?"

Delilah squints one eye while considering. "Yeah, sure."

Raven resurfaces from Trey-land. "I'll come."

He chuckles. "Travel in packs. Fucking pack animals."

She flicks him. "You'd feel really bad if I slipped and fell without anyone there to save me."

Trey gives her a look. "Because that's why you all go together."

Ravens hops off her seat and waves him off. "We'll never share our secrets."

They link arms and giggle while disappearing into the crowd. I finish off my beer and feel when Trey's attention turns to me. We exchange silent glares, neither backing down from whatever the hell this standoff is about. He jabs a thumb toward the parking lot, and I can only imagine what he's going to spew.

"Krue, your truck sounds like shit."

"How the hell do you know?"

"Is that a joke? I can hear that rusted pile of junk coming from a mile away."

I clack my teeth together. "Get some earplugs. We can't all afford to buy brand new," I say, referring to the shiny pickup he's been driving. That beast is hard to fucking miss in this town.

Trey glances down, maybe pondering that possibility. "Bring it by Jacked Up," he offers.

I lean back in my chair. "No, thanks. I'll pass."

Trey grunts. "Too good for my garage?"

"Last I recall, as in twenty minutes ago, we hate each other. Why the fuck would you help me?"

He lifts a shoulder. "Water under the bridge. We're solid."

I send him a look. "The hell we are."

"Don't be a dick, Krue. We'll be seeing plenty of each other if you're planning to date D again. I'm not going anywhere. Raven has promised me forever. What's your status?" he asks with a sneer.

He's getting under my skin, needling me with sharp barbs. But I'm not giving the reaction he's aiming for. "Still an asshole, huh?"

"Meh, not as bad since Raven came around. But this leopard didn't lose his spots." He smirks.

"Hope she catches those true colors of yours."

"Not sure why I'm wasting breath on you," he mutters while standing up.

I tense in preparation for his next move. "Good fucking question."

Trey surprises me by walking away from the table, effectively ending the conversation. Fine by me. I'm about to order another drink when Delilah weaves through the throng. The altercation with Trey vanishes as I get lost in a haze of blonde hair and seductive curves. She hovers in my space and smiles, but doesn't say anything. A sense of peace settles in my gut as I soak in her warmth. Something needs to give, or I'll maul her.

I jerk my chin in the direction Trey went. "That guy? Really?"

Delilah huffs. "Raven loves him. He's grown on me. A little." She shows a sliver of space between her thumb and finger.

"For real? What the hell?" I demand.

"He's not so bad once you get to know the real him."

I peer into her green gaze. "Did he brainwash you or something?"

She laughs and rolls her eyes. "I was a super bitch to him when they started messing around. It was wrong of me, and I realized that . . . eventually. Give him a chance."

"Do you have more of those to hand out?" I ask, forgetting about Trey altogether.

An adorable crease forms between her brows. "Huh?"

"Chances. I could use one."

"What do you call this?" she says and motions between us.

I pretend to think on that, but can hardly stop a smile from forming. "A decent start?"

Delilah bites her lip. "Well," she starts and shifts closer. "Wanna check out the rooftop?"

The sprouting hope grows a bit taller inside me. "I thought you'd never ask."

# TWELVE

## INTENTIONS

## ZEKE

I PARK MY ASS ON the row of concrete blocks and take another enormous bite of pizza. Devon was kind enough to order lunch, and I'm not letting any go to waste. I take a huge gulp of soda and sigh as the cold liquid relieves my throat. A dessert from Jitters is the only thing that would make this meal better.

"Holy shit, are you smiling?" Lewis shouts out of nowhere.

My expression falls away when he plops down beside me. "Not sure what you're talking about," I grumble with my mouth full.

"Ah, hell. Didn't mean to embarrass you. Don't stop on my account."

I roll my eyes. "You're a dick. Any reason you're interrupting me? You should focus on eating or get back to work."

Lewis grips my shoulder. "I miss you, man. You're not around the cabin as much. Is that blonde honey keeping you busy?"

I drop the half-eaten slice on my plate and fix him with a glare. "Don't fucking talk about her like that."

His eyes expand, showing far too much white. "Oh, shit. This is serious, huh?"

I turn away with a scowl, returning to my food. "Pretty sure there's a better use for your break than all this talking."

"Dude, this is friendly conversation. Does your girl have hot gal-pals?"

My stomach lurches, and the reaction is not from the greasy goodness. Could Delilah be mine again? The thought gives me pause, but then I remember what Lewis asked.

"If she does, I wouldn't set you up with them."

"What the hell? We're friends. You're supposed to be my wingman."

I snort. "Not likely. You just want a quick fuck. Do you honestly think I'd hook one of Delilah's friends into a situation like that? Pretty sure it wouldn't go over well."

Lewis lowers his chin, appraising me with cool eyes. "How is that different from what you're doing? We're in the same position, my man. When the job is done, we move on."

His words are a cruel smack to an already sensitive subject, and I try not to wince. Thinking about leaving is a dull blade slicing into my wounded flesh, but that's reality. After my discussion with Delilah at Boomers, it doesn't seem like she cares if I stay or go. But that could be an act.

I stay silent, feeding Lewis's assumptions. "That's what I thought," he says. "There's nothing wrong with keeping her bed warm while you're in town—"

"It will never be that way with her," I cut in. My low tone is full of warning, and he takes the hint.

He nods. "Of course not. My bad, Zeke."

Rather than responding, I stew in silent fury. I finish off my lunch, but all the joy is gone. All I taste is wasted time and opportunities. Fucking Lewis and his big mouth ruin everything.

Before I can storm off to my station, Devon ambles over. "Great work today, guys. Concrete is shit work but you make it look easy. Even in this heat, we're ahead of schedule."

"Thanks, boss," I say and shake off the suffocating pressure that's closing in.

"Yeah," Lewis agrees. "Appreciate that, Dev."

Devon turns his sole focus on me, his weathered skin wrinkling with a grin. "Other than arguing with Lewis, you seem to be in decent spirits."

I give him a bland stare, blinking slowly. "What do you mean?"

He claps my back a few times. "I'm aware of your reservations regarding Garden Grove, but this place has done wonders to you." Devon pauses for a moment before adding, "Or maybe a certain someone has."

Lewis chuckles loudly next to me. I shoot him a scathing glare, telling him to keep his loud trap shut.

"It's her, not the town," I finally admit after all. There's no use denying it, and I don't want to.

Devon rubs his stubbled chin. "The pretty blonde, right? I'd change my attitude for her, too." I grind my teeth, and he laughs, "Just joking, Zeke. She's young enough to be my daughter."

My phone dings, and I'm thankful for the interruption. I stand and pull the cell from my pocket, tapping the screen.

Trip: Hey, Zeke. Don't mean to bug you, but I've got a favor.

And just like that, my mood springs straight upward. A smile automatically lifts my lips as I quickly type a reply.

Zeke: Good timing. I'm on lunch break. What's up?

Trip: Ugh, I hate to even ask. A shelf at Jitters broke, and it's a serious eyesore. Is there any chance you could swing by after work?

Lewis hoots. "Ah, the happiness returns. Must be your girl," he says and wags his brows.

"Fuck off," I growl while calculating the hours until quitting time. Too damn many. I jab at the screen in frustration, but I'm hesitant to press send.

"What's she saying? Is there a problem?" Devon asks, seemingly aware of my irritation.

I shrug and keep my chin tucked. "Something busted at her shop. She's hoping I can fix it."

"Go ahead," he offers without pause.

My head whips toward him. "Now?" I ask. "I've got a whole afternoon shift left."

Devon scoffs. "What're we doing? Waiting for concrete to settle. The other guys can finish smoothing shit out. You can take off early today. Not like you ever ask for anything."

I nod eagerly, knowing better than to question his generosity. I drag a sweaty palm against my filthy jeans while trying to piece a plan together. After appraising the condition of my work clothes, I realize taking a shower would be wise. I don't want to waste precious moments, but showing up sweaty and dirty won't grant me any leeway.

"You'd think I just invited him on a private tour of the Playboy Mansion," Devon jests and elbows Lewis.

The barb doesn't bug me in the slightest because all I hear is Delilah needing me. She sought *me* out when something went wrong. I'm the one she wants help from. True pride inflates me for the first time in years.

I have to force my feet to slow down and walk off the property. After rounding the corner and out of sight, I begin to jog. If the guys caught me rushing off to Delilah, I'd never hear the fucking end of it. Not that I give a shit what they think or say, but hearing their constant jabs taunts my temper. I'm trying to change my ways, which includes keeping a lid on that shit.

I've never been more grateful to be staying at The Mossy Den. The short block is no match for my fast stride. After a fast rinse, I throw on clean clothes and grab my keys. With new found purpose surging through me, I hop in my truck and drive to Jitters.

When I walk through the door five minutes later, Delilah seems surprised to see me. She appraises me with wide green eyes from behind the counter. Her pouty lips are parted, and I imagine kissing her shock away. When she glances at my toolbox, a dimple instantly dents her cheek.

"Hey," she greets. "Didn't expect to see you until much later."

I freeze in front of her. In my haste to hustle over here, I never responded to her last text. I scratch at the burn across my nape and exhale heavily.

"Guess I forgot to mention Devon let me leave early," I tell her with a grimace.

Delilah giggles. "Zeke Kruegan, are you blushing?"

I shove my fumbling hands deep into my pockets. Being called out by anyone else would be asinine, but I like Delilah noticing how she affects me. I ignore my scorching skin and shoot her a wink. "Maybe?"

She sucks in sharply, a matching flush creeping up her neck. "You're trouble."

"Thank you," I mutter.

Delilah sags against the display case while her lazy gaze slowly traces me. I take this moment to enjoy the beauty before me. Her long hair is swept up into a braided knot that looks complicated yet effortless. A few wisps frame her tan face, and I picture my finger wrapping around the tendrils. Delilah isn't wearing much makeup. The familiar spattering of freckles on her nose are a map to better days. I press against a cramp in my chest that's making it hard to breathe. The twitch in my hardening dick isn't helping. She's so damn gorgeous . . .

Delilah suddenly straightens with a jolt. "Uh, about the shelf," she croaks.

I shake the lust from my brain. "Right, yeah." I glance around the shop and notice the crooked beam along the wall. "Did the brackets come loose?"

Her mouth twists. "I have no idea. All of a sudden it just . . . fell."

I nod. "Okay. Should be an easy fix. Wanna lend a hand?"

"Of course. I really appreciate this, Zeke. Thanks for dropping by, especially on your free afternoon." Delilah walks out from behind the counter and meets me under the lowered shelf.

I wave her off. "No problem at all. What else am I good for, right?"

"Fishing for compliments?"

I shrug. "Never hurts to try."

She grips my forearm and gives me a squeeze. My eyes nearly cross from the shock of pressure blasting into me. One gentle touch from her is apparently all it takes and I'm ready to go.

"You seem very . . . capable. I'm glad to have such a strong man on call," Delilah coos.

I cough into my fist, trying to get this stupid arousal under control. "Thanks."

She smirks. "My pleasure."

I focus on the task, running a palm over the splintered wood. "Looks like the screw split the board. Where did you get this?" I point to the shelf.

"Oh, it's reclaimed barn wood. I got some at a craft sale."

"Makes sense. Those materials can break down faster due to age. I have stronger bolts that won't cause more damage," I explain while searching through my tools.

Her forehead scrunches as she watches me. "Sounds like a plan. I'm not good with this stuff."

"Who usually handles repairs for you?"

"My dad is fairly handy. And Trey has done a few things in the kitchen for Raven."

"But now you have me." It's not a question, but I want

Delilah's confirmation.

"I do," she murmurs without hesitation. Her green gaze latches onto me, exchanging years of longing love with a single glance. I'm lost in this powerful grasp and my head dips lower. Delilah gasps, and I assume the trance is broken, but her face tilts up putting those delectable lips inches from my mouth. I feel her rapid exhales, the warm puffs giving me chills. I soak her in, shifting to close the gap when a loud crash explodes beside us.

Delilah jumps, and I flinch, the noise effectively popping our bubble.

"Shit," she whispers. "That scared the hell outta me."

The guilty object rolls into a neighboring table. Thankfully, the canister is made of some kind of metal so it didn't shatter. I reach down to pick it up and set it on an empty chair. I glare at the shiny cockblocker before facing Delilah again.

"Close call," I mutter.

"Yeah," she returns. That lovely blush is coloring her skin again.

*No more fucking funny business.* Otherwise I'll have blue-balls for a week.

I clear my throat. "Can you hold this end while I get the bolts secured?"

Delilah moves into position, hoisting the beam without much effort. It only takes a couple minutes for me to fasten the rivets and secure the shelf. I rattle the wood to make sure. It doesn't budge.

She whistles. "I'm impressed. Great job, carpenter."

I smile and wipe the specks of sawdust from my palms. "All in a day's work. I'm more than willing to be on retainer for any repairs."

"Aw, thanks. We've been open less than two years, and everything is fairly new, so there shouldn't be much. But it's good to plan ahead."

I turn toward her after packing up. "What happened to Nova Tova? I thought that boutique did pretty well. Hell, you alone kept her in business."

Delilah sticks her tongue out. "She had cute stuff, so sue me. Georgina, the owner, had a better offer. Pretty sure she moved to Tantiga Park. Bigger city, more clients.

"Who lives upstairs?"

"I do," she answers simply.

A stream of late nights with her, closing up Jitters, flash before my eyes. We'd stumble to the loft after I've fucked her over every surface down here. Shit, that's fucking hot. I yank on my shirt, the fever spreading like rapid fire.

"That's convenient," I manage to choke out.

Delilah gives me a funny look. "You all right?"

I grip my throat. "I've got a little something stuck. No big deal."

"You sure? How about some water?" she offers and starts walking away before I can answer.

"That sounds nice."

Delilah pours me a glass, and I step behind the display case to accept it. I'm tired of being separated by that damn counter. She doesn't kick me out of her domain so I relax against the wall. I chug greedily and slide the empty mug along the glass top.

She shuffles her feet, clad in pink flip-flops. "So, what do I owe you?"

I jerk back slightly. "Seriously?"

"You helped me out. I don't wanna take advantage.

"Trip, we're square. Trust me."

"I have plenty of cupcakes or coffee?" Delilah prods.

I bite my bottom lip. "A date sounds better."

She blinks quickly. Her mouth opens and closes several times, but no sound comes out. Finally she stammers, "Uh, well . . . I wasn't expecting that."

"No pressure. We can grab a bite or some drinks, just *as friends*." I tack on the last part to appease her, though it's tough to spit out.

Delilah studies me, maybe weighing the options. "Well, I'll be busy with Garden Daze this weekend. After that?"

My heart lurches at the possibility she's handing me. I can't agree fast enough. "Definitely. And I'll see you there. We'll make sure to stop by your booth."

She crosses her arms. "We?" I suspect a hint of jealousy in her tone, but it's probably my imagination.

"I'm going with Ryan on Saturday."

She grins. "Oh, it'll be nice to see him."

A flicker of darkness skitters through my stomach. "Yeah, he's a good guy."

"There's quite a few of them 'round these parts," Delilah quips.

I squint at her. "I'm beginning to wonder if you're making me jealous on purpose."

She shrugs. "You're clumped in there somewhere. At least you used to be."

"I'll earn that title back," I promise.

Delilah points to the repaired shelf. "You're off to a fantastic start."

"Yup. And you'll be seeing a lot more of me."

"I could get used to that," she whispers, and I grow ten feet taller from those words. She leans closer and asks, "Where will we go? Next week, I mean."

"Can I keep it a surprise?"

She peeks at me from under lowered lashes. "I've always enjoyed those."

"Don't worry, I remember."

The smile Delilah gives me is worth all the air in my lungs. "Good," she murmurs.

I shuffle forward until there's a single foot separating us. I take a chance and reach for her hand, lacing our fingers together. She doesn't pull away. Instead Delilah flattens her palm against mine, letting our skin connect for a blissful moment. We stare at the bond reviving between us. The silence stretches for a bit, and I fear overstaying my welcome—or crossing whatever imaginary line is drawn between us. I've already taken enough liberties and don't want to push my luck.

After a gentle squeeze, I pull away, and Delilah releases a breathy sigh. When I glance at her, she's watching me expectantly.

"I should probably go," I say.

She nods. "But I'll see you soon?"

I knock on the glass, smiling wide. *"It's a date."*

# THIRTEEN

## READY

## DELILAH

I SCAN THE CRAMPED FRIDGE, searching for available space to store another pitcher. I'm not finding any, and Raven isn't done yet. A quick survey around the chaotic kitchen confirms that. Every inch of countertop is being used, which has me concerned about where all these desserts are going. My beverage containers don't take a lot of space so I can keep the rest upstairs. I double-check our walk-in but find the same result.

"Uh, Rave? I think you went overboard this time," I say while shutting the cooler door.

"Nonsense," she replies. "We'll sell out. I'll make sure of it."

"Especially if Marlene stops by. She can't deny your master baking," I laugh.

"For how much trouble that lady stirs up, she's actually a very loyal customer."

"That's why I haven't cut her off. *Yet*," I add for good measure. I make my way over to her, inspecting the array of colorful creations littered all about. "I'm finished with all my pre-blends and mixes. What can I help you with?"

Raven brushes stray hair from her forehead. "I'm almost done. Then we can relax and rest up for tomorrow."

I purse my lips, giving her a side-eye. "And you're putting all these . . . where?"

She snorts. "Don't look so worried. The torte and cookies don't need to be kept cold. They'll survive the night."

"If you say so."

"You didn't dub me the master baker for nothing," she reminds me.

"That's a valid point." I point to her shirt. "But I'm not entirely convinced this was the best slogan."

Raven glances down at the writing across her chest. *"Master-baking, anyone?"* she asks the question aloud.

I have to clamp my mouth shut to contain the cackle. "I admit it's hilariously punny. After two bottles of wine, it seemed like a great idea. But in the light of day, it might be a tad too . . . *saucy*. The old birds will be scandalized."

"Good," she huffs. "Serves them right."

"True, true. It's a killer tagline for you. Maybe we should make stickers," I suggest.

"And buttons," she adds.

"All the things. Maybe you should whip up some erotic lollipops while we're on this crazy-train."

Raven shoots me a disapproving scowl. "That's taking it too far."

"Oh, I've found the limit," I announce.

"You're a nut, which reminds me. Where are your shirts?"

I scrunch up my nose. *"Brew My Beans* didn't have the same quality. You'd steal the show regardless."

Raven smirks, not arguing in the least. "Your iced coffee and smoothies are tasty, though. They pair well with my frosted delights."

I point at her. *"That's another tee in the making!"*

*"I'm just that good."* She dusts off her shoulders.

*"It's why I keep you around,"* I say, and she bumps me with her hip.

*"Lucky for you, I'm not offended."* A suspicious sparkle twinkles in her blue eyes. *"So, are you excited?"*

*"Of course. The Daze is always fun."*

Raven pokes my side. *"You know what I mean."*

*"Do I?"*

*I totally do.*

Her lips flatten. *"Don't be a butt. Have you talked to him?"*

Somersaulting butterflies tumble in my stomach when I think about Zeke's recent texts. Over the last few days, he's become bolder. I like him that way. A lot. He's reminding me of everything I've been missing. I should keep my guard locked in place, but that's not what's happening.

Raven snickers. *"That good, huh?"*

I avert my gaze, and the apparent tell written all over me. *"Yeah, yeah. He's been fine. It's nice to have him back, for however long that might be."*

I need to keep telling myself Zeke is leaving. He isn't staying in Garden Grove permanently. It's the only protective shield I have left.

*"Too bad I wasn't here to witness him busting in to save the day."*

*"A shelf broke. Nothing exciting happened,"* I mumble.

*"Except the touching,"* she chirps.

I lean against the counter and exhale. *"You're making it sound sexual."*

*"Wasn't it?"*

There's no denying Zeke's steam-factor. I willingly admit, *"When he grabbed my hand, I about fainted from the tingles."*

Raven does a little dance. *"Oh, yeah. Those are detrimental* for the lady bits."

"Yup, that was the highlight. Serious swoon moment," I agree. My voice has gone all breathy, and he's not even nearby.

She puts a fist under her chin, looking all dreamy. "Hot carpenter to the rescue. Was he wearing a toolbelt? With a big hammer?"

"I'm regretting telling you about this."

"Just let it happen, D."

I huff, but I'm already surrendering. "He was an impressive sight, trust me. I needed a cold shower after he left."

And I'm not lying. When Zeke walked into Jitters, freshly showered and on a mission, I almost swallowed my tongue. Good thing the air conditioner was already cranked to max because I was instantly overheated. He strutted toward me like a true hero ready to save the damsel in distress. When Zeke blasted me with that trademark grin, I was putty in his talented fingers. I don't want to think about the come-hither vibes radiating off me. He must have felt them. Pretty sure I would have agreed to anything he suggested. Thankfully, Zeke only wanted a date. That's an easy start.

"Oh, Rave. I'm so far gone," I groan.

She pats my shoulder. "That's a good thing. It's all going to work out, D. Everything changed with Trey after The Graze, remember? These festivals are magic-makers."

"You two are a totally different story."

"Zeke wants you something fierce, D."

I shake my head. "That's never been the issue."

Raven's brows furrow. "So, what is? It all seems simple to me."

I comb through my tangled hair. "Once Roosters is done, he'll be gone again. Off to the next job. He practically spelled that out when we were at Boomers."

"Well, have you asked him to stay?"

"No way. That's not happening. I'm not putting myself in that position again."

"You could just go with the flow."

"That's rich coming from you."

She giggles. "I know, right? But it ended up real swell. Maybe it can be your motto, too."

I frown. "It's not that simple for us. There's a lot of pain and history standing in the way."

"Doesn't he have a drill or a chainsaw to destroy all that crap?"

"This is serious, Rave. I'm not really sure how he's changed in the last five years. There might be bigger demons than I can handle." My stomach cramps when I consider the shit he's been through. I'd always been his rock, without question. Even though I'm trying to be smart about this, my resolve to remain cautious is nonexistent.

Raven wraps an arm around my shoulder. "Give him a chance to tell you."

"I will." And that's the truth. I could never turn my back on Zeke.

"But?"

I roll my eyes. She knows me too well. "That doesn't mean we're driving off into the sunset and living happily ever after."

"There's a chance, though."

"Sure, the possibility is always lingering."

"Just don't give up before trying to let it happen. Zeke seems like a really great guy."

A smile tugs on my lips. "He really is."

She makes a noise that's all smugness. "It's obvious you still care about him."

"I already agreed to a date. I'm not handing over my heart on a platter."

"At least you're thinking about it."

"Hard not to," I mutter. "Love is thicker in the air than sugar around this place. That's saying something."

Raven just nods, then a cringe tightens her features. "Next on the agenda is patching things up between Zeke and Trey. There's some serious animosity." she says.

I wince in return. "That's gonna take time. Their rift dates back to middle school when Zeke first moved to Garden Grove. It definitely wasn't helpful that Trey and I didn't get along."

"Ah, right. Thankfully, we've smoothed things over in that respect."

There's days I still want to knee him in the balls, but I don't tell Raven that. Instead I ask, "Will Trey be around tomorrow?"

"Oh, yeah. I told him there'll be a Dirty Mechanic with his name on it, so he'll show up at our stand eventually. He's helping Jack with the vintage auto parade in the afternoon."

Trey's uncle has a wicked collection of classic muscle cars. My interests veer far from anything with four wheels, but those beasts can make anyone's engine purr. There's a reason why people travel across the state to have their vehicle serviced at Jacked Up. He's extremely talented, and his garage is crazy amazing.

I make a trail through a pile of flour on the table. "If Zeke shows up, I'll talk to him about Trey. Hopefully, they can learn to play nice."

"It would be nice for our guys to get along. Hanging out together would be a lot less awkward," Raven says.

I slice through the air. "Zeke isn't—"

"Oh, stop. You know what I mean, D."

Some of the fight falls away, and I breathe a little easier. What's the point of constantly swimming upstream against the rapids? I can let my guard down with Raven. "Okay, I'll quit being negative."

"Was that so hard? Now, let's get Trey and Zeke on board."

"Maybe we can all grab a drink afterwards," I suggest.

"We'll need a few, I'm sure. It's supposed to be really hot tomorrow," she practically whines.

"That's why I'm confident my smoothies will be a hit."

I didn't tell Raven about one of my specialty items for The Daze. It will be a surprise for everyone. My form of a peace offering, a caffeinated olive branch just for Zeke. To make up for the broken-heart cupcake, and plenty else. Warmth spreads through my limbs just thinking about his reaction.

Raven takes a sip of a taster I have sitting out. I giggle when she winds up drinking the entire thing.

"You've got mad mixology skills, D. These blends are tasty." She smacks her lips.

"Aww, aren't you sweet. Maybe I'll add a few to the regular menu."

Raven nods, then scans the endless dessert buffet laid out in front of us. "Okay, let's be real. I might have gone overboard."

I giggle and cover my face. "Glad to hear you admit it."

"Yeah, yeah. Keep laughing. You'll be the one helping me haul all this outside."

I recall the countless trays lined up in the coolers. "Call for backup—there's a master-baking emergency."

We explode into cackles and stumble out of the kitchen. Cleaning can always wait.

# FOURTEEN

## DAZE

## ZEKE

WHERE DID ALL THESE PEOPLE come from? Last I checked, Garden Grove was a really small town. Based off this crowd, I'd assume the population has recently doubled. Main Street is a fucking zoo.

Once the parade ended, organized chaos erupted to set up for the lunch crowd. It was impressive to witness how quickly the road was converted into a seating area. Everywhere I look is flooded with hungry folks seeking out their next meal. I don't blame them considering it smells like the finest meats are being smoked. Barbeque has always been my favorite, but I could care less about what they're serving.

Right now, my mouth is watering for a different flavor. I've got my eye on the prize, and she's currently smiling far too wide at a male customer.

"Krue, slow the fuck down," Ryan complains next to me. "Don't you wanna grab some grub from BBQ Shack?"

"I'm not in the mood for food."

He follows my line of sight and hums knowingly. "Ah, you've got coffee on the brain."

"Something like that," I mumble. I have one goal in mind—reaching Delilah and parking my ass next to her for the remainder of Garden Daze.

"All right, I guess my stomach can wait. I don't wanna miss whatever is about to go down."

My steps falter, and I pause momentarily to look at him. "What do you mean?"

Ryan adjusts his ball cap before meeting my stare. "You're practically foaming at the mouth, bro. Delilah is about to get mauled, or the man talking to her is gonna be knocked out. I give it fifty-fifty odds."

My attention swings back to her and the moron who's taking his sweet time ordering. "I won't hit him."

"But you want to."

"Fuck, yeah. He's drooling all over my . . ." The words trail off. I've got no claim to Delilah. She's free to talk with whoever, but that doesn't mean I have to like it. Just thinking about her flirting with other guys sets my blood to a boil.

I flatten my lips and blow out a forceful exhale, trying to regain some semblance of calm. Delilah is finally giving me a shot. I don't need to blow the chance before getting it.

Ryan claps my shoulder. "Don't worry. She'll be your everything again soon enough."

I shake off the tension in my muscles. "Thanks, man."

He nods. "That's what I'm here for. I'll ditch your ass if we don't hurry this up, though. I'm starving."

"I'll buy you a cupcake," I offer.

His brow furrows. "Thanks?"

I blindly gesture toward the booth. "From Raven, the one who works at Jitters."

Understanding loosens Ryan's expression. "Oh, right. I've

heard she's a whiz in the kitchen."

Just then, Delilah laughs and the tinkling noise carries over to me like a jackhammer. I practically sprint to cover the remaining distance to her stand. Ryan chuckles behind me, but I'm not listening. She's hogging all my senses as I propel forward.

Delilah notices me approaching, and a megawatt smile curves her mouth. My lungs quit functioning when I forget how to breathe properly. The lack of oxygen makes me dizzy and my knees threaten to buckle. She's too damn stunning, and it hurts to stand this close without touching her. She tilts her head, and a cascade of blonde waves spills over her shoulder. I want to feel the silky strands against my rough fingertips. Delilah's beautiful eyes crinkle in the corners, and I would happily stare at those barely-there creases all day. I don't care if that makes me a pussy. I'll gladly hand in my man card to have her look at me like this.

She tucks some shiny hair behind her ear. "Hey, Zee."

All coherent thought screeches to a halt when that name falls from her lips. I can't believe my ears and almost ask her to repeat it. I lean in, more than willing to vault over the table separating us. Instead I choke out, "Hey, Trip."

Delilah's grin stretches wider, and I have to bite down to keep my tongue from lolling out.

"I'm glad you made it," she blurts.

"Me too," I say, at a complete loss for what else to say. With Delilah staring at me, words seem extremely inadequate. Kissing her has never been a greater need, the demand screaming through my veins. I want to show her what she's doing to me. My vision narrows further, blocking out the booming crowd and ruckus.

From beside me, Ryan clears his throat. "It's cool. Don't mind me."

Delilah's lashes flutter, breaking the trance she's caught me in. Her gaze darts to him, and she startles slightly. "Oh my gosh! Hey, Ryan. It's been a long time."

He offers her a lame-ass wave. "What's up, D? You seem to be doing well here."

I grind my teeth as their pleasantries continue. I want to punch him for interrupting and stealing Delilah's attention from me. Yet it's probably for the best. With her sole focus locked on me, my control was nonexistent. Any signal from her would have sealed the deal and escalated our situation quickly. The dull throb in my dick reminds me I'm probably pitching a tent—in public with the entire town present.

While Delilah is still occupied, I lean against the counter to adjust and hide the evidence of my arousal. I have no desire to show off my shit to any nosey neighbors.

"Isn't that right, Zeke?" Delilah randomly asks.

Awareness slams into me. "Uh, what?"

*I sound like an idiot.*

She rolls her eyes. "We just talked about getting everyone together for a night."

"And I heard nothing about it," Ryan adds.

I jab his chest. "I texted you about this last week. You didn't seem to care one way or another."

"You didn't mention Emery would be included."

"Well, we don't know if she'll be around for sure. For your sake, I'm hoping she is," I respond.

"If there's a chance, you say so," he retorts.

"Sorry, man. There's a possibility your girl might be in town soon."

He grunts but doesn't dispute the term. "Whatever. Keep me in the loop, yeah?" Ryan looks between Delilah and me. "I'm glad you two are figuring shit out. You're meant to be."

Her eyes expand to saucer-size. "Uhhh," she says.

While at the same time I cough into my fist. "Slow down, Ryan." But secretly I'm high-fiving the fuck out of him.

"Oh, yeah? You just called Emery my girl. At least you know

D likes you, or used to."

Delilah groans. "Ryan, we all know she has the hots for you. Let's be honest."

"Would it kill her to show it?"

I grip his shoulder. "All right, see? Let's all take a step back. We're here to have fun."

He messes with his hat and turns to me. "Wanna go get food?"

I scratch the scruff along my jaw. "Nah, I'm good."

"I bet you are," he mutters with a grin.

"Want a cupcake?" I point to the ridiculously large display behind Delilah.

He peers at the spread. "I'll circle back after lunch. Pretty sure you're not moving."

"Damn straight," I agree.

Ryan salutes and wags his brows. "You two stay decent and keep your clothes on."

I laugh at his retreating form, the joyful sound becoming more common with each passing day. If I sit and think about it, my temper has been receding further into the background. I'll never complain about these turn of events.

Delilah is blushing something fierce when I look at her. "What's got your cheeks all red?"

She fans her face. "Thanks for calling me out, ass. It's over ninety degrees. There's good reason to be flushed."

I wink. "Or you're thinking about getting naked with me."

Delilah sputters. "Don't start, Zeke. We haven't even been on our date yet."

"Is that the prerequisite?" I'm pressing the boundaries, and it feels damn good.

She crosses her arms, studying me with sparkling eyes. "How have you been?"

"Good, good. Staying busy, can't complain." But I want to.

So long as she's not mine, I'll have a long list of shit to change. It doesn't help that my thoughts rarely stray from her, in a rather obsessive manner. I can't go five minutes without Delilah's gorgeous face filtering into my mind. That's not one of the issues I'd ever fix, though.

Delilah twirls a strand of golden hair around her finger. "You look . . . *good*," she purrs.

Warmth travels up my neck, and it's not from the stifling temperature. "Yeah?"

"Uh huh." She bites her lower lip. "Have you saved any other helpless shop owners lately?"

"Nah, that's just for you," I say with a smirk.

"Really?"

"Uh huh," I repeat her phrase.

"Well, I've got something special for you."

"Now?" My imagination immediately runs wild. I bump up against the table when my cock twitches. I'm like a fucking teenager with this instant hard-on bullshit.

Delilah very deliberately peruses my body, every inch of me feeling her visual inspection. I don't mind the blatant ogling one bit and almost ask if she wants me to spin slowly. Before I get the chance, her eyes snap up to mine and the blazing heat in them steals my voice.

Suddenly Delilah says, "Yep, right now," and turns away.

She busies herself behind the counter, making a drink from the looks of it. I let her work, happy to watch her graceful movements. When she reaches to grab a few objects from the shelf, a sliver of tan skin shows between her hem and waistline. My fingers crave her silky softness. I want to trace along that exposed patch until she shivers. All too soon, she shifts and hides that strip of heaven from me. Next time I'll have to move faster.

I'm distracted from that possibility when Delilah places a

plastic cup in front of me. It's filled to the brim with a blended beverage, frosty and cold to the touch. My dry throat yearns for a taste.

"What is it?" I survey the light orange liquid, which reminds me of creamsicle.

"Try it," she urges.

"There's no coconut, right?"

She rolls her eyes. "No, I was messing with you about that. You'll like this. At least, I hope so."

"That's all the reassurance I need." I chug half the glass in one gulp, greedy for the cool relief. The rich flavor bursts on my tongue, and I moan loudly. I wipe over my mouth and say, "Holy shit, this tastes like Thanksgiving dessert."

Delilah's smile is blinding. "Ah, I was hoping you'd think so. It's similar to the pie recipe you always loved."

"Pumpkin?"

She nods and tics items off her fingers. "There's vanilla yogurt, banana, cinnamon, toasted pistachios, and pumpkin purée. I, um, call it . . . Miss Me."

Wind echoes in my ears as I get lost in the meaning. I should be concerned that my heart is pounding so fast. I might wonder how obvious my surprise is. But all I can do is stare at my beautiful girl. This moment is heavy, packed full of importance, and I don't want to miss a second of it.

I finish off my drink and lick my smoothie-coated lips. "Do you, Trip?"

"I do. Really, truly. I'm glad you're back, Zeke."

For the first time in five years, the struggle lifts off my shoulders. "Me too. So damn much."

Delilah is everything I've always wanted. Scratch that. She's all I *need*. I reach for her hand, taking the liberty she allowed me before. This is the one boundary we've crossed so far. Otherwise we've been frustratingly platonic. There's been a shift today, though. If looks were actions, Delilah would have me undressed and stripped naked. I link our fingers on the table and sigh. She's going to be mine again.

She giggles. "I'm even more excited for Monday."

I study the joy on her features. "It's gonna be the date to end all dates," I tell her.

"Should I be nervous?"

"No way. Be ready for the swoon."

Delilah's free hand flutters to her chest. "I can feel it already."

I squeeze the one still locked against mine. "Good. That's the point."

She looks down briefly before peeking up through her lashes. "Knock, knock," she murmurs.

She's playing our game? I can't stop my jaw from dropping. I lick my lips and ask, "Who's there?"

"When where.

"When where who?"

Delilah tugs me a bit closer. "Tonight. Dagos. A bunch of us are going."

I grin. "Thanks for the invite, Trip. Count me in. Always."

# FIFTEEN

## DATE

## DELILAH

THE LOUD KNOCK ECHOES OFF the wood, driving straight into me.

"Be right there," I call out. My heart gallops faster with each step I take. When I open the door, Zeke is there with a bouquet of beautiful hydrangeas. A dopey grin lifts my lips.

He smirks and passes me the flowers. "Damn, I've missed this."

I bury my nose in the nearest blossom and inhale. "What's that?"

"Picking you up. Having you happy to see me. Witnessing that smile on your face when it lights up the room, and knowing I put it there." Zeke scrubs over his mouth and adds, "Spending the night together."

My lower belly tingles, the impact of his words a direct hit. "You're not messing around with the swooning."

He rocks back on his heels. "Not even a little bit."

I lean against the doorframe and take in all his manly glory. His spicy-crisp scent overpowers all else, the sweet floral aroma already forgotten. I'd take Zeke wearing a white tee and khaki shorts over a billionaire in an expensive suit any day of the week. I rub my legs together, hoping that my extra primping and polishing will pay off. My skin prickles while his stare eats me up. I gladly take my fill of him, too. My gaze settles on his flip-flops and I'm reminded of our countless trips to the beach. That gets me thinking . . .

"Where are we going?"

"It's a secret."

"Still?" I prod and he bobs his head. "Well, am I dressed okay?"

Zeke gives me a dragged-out once-over, spending extra time on my boobs. I don't mind the attention. Not even a little bit. His intense focus has me flustered, and I need to occupy my mind elsewhere.

I step out of the walkway, granting him permission to enter. "Let me put these in water." I give the hydrangeas a little shake.

"Are you wearing a swimsuit?" His arm brushes mine when he passes into the room.

I purse my lips. "Why would I be?"

"It's summer?"

"And what do you call those?" I point to his shorts.

Zeke tugs on a pocket. "These double as trunks."

"Ah, clever."

"I can take care of the flowers while you change," he offers.

"Vases are above the sink. I'll be right back. Make yourself comfortable," I say before darting down the hall and into my room.

Zeke calls out, "Do you live alone?"

"Uh, yeah," I respond while quickly stripping off my tank and skirt. "Raven stayed here for a bit, but now she's with Trey."

"It's a nice place. You've really made it a home."

I smirk and adjust the triangle cups over my chest. "Thanks, but don't get any crazy ideas."

Although the idea of Zeke living here doesn't unsettle me in the slightest. My defenses have clearly left the building, and I'm in big trouble.

After getting dressed, I make my way to the kitchen and Zeke places the arrangement on the table. He twists to look at me and zooms in on the neon pink strings around my neck. "I like your choice of attire."

"You haven't seen it yet."

"My imagination is filling in the gaps. Should we go?" He motions to the door.

I grab my purse and usher him out, locking up once we're in the hallway. We walk down the stairs, and Zeke grabs my hand. I squeeze his fingers in response, and we share a breathy sigh.

"You make life better," he tells me.

Giddiness tickles up my arm. "Yeah?"

Zeke hums. "It's easier to be positive when you're with me. It's always been that way. You're like my good-luck charm or something."

I'm sure there're stars in my eyes. "And you're a sweet talker."

He leans down. "You're beautiful," he whispers close to my ear.

Before I can respond, my feet skid to a halt on the sidewalk. I widen my eyes at the vehicle parked along the curb.

"Oh, wow. You still have Bertha." The awe is clear in my voice. This baby holds more memories than I can recall.

Zeke grunts. "I could never part with her."

I try not to get jealous of his devotion to this hunk of metal. I walk forward and pat the rusty side panel. "I've missed you, old girl."

"Fucking truck gets a better welcome than me," he grumbles beside me.

I swing my attention to Zeke. "What's that?"

He shakes his head. "Nothing at all." The hinges complain

loudly when he opens the passenger door. "Your chariot awaits."

I grin at his chivalry. "Thanks, Zee."

While I get settled, he makes his way around and gets in. He cranks the key and the pickup rumbles awake. Like, actually vibrating in place. I grab the oh-shit handle just in case.

He laughs at my precaution. "Afraid?"

"Um, no. Should I be? It seems the lady is upset about moving," I point out.

"The hiccups don't bother me. She has good bones and a lot of miles left to give," he says.

I glance out the window, watching people stare as Bertha literally roars by. "You might have a few folks concerned, though."

Zeke shrugs and keeps driving without a care. I have a strong inkling we're heading to a lake, but there are several to choose from. We remain silent, as in no conversation is happening. That's mostly due to the horrible grinding noise coming from under the hood.

A few minutes later, I start laughing uncontrollably. "Seriously, Zeke? She's practically begging for a tune-up."

He squints at the road and bends toward me. "What's that?"

"Exactly," I huff. "You can't hear me over . . . *that*." I flail my hand all about. The sound is deafening around us.

"Guess I've gotten used to the noise. I haven't thought much about it since no one rides with me." He smirks in my direction. "That might be changing now."

"You should take Bertha to Jacked Up. Trey will fix her for you." This could be another opportunity to bridge the gap between them.

"He offered."

That surprises me. I turn in my seat and face him. "Why didn't you take him up on it?"

Zeke shrugs. "Because he's an asshole."

"We've talked about this."

He blows out a breath. "Guess I can give him a shot."

I almost applaud his willingness, but hold off. "Do it for my sake. And Raven's. It's very stressful having boyfriends that don't get along."

"What did you say?" he immediately asks.

I furrow my brow, unsure why he's so interested. "It's difficult for Raven and me with you two hating each other."

Zeke clucks his tongue. "Not that part."

Realization dawns, and my face heats. "Shit," I mutter and wave away my slip. "Just an expression. Don't read anything into it."

I don't regret giving him that title. In fact, my stomach flutters when I repeat it silently. That's a reason for worry. I don't want to reveal how easily my shields are folding.

His brows bounce. "I like it."

"We'll see how today goes. This doesn't mean anything serious. I'm still not fully forgiving you," I tell him with as much strength as I can muster.

"I've pulled out all the stops today," he says as we pull into the lot for Grove Park.

A lump rises in my throat when I consider why he chose this spot. "Enough to make up for five years?"

"I'm trying, Trip. Give me that."

"I am, but it will take more than one date to wrap me back around your pinky."

"That was never the case to begin with," Zeke grumbles.

"Little do you know," I retort.

We get out, and I stare off into the distance. I'm all too aware what's waiting beyond those trees. Zeke grabs a basket and bag from the truck bed.

"What's all that?" I ask, distracting myself.

"Just some means of assistance."

"For the wooing?"

"Yup."

I reach for the tote, and he passes it over. Zeke clasps our free hands together as we start walking down the dusty trail. "I've missed this area," I say softly.

His forehead crinkles. "What do you mean? You live five minutes away."

"I don't visit this part often."

Zeke nods knowingly. "I wouldn't either."

We stroll in silence, giving the past a moment to intrude on the present. There's so much history in these woods, but even more on the beach. We stop at the clearing, where dirt turns to sand. I glance to the left and see our etched heart, like a beacon calling us home. The ink along my upper back burns like the day it was drawn. Emotion stings my eyes, and I suddenly find it hard to remain standing. I grip Zeke tighter for support. I knew where we were going but didn't properly prepare for the onslaught of pain this cove would bring.

My voice is shaky when I ask, "Why did you bring me here? Of all places."

"I want you to remember the good," he soothes.

"I could never forget."

"Let's sit down." Zeke takes a blanket and lays it on the ground. I easily collapse, trying to find comfort in the soft fabric. He settles in next to me, close enough to touch, but I still have an inch of distance. I'm thankful because it gives me a second to wipe the jumble from my brain.

The humidity broke at some point, and a cool breeze swirls around us. I point to the sky. "Looks like a storm is brewing."

Zeke glances up. "We'll be fine. If it rains, we can swim another day."

Thinking about coming back here that soon twists a knot in my chest. "Maybe."

He points over my shoulder at our tree. "Remember when

we carved our love into that trunk?"

I snort. "In more ways than one."

He chuckles but continues. "How about that rock? You'd lie there for hours getting tanned while I'd catch fish for dinner."

"I know what you're doing, Zeke."

"Is it working?"

"No." But it most definitely is.

Zeke shifts closer, eliminating that sliver of space between us. "Should I keep going?"

I bite my wobbling lip. "Sure."

"I miss our dreams of the future. Remember those?"

"We were foolish," I say.

He ignores my pessimism. "I miss sneaking out my window to meet you. Those stolen kisses kept me going on the worst nights."

My nose stings, and I rub at the burn. "Dammit, Zee. You're digging where it hurts."

His fingers drift along my knuckles. "I miss our jokes. The sound of your laugh plays on repeat in my head."

A rumble rises from my throat. "Then why did you leave me?"

"I had to, Trip. You know that."

"I guess, yeah," I mumble.

"Tell me," he urges. His blue eyes shine in the sunlight reflecting off the lake. I allow myself to get sucked into those glistening depths.

"What do you want to know?"

"Have you missed me?"

"Only with each breath I take."

His thumb trails down my face. "Remember the night you gave me everything? Right on this beach?"

I hold his intense stare. "Like it was yesterday. But you broke a promise."

"I'm trying to be romantic, Trip."

"And I'm being realistic. I have to protect myself."

"From what?"

I gesture between us. "This isn't a guarantee. I don't have much trust left to spare."

"I put that hurt there," he says and brushes under my eyes. "The distrust has buried your belief. I'll bring it back, though."

"Yeah? Then tell me why I wasn't good enough. You should have come back for me, no matter what."

Zeke is quiet for a minute. Finally, he says, "I did."

I shuffle backward. "What's that?"

He rubs over the scruff coating his jaw. "No one knew about it. This was a few years after I'd left. I wanted to check on you. I laid low and poked around, staying out of sight. Turns out you weren't in Garden Grove."

"College," I say, filling in the blanks.

"I guess? Regardless, that solidified my decision. You were off living and didn't need me. It was a tough pill to swallow, but I was glad in the end."

"That was a shitty assumption."

"Yeah, Trip. I fucking know. I've made a lot of really stupid mistakes. We're moving forward, right?"

"You ruined me," I croak. When he reaches for me, I dodge his touch.

Zeke's brow furrows. "Trip, I thought—"

I slash through the air, cutting him off without a word. I stand in a flurry, more than ready to rip this flimsy Band-Aid off. Zeke follows suit, launching up in one fluid motion. For weeks, this tether between us has been pulling taut. With each beat, the strain gets tighter, threatening to snap. It was bound to happen eventually. A crushing wave of sadness slams into me, drowning me on the spot. I can't breathe or escape or understand how the hell we got into this position.

With a crack of thunder, drops begin falling from the sky. Go fucking figure. The only thing missing from this shitstorm was rain, so at least there's a cherry on top. In seconds, I'm completely drenched, and not in the good way. My sloppy state feeds the fury, adding weight to the breaking point.

I shiver against the cold splatter, but outrage burns across my skin. "You broke us, Zeke!" I yell through the whipping wind. "You shattered me and wrecked yourself too by the looks of it. I hope staying away was worth it."

He stalks into my personal space. "I did it for you!" Zeke roars.

I fling the wet hair off my cheeks. "Oh? You walked out of my life, broke my heart, and destroyed my faith in love for *my benefit*? That's so sweet."

Zeke's eyes flash, like a streak of lightning. "It's about damn time I fixed us."

# SIXTEEN

## CRASH

## ZEKE

WHILE DELILAH CRUDELY LISTS MY crimes against her, I obliterate the space between us. I hate the way she's looking at me, like the man in front of her is a stranger. But in many ways, I am. We're solving this shit once and for all, right the fuck now, and I know exactly how to make that happen.

Before she can blink, I have Delilah hoisted into my arms and pressed against our tree. There's a reason we chose this one—the smooth bark is forgiving on her back. A boom of thunder explodes, and we crash together. Our angry words die as my mouth slams against hers, punishing and brutal.

I feel the instant Delilah surrenders, her resistance melting away like snow in the sun. Her lips open for me, and I moan while our tongues twist together. I take full advantage, plunging deeper. This time she greets me, giving back what I'm taking. Our movements are a frantic blur, yet we can't get naked fast enough. The furious rain pelts against our heated skin, ensuring we don't go up in flames.

Delilah rips her mouth away and begs, "Please, Zee. Don't make me wait." Her legs cinch around my waist, and she bucks against me.

"Fuck, Trip. You're too damn sexy. I'm never gonna last."

"Who the hell cares. Just get inside me," she pants.

Delilah's skirt is the greatest blessing. I'm granted fast access between her thighs with a flip of denim. Her flimsy bikini bottoms are no match for my strength, and I tear the fabric with a savage jerk. I manage to shove my shorts down just far enough without losing the grip on her hip. In the next breath, I'm sliding inside her, joining us as one.

"Holy shit." Delilah's wail pierces me while her nails dig into my shoulders.

I grind my teeth, firing off a round of expletives. Delilah is so damn tight, and it feels like our first time all over again. Her strangle hold on my dick is unforgiving as I piston in and out. The pinch of pain fends off the release that's already rushing forward.

"You wanna scream and yell? Let me hear you," I demand.

"It f-feels so d-damn good," she stammers.

I grunt and punch forward. "More."

Delilah claws into my neck, the skin there screaming, but I hardly feel it. "You're so fucking big, Zee. I almost forgot how far you stretch me. You're gonna split me in half," she whimpers.

I hum along her tilted jaw. "You'd love that."

She nods. "So much."

"I'm gonna make sure you're still feeling me tomorrow," I growl.

"Y-yes! Please," she moans.

Delilah pushes down, grinding into me. I thrust harder in response, wanting to give what she's seeking. This needs to be good for her, but I'm ready to blow. My skin is sizzling, and I feel higher than the stormy clouds. I grip her ass cheek, using my hold to propel faster and deeper. I'm hammering her with brutal force and for a split second, it seems too rough. But when Delilah screams for more, my second-guessing vanishes with another powerful thrust.

This is sex with a purpose—to reclaim what we've lost.

Soft touches and sweet words don't belong here. We're screwing the anger out and releasing our pain. Years of pent-up feelings are pouring down with the rain. The slap of skin surrounds us, the sound filthy and erotic. Delilah scratches down my back. I grip her ass so tight the skin is bound to bruise. She squeezes me past pain, and I jerk her closer in response.

"Fuck," I snarl. "You want it to hurt?"

Delilah's breath hitches with rapid inhales. "I just need to know this is real."

I bite her collarbone. "Nothing has ever been this real."

She bends back until wet hair tickles my hand on her hip. "Never stop," she pleads.

"Have you missed *this*?" I ask, accentuating the question with a forceful plunge.

I watch her throat move with a harsh swallow. "E-every day."

I bring Delilah flush against me, setting an unbreakable rhythm. She slips back and forth, riding me so fucking good. I stare into her forest green eyes when they collide with my sky blue. Then focus on her open mouth. I slow down for a moment and suck her bottom lip between my teeth. Delilah gasps, and my gaze bounces back to hers.

"You're mine, Delilah. Always have been."

She clutches fistfuls of my hair and steers me closer. "Yes," she murmurs.

I bury my nose into her neck and inhale, groaning at the sweet scent. I assault her delicate skin, alternating between nips and licks. My hand latches onto her hip while the other sticks to her ass like glue. She squirms in my hold, moaning so loudly my ears are buzzing.

"Say it," I demand, needing to hear it.

"I'm yours," Delilah says. "All yours. Always."

That flips a hidden switch I didn't know existed. All at once, I melt and turn to stone, an electrical current blasting into me at an alarming rate. I discover another level and surge forward even stronger.

"I've got you, Trip. You'll always be mine, dammit."

"No doubt," she whispers against my cheek.

Once upon a time, we were fumbling rookies without a clue. The years have changed us in this way, too. We aren't questioning anything in this moment. There's no hesitating or sloppy missteps. We're not afraid to devour each other. My strokes are sure and confident, her body welcoming me deeper. Desperation jolts through me when I buck upward, driving her further against the tree.

"You're so fucking wet," I mutter. And she is. My cock glides in before dragging out with zero resistance. Delilah's legs are spread impossibly wide, but she doesn't complain. Quite the opposite as she manages to arch further, giving me the freedom to adjust and hit a new angle.

"Make me come," she wheezes.

I circle my hips and rub faster, trying to hit her clit. Delilah's loud gasp lets me know I've struck gold.

"Yes, there! Holy shit, yes!" Delilah has never been more agreeable.

"I can't hold off much longer."

"Me either," she pants.

"That's my girl." I've never been more thankful for her quick trigger than this moment. Lust thrums in my veins, overpowering everything else. The need to conquer every piece of her possess me, and I slam forward even harder. Blinding heat scorches up my spine, and my eyes cross from the mounting pressure. The bomb inside of me explodes, utter destruction to my grasp on reality. I clench my jaw while unbearable pleasure rips at me. Delilah's clenching so fucking hard that I feel every wave while she shudders in my arms.

I erupt with a roar at the same time Delilah screams, "Oh, oh! K-keep going. I'm g-gonna . . . Yesssssss!"

We're clutching each other so tight, no space exists between us. I jolt with each shot, giving her all of me. Delilah's entire body is locked up and tense. Mine is the same way. When the searing white light clears from my vision, I rest my forehead against hers. Our panting breaths mingle with each forceful exhale. In the midst of everything, I realize it's no longer raining, and Delilah's bliss is sparkling across her damp skin.

"Holy shit," Delilah sputters.

"Damn," I blow out. "Sorry if I was too rough."

She shakes her head against mine. "Never apologize for that."

I take a few steps back, and Delilah loosens her grip. I slowly lower her to the ground. When she's standing, I go to yank up my shorts and stop short with a curse.

"What's wrong?" she asks.

I release a heavy breath. "I didn't wear a condom."

"Oh," she says simply.

When I look up, she's biting her lip and avoiding eye contact. "I fucked up, Trip."

"It's okay," Delilah murmurs.

I stare deep into her, finding the truth reflecting there. "Yeah? We're safe?"

She nods and tucks some hair behind her ear. "I still have an IUD. No worries."

I scrub the back of my neck, unsure how to bring up the other concern. I swallow bile just thinking of her with someone else.

"But what about . . ." I trail off, hoping she gets the hint.

Delilah's foot digs into the muddy ground. "Uh, well . . . I'm clean, if that's what you're implying."

I wait a beat before responding, my face heating with the impending confession. "Okay, good. Same here." I clear the sand from my throat. "There isn't any threat considering I haven't slept with anyone in years."

Her head jerks up. "Really? Wow. I never would have guessed that."

I chuckle, a little pressure easing off my chest. "Why? You assume I was fucking around?"

"I didn't think that was a possibility. You're super-hot, like a walking advertisement for getting laid. This is the prime of your life and all that. How did you manage this?"

I shrug her words off. "Because I've only wanted one girl. If I couldn't have her, there was no point in trying."

A strangled cough escapes her. "Oh my God."

I smirk at her reaction. "Crazy, huh?"

Delilah gasps. "Wait. Are you really saying—"

"I haven't had sex since we made love under the stars five years ago," I finish for her.

Her lips part as she studies my expression, seeking and searching. Her eyes glisten in the low lighting and she blinks quickly. "I'm trying to figure out what to say," she tells me honestly.

"Does this change your mind about me?" I joke.

Delilah sniffs. "Just the opposite, Zee. That's the most romantic thing I've ever heard. It also makes it easy to admit I haven't slept with anyone either."

Shock barrels into me and I gape. "No way, Trip."

"There's only been you for me," she continues. "I've been close, sure. But when the moment came, I could never share myself with someone else." She laughs, the noise hollow. "I hated that weakness. I was holding out for a man who might as well be a ghost."

Delilah gathers her hair and drapes it over one shoulder. She turns slightly until her tattoo is in full view, exposed to me in more ways than one. Her fingers tremble when they brush over the patch of colorful ink. Suddenly I can't take a decent breath, my throat squeezing in a vice.

"This is my tribute to you . . . and us. I created the design and had it done on my eighteenth birthday. Even when you didn't come back, I never regretted the decision. I want you with me always," Delilah explains.

I stare at the array of blooming hydrangeas, begonias, and camellias. Those are her favorites. But the letters in the center of it have me gasping. Hidden within a few petals are our nicknames, curved into a heart. We're permanently marked on her body in an ultimate gesture of devotion. I feel like my lungs are failing. How can this be real? Why would she do this for me?

In the next second, she's wrapped in my arms. The hug is fierce and expresses all the emotion bubbling through me. "I love you so fucking much," I murmur.

She lifts her face to look at me. "I love you, Zee. Always."

"This is all so . . . unbelievable." The awe easily slips off my tongue.

"I know we planned to get tattoos together, but I couldn't wait. I wanted to surprise you, and better late than never. Mission accomplished, I guess."

"Will you go with me to get one?" Getting her name scrawled across my ribs is suddenly all I can think about.

Delilah nods. "Of course, but don't feel obligated."

I shake my head. "I've never wanted anything more."

"I can design something for you. I mean, if you're sure."

My eyes sting and I smile. "You're all I've ever seen, and that will never change."

Her nails dance along my jaw. "Same for me. I've missed you so much."

I kiss Delilah's cheek, tasting the salt of tears long overdue. She's finally letting me see her again. I hold up my hand and she places her palm against mine, our fingers forming parallel lines. Hopefully we're going in the same direction.

My lips sweep along her forehead. "I've never stopped loving you, Trip. Even when I made the choice to stay away, you were always on my mind. In some warped way, I was trying to protect you. That decision had nothing to do with my feelings for you."

She shivers, and I drag her tighter against me. "I wish you'd found a way to tell me that," she whispers.

"I know, D. But it's gonna be better now. I'll regain your trust and fix everything." I press her palm to my ribs, moving our joined hands along the ridges. "These wounds have healed," I start, referring to the countless sprains and breaks I faced under my father's hand. I drag her fingers up until she's touching my temple. "But there's still a battle happening in here."

She brushes my hair away. "I miss the hope in your eyes. Let me show you the good again."

I lean into her touch. "I want that. I miss the guy from five years ago."

"Me too. But he's still in here," she says and strokes over my left pec.

I kiss her softly, pouring so much between the brief press of our lips. "You're so beautiful, baby."

Delilah snuggles closer. "You're beyond words. I can't believe this is happening."

We're quiet for a few moments, just content with being intertwined. But when Delilah trembles, I realize the temperature has dropped significantly. "Should we go? I'd love to hold you all night, but we're soaked."

She pats the wet fabric stuck to my chest. "I don't mind you this way. You're extremely sexy. So ripped," she purrs, and her hand slides down my torso.

I pause her descent. "Keep going and you'll be against that tree all over again."

Delilah tries to escape my hold with a light tug. "Promise?"

"Absolutely, but not here. I want to worship you in a bed."

"Round two?"

"At least. I think we've fucked the anger out of our systems. We needed to blow off some steam, huh?" I chuckle, and she wrinkles her nose. "From now on, it's about spreading the love."

Delilah hums. "We have a lot of making up to do."

I bump our hips together, letting her know I'm more than ready. "Your place or mine?"

# SEVENTEEN

## YOURS

## DELILAH

I WAKE WITH A JOLT, my eyes flinging wide open. It takes a few moments for the memories of last night to break through the fog. I stretch, and a dull ache pinches between my legs, offering a lovely souvenir. A satisfied moan escapes my curved lips at that.

I press my mental rewind button and review our methods for testing the box springs. Zeke proved he still knows my body better than I do. And I was all too happy to let him show me, over and over. My smile grows when I glance at him lying naked beside me. I'm content to continue lounging and replaying the sexcapades in my head. Until I get a glimpse of the clock.

"Shit," I whisper-yell into the fading darkness. I have to get a move on and haul ass downstairs. I'm already running behind. After another look at Zeke's resting face, I swing my legs off the mattress.

His raspy voice halts my movements. "Making a fast getaway?"

I grin at his accusation. Without turning around, I explain, "I have to work."

"No rest for the owner, huh?"

I peek over my shoulder, which is a mistake. This time my gawking involves his entire . . . package. Zeke is sprawled out with the paper-thin sheet hanging low on his hips. One muscular arm is behind his head, propping him up. That bulging bicep beckons me, sparking a highlight reel of his virility and strength. My toes curl into the plush carpet, and I try to ignore the buzz racing through me. Then Zeke's fingers on the other hand begin making a slow trail along his flexing abs. Down and down until he's tracing the hem on the fabric barely covering his growing erection. The outline of all that hardness is on full display, and I want to be the one touching. My mouth waters and getting out of bed has never been so difficult.

"Why don't you call in?" Zeke's tone is still extra gruff and scrapes over me like sandpaper. I shiver involuntarily. I force my hungry gaze up, settling on his smug expression.

"The boss doesn't get sick days," I say. "I didn't plan accordingly and ask someone to open for me."

"Hmm," he purrs. "I could help you with that."

I bite my lip while a scorching flush blankets me. I've lost count on the number of orgasms he's delivered. But either way, my hoo-hah is wrung out. "Not sure I could handle another round," I tell him honestly.

"But I'll miss you," he says while dragging a finger down my spine.

"You'll miss the sex," I tease.

Zeke loops an arm around my waist and yanks me into him. He murmurs into the crook of my neck, "I always miss everything with you."

I melt against him and seriously consider blowing off Jitters. "Why are you so wonderful?"

"Because I love you," he hums along my skin. Zeke begins peppering me with soft kisses. Between the assault to my resolve, he adds, "I want to win you back." His sweet touches are my undoing, and I twist to face him. His blue eyes gleam, and I fall a little deeper at the happiness swirling there.

I cradle his jaw in my palm. "You're well on the way, Zee."

He presses his lips against my wrist. "I won't stop until you're really mine again. Completely," he states with conviction.

I blink at his words, wanting that more than anything. But there's a very large issue looming over our heads. I don't want to bring up his temporary situation in Garden Grove, but it's an extremely huge factor in how this will pan out for us.

Thinking about Zeke's eventual departure pops my bubble of bliss. I don't want to assume he'll stay, or be the one asking him to make that decision. It doesn't matter that the plea is waiting to drip off my tongue at any given moment. We're making up, but still on shaky ground.

Each time I've built up the guts, my throat squeezes shut and the words can't pass. Fear of rejection holds me back, terror of hearing his plans. Or perhaps dread that he's leaving regardless of what I say. I don't want to break us with the truth.

"I'm so screwed," I murmur.

"I didn't hear you complaining a few hours ago." He chuckles.

"I'm serious, Zee. We're acting like things can pick up where they dropped off. It's not that simple."

He sits up and cuddles me into his side, lacing our fingers together. "Here's the truth I know, Trip. The days are painfully lonely. But the nights blind me with unbearable misery. I'm not sure there's ever been an escape without you. I need you in my life, plain and simple."

I blow out a heavy breath. "If we stay on this path, wherever it leads, I'm going to get attached to the idea of you being around. But what happens next? I'm scared of the unknown. You have to understand that."

Zeke tilts my chin up until our eyes are locked. "I do, Trip.

And I'd never hurt you. All I want is to shower you with love."

The lump in my throat makes it difficult to swallow. "For how long? Until your job in Garden Grove is done?"

He shakes his head but doesn't give a definite answer. "Let's not worry about that today."

"How can I not?"

Zeke brushes a kiss to my forehead and ignores my concern. "I miss you caring about me."

"And I miss you being around permanently," I retort.

His body turns to stone beneath me, and he hauls me closer. "Fuck, D. I do, too. Each and every second. I'm not planning to leave again, okay? I'll figure this out."

I believe him, but a crumb of doubt feeds the broken part of me. My temples begin to throb, warning me of an impending headache. I need coffee, stat.

"I really need to get up," I mutter.

Zeke's relaxed demeanor returns with a smirk. "I'm already there, baby."

I can't help but laugh. "You're a goof."

"Whatever keeps the tension away," he whispers into my hair.

I press my nose into his neck, inhaling woodsy masculinity. "You smell so good."

"Remember that when you're lonely at Jitters later. We could stay wrapped in each other instead."

I make a frustrated noise, hating how much better his alternative sounds. "Speaking of, what's up with your job? Aren't you supposed to be working?"

Zeke grunts. "This week is all fucked up. We're supposed to start framing but most of the wall studs were damaged in shipment. That issue has forced a pause in the progress. I'm not complaining because the delay is allowing me to be here with you."

"So, you have the day off?" My voice is too damn giddy.

I feel his lips curl against my cheek. "I have to swing by the site for general shit, but nothing major. We don't get paid our regular wage, and that sucks, but it's only a few days. Figure there'll never be a better reason to play hooky. Spending time with you is the best excuse."

I hum and rake my gaze along his bare torso, taking advantage of his nudity. "A forced vacay?" I manage.

Zeke chuckles. "Seems that way. I can help you get things started downstairs. What do you need?"

I bob my head along his chest. "I don't want you to waste precious free time in my shop. You've helped enough. Go have fun. Call Ryan or whoever."

"Nah, he's probably working. I'll gladly offer a hand . . . or something else."

"What are you implying, Mister Kruegan?"

"Maybe we can have a quickie in the kitchen," he suggests.

I choke on an inhale. "Oh, no way. That's Raven's domain," I say with a shudder. "Trey has marked his territory all over in there."

Zeke's upper body curls with a fake wretch. "Gross."

"Right? I made her triple-bleach every square inch. Pretty sure she learned from that mistake."

My fingers dance along his abs. "How about you help me open the store? Then you can take Bertha to Jacked Up."

He groans. "She's fine."

I scoff loudly. "That truck is most definitely not okay. Pretty sure the engine is about to fall out from all that rattling."

Zeke rolls his eyes. "I'll think about it. I'm not guaranteeing anything."

To me, that's a yes. Why not press a little further, right? "Take Trey out for a beer while you're at it."

"Don't push your luck, Trip."

"There isn't much else going on, so why not?"

"This seems like a setup. Are you trying to start a bromance?"

"Would that be so bad?"

He pulls away and looks down at me, feeling my forehead. "I think you have a fever. Let's stop talking about other men while you're naked in bed with me."

"Good plan," I say with a nod. I lean up to brush our noses together, the soft touch igniting a fire in my lower belly. "You're the only one I want to talk about."

"That's better," he grunts.

Our lips meet in a kiss. I'm about to deepen it when responsibility clangs in my brain. I break from the embrace with a pout. "I need to get dressed. Reality calls."

Zeke smacks my butt when I scoot off the mattress. He follows suit, standing on the opposite side. I take a long, leisurely scan of his body. His hair is perfectly mussed and well-loved thanks to my wandering fingers. As my gaze sweeps lower, I get caught up in sculpted shoulders and defined biceps that lead to sinewy forearms. Zeke has muscles stacked on top of each other. Damn, construction certainly pays off. I'll have to write a thank-you note to his boss for working him so hard.

He faces me and widens his stance. "You keep looking at me that way, leaving this room won't be an option."

I yank my eyes off his morning wood. How the hell did my pesky attention get down there so fast? I wipe across my chin and mumble, "Yeah, right. Sounds good."

He laughs. "That makes no sense."

I motion toward him and all his naked glory. "How am I supposed to think straight with your dick saluting me?"

Zeke shrugs. "Easy. You don't." His thumb swipes at the corner of his mouth. "You missed some drool."

I stomp around the bed and stand in front of him. "Stop tempting me."

He gestures to his impressive hard-on. "Nothing to be salty about. The feeling is definitely mutual, Trip."

I throw my hands in the air. "My good sense is going up in smoke. All I can think about right now is sex."

"Damn, I've missed you. C'mere," he says with a crook of his finger. He prowls forward, and I step out of his reach.

I'm in desperate need of a distraction before my legs find their way around his waist. "Let's get going, Zee. When Marlene catches sight of you in Jitters, this will be front page news. You've gotta be presentable."

He grumbles. "Good deflection, but tell me something I don't know."

I tap a finger to my lips, and a thought hits me. "Okay, I've got something super odd. These women came in the other day and were talking about dolphins. Apparently, males are crazy horny and total sex fiends." Zeke just raises a questioning brow, so I continue. "Apparently there was a trainer who jacked off this dolphin to get him to . . . perform. No pun intended. Or maybe big time implied," I giggle out.

He tilts his head. "Is that true?"

"I dunno. They were discussing it. The one girl sounded pretty serious about it."

"That sounds like a made-up story, Trip."

I wave him off. "Either way, it's funny to think about."

"That'd be one smart fish," he says.

"Dolphins aren't fish, you dork."

"That's the issue you're pointing out here?"

I snort. "Touché."

Just then I realize we're having this random-ass conversation buck naked. It's startling to know how comfortable I am already, like we've always been together. The years spent apart disappeared in a hot second while we were getting intimately reacquainted. But I've always been this way with Zeke. That's a huge reason I never bothered trying to find someone else. What would be the point?

I study him quietly and make a snap decision.

*Fuck it.*

I bite my lip and murmur, "Another fun fact? Showering together conserves water. Wanna be environmentally friendly with me?"

Zeke's blue eyes sparkle. "I thought you'd never ask."

# EIGHTEEN

## DELIVERY

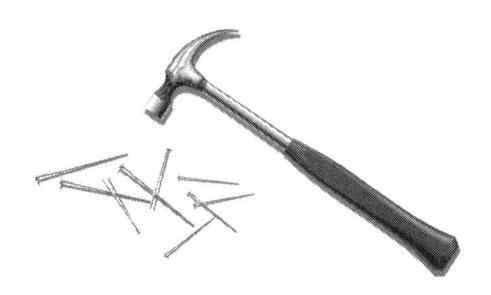

## ZEKE

IN BETWEEN THE POP FROM the nail gun, I hear a few whistles and catcalls from across the yard. Some unsuspecting woman must be strutting by, and the guys are taking notice. I roll my eyes at their predictable antics—playing into the douchey construction-worker role perfectly. I'm about to yell at them for being immature assholes when her voice rings out.

"Is Zeke around?"

My task is immediately forgotten, and I'm hustling across the grounds to where Delilah stands. It's no fucking wonder the crew is all worked up—she's wearing next to nothing. With her hair twisted into a bun, I get an eyeful of tan skin from every direction. Her toned legs are on full display in a tiny pair of cutoffs. The strapless crop-top leaves little to the imagination. A Hooters server would be considered modest in comparison. On any given day, Delilah is any man's walking wet dream. But looking like this? She just dropped fresh meat into a rabid bear den.

*Dammit.*

I'm ready to tear the limbs off each gawker. These wankers don't stand a chance and need to back the fuck up. Every piece of her fine ass belongs to me. But then Delilah raises her gaze and meets mine. She's beaming at me, a blinding smile stretching over her face. The fury in my blood cools as I get lost in her green eyes. Delilah makes me feel like I'm floating.

The spell is broken when Kayne moves a little too close. I plow forward, prepared to steamroll everyone in my path.

"Get back to work," I growl at her audience of admirers.

Lewis is in the front of the pack, go fucking figure. His shit-eating grin has my molars grinding. "Zeke, my man. Where've you been hiding this gorgeous honey?"

Delilah bites her lip, trying to trap a laugh. I find no humor in this, at all.

I crowd his space while he stokes my temper. "Remember when I said don't talk about her like that?"

Lewis nods toward Delilah, apparently connecting the dots. "Ah, is this *the one*?"

"Who the fuck else would she be?"

He holds up his palms. "Got it, loud and clear."

I focus on my girl, trying to forget anyone else exists. "Hey, Trip. This is an unexpected visit."

Her delicate fingers walk up my rigid arm. "Hi, Zee. Good, because I wanted to surprise you."

Lewis whistles. "Oh, shit. This is serious."

"I told you to get lost." I manage to keep my tone level.

He chuckles, hitching a thumb my way while speaking to Delilah. "He's all bark and no bite. I've made it my job to test his limits. So far, I'm still unharmed."

She giggles. "Good to know Zeke has someone watching out for him."

A rumble builds in my chest. "Enough chit-chat." I glower at Lewis.

He winks at Delilah, begging for an ambulance ride. "It's been a pleasure making your acquaintance. Or whatever this was. I'd say Zeke is in good hands with you." Lewis wags his brows at me before wandering off.

I tug Delilah close in an attempt to shield her from the prying glances. I steer us to a shady corner of the lot that's relatively abandoned.

"He seems . . . nice," Delilah comments.

I ignore her assessment. "Are you trying to get me arrested?"

Her forehead pinches. "What are you talking about?"

"Couldn't you have covered up a little more?"

She looks down, inspecting her lack of attire. "With what?"

"Maybe a parka?"

Delilah huffs while fanning her face. "Zee, it's over ninety degrees and midday. You're lucky I'm wearing any clothes at this point."

"I want to bash in all their faces just for seeing you like this. You've turned them into a bunch of slobbering idiots," I mutter.

"Are you jealous?"

"Extremely," I admit without hesitation.

"I like you all growly and possessive," she purrs against my jaw.

"You're testing my control, Trip."

Her hand drifts up and settles against my neck. "Hmm, and you're sexy."

My cock twitches, and I grunt. "Better be careful. I'm a few seconds away from tossing you over my shoulder and finding the nearest flat surface."

"Hmm, that sounds super-hot."

I cough into my fist. "Why are you teasing a starving man?"

Delilah crosses her arms. "Hardly. We had sex twice last night."

I drag her in by a belt loop. "That was too long ago."

She nibbles on my chin. "Guess we know what's happening later."

"Why wait?"

I back Delilah against the equipment trailer, looking over my shoulder to make sure no one is watching. My hand roams under the indecent hem of her shorts. I grip her bare ass with purpose and yank her into me. She gasps when I grind my dick against her.

"Easy access, huh?" I mumble along her temple.

"You could say that," she wheezes on an exhale.

"I'm on the fucking clock with a raging hard-on. Was this what you wanted?" I ask and rotate my hips, letting her feel exactly what she's doing to me.

Delilah moans and claws at my hair. "That wasn't my original intention."

"Oh, no? What was it, then?" I demand before kissing her throat.

"Uhhh," she pants. Her head lolls to the side, offering me more for the taking.

I greedily suck along her sweet neck, happy to oblige. "Trip? Why'd you stop by?" I murmur.

Delilah chokes on a groan. "I wanted to bring a little something for your boss and the others."

That cools my jets and I pull away to study her face. "And what exactly are you giving them?"

She smacks my abdomen. "Nothing like that. Jeez."

"I'd fucking hope not."

Delilah laughs, but the sound trails off when she sees my serious expression. "What's wrong?"

"I don't wanna share your attention."

She scoffs. "Puh-lease, I'm only dropping off cookies. If anyone is being passed around, it's Raven," she whispers out the side of her mouth, "Don't tell Trey."

"Why did you wanna do that for them?"

"As a thank-you?" She looks sheepish, and the blush coloring her cheeks is adorable.

I stroke a finger down her flushing skin. "You're too much. They'll appreciate it, though. Probably want to eat *you* up too while they're at it."

Before she can comment further, Devon calls out from behind us. "Hey, Zeke?"

With a groan, I release my hold on Delilah's ass and take a step back. "Yeah, boss?"

"I heard you were hiding someone out here." He strolls over, officially putting an end to my private party with Delilah.

I huddle her toward me. "We just wanted a moment of alone time."

He sticks out his hand to Delilah. "Hey, there. I'm Devon. It's nice to meet you."

She slips her palm into his for a quick shake. "My name is Delilah—"

Devon cuts in. "Oh, you need no introduction. This one doesn't stop blabbering on about you."

I almost laugh at that pile of bullshit. I rarely say more than a few words in any given conversation. Unless I'm talking to Delilah. She's a different story. An extra wide smile stretches her lips, and I decide to keep the truth locked up indefinitely.

"Oh, really?" she asks with a quirked brow.

I offer a shrug. Devon snorts, no doubt knowing how hard I'm biting my tongue. Delilah looks between us, most likely trying to figure out the silent exchange.

He claps and takes a step back. "Anyway, I didn't mean to interrupt. Just wanted to say hello."

"Oh, you don't have to go. I can't stay much longer and actually have something for you," she tells him.

"Wasn't expecting that," he muses. "Whatcha got for me?"

Delilah holds up a finger. "I'll be right back."

As she's dashing off to her car, Devon makes a noise of appreciation. "You've got quite a catch there, Zeke."

"Don't I fucking know it."

"Better hold on tight and never let go."

"Planning on it," I reply.

He nods. "Good thing you came back to Garden Grove, huh?"

I grunt. "Yeah, yeah. Gloat all you want. This was a great choice, and you won't hear me complaining."

"Damn fucking straight. Always remember the boss knows best."

Delilah is heading our way and walking far too fast. Her tits are swaying with the rapid steps and a nip-slip is a serious possibility. I groan while fighting the urge to cover Devon's eyes. At least the container she's carrying covers most of her torso.

"Here you go," she says and passes him the white box.

He shakes it and asks, "What could this be?"

She laughs. "Nothing too special. Just some dessert from my shop, Jitters. My friend is a baker and makes everything from scratch. I wanted to say thanks for all you've done."

"I didn't know fixing up this bar was cause for receiving treats," he jokes.

Delilah glances at me. "I don't really care about what happens with Roosters."

The grin I offer in response can be seen from two counties over. This girl gets to me.

"Good answer," Devon says. He lifts the cardboard flap and peeks inside. "If I wasn't already convinced, this seals the deal. This woman is a keeper, Zeke."

"Thanks for the approval," I say with sarcasm thick in my voice.

"I like you," Delilah tells him.

"That's nice to hear because I hold a lot of weight in decision-making." He rocks back on his heels, sending me a smirk.

I grunt. "Is that so?"

Devon rolls his shoulders. "You wanna steal him away, right?

I can already tell how this will go."

Delilah looks like she's been caught robbing a bank. "Um, well, we haven't talked that much about it," she mumbles. Her pleading gaze swings to me, begging for a rescue. I'm just as caught off guard and not much help.

Devon hoots. "You kids. So in love. It will be a challenge to keep you two apart. The struggle might as well be painted across your shirt. There's plenty of time before decisions need to be made. I'm sure we can work something out," he says to me with a slap on the back.

I feel like wiping my brow in relief. He just saved me the trouble of having to bring up quitting. There's no way I'm leaving Delilah when the job is done.

"Thanks, boss. You're a lifesaver," I say and truly mean it. Devon has done so much for me, and letting me off the hook easy is another item on the list.

He drums his fingers on the box. "Just doing my job, same as you." With that, he gives us a salute and walks off.

It feels easier to breathe, a cinder block lifting off my chest. We don't need more obstacles in our path, and this was a big hurdle to clear. Our outlook should be smooth sailing from now on. I move closer to Delilah, linking our fingers tight. "Let's have some carefree fun this weekend. Like the old days."

She tilts her head, giving me a shy smile. "There're so many options. What do you have in mind?"

"I miss taking you out for ice cream. And picking fresh blueberries. We need to visit that abandoned red barn off I-65. Maybe have dinner at Mel's and sit on the patio. We can sit on the same side of a booth."

"I'd love to do all of that, Zee." Delilah's soft lilt wraps around my heart, and I tug her against me.

"There's so much to miss, but not anymore. We'll do everything together again."

"That's all I've ever wanted," she whispers. Delilah tilts her chin up, and I answer with a kiss.

I pull away and lightly spank her. "Now get your sexy ass home and put on some snow pants or a trench coat."

She licks her lips. "Isn't your lunch break starting soon? Maybe you should help me pick out something *more appropriate*."

I prowl forward with a growl and she turns away with a playful squeal. I scoop her into my arms and jog to her car. "We've got thirty minutes. Better make it count."

# NINETEEN

## ROOMIES

## DELILAH

ADDISON TOPS OFF MY WINE, pouring too much so the red liquid almost overflows. She doesn't seem to notice since her laser-focus is set on Raven's full glass. We all have a mutual appreciation for booze, but Addy is being extra pushy tonight.

As if to confirm my suspicion, she snaps, "Do you see a problem with this bottle?" She jostles it in front of us. We don't dare respond. "It isn't empty yet," Addison bites out.

I grimace at her snarky tone while Raven snatches her own cup and takes a healthy gulp.

"Didn't mean to piss you off. I'm not much of a wine-drinker," Raven murmurs.

"I have vodka in the freezer," Addison says and blindly gestures toward the kitchen.

Raven glances at me, and I shrug.

"It's Wednesday," she tells our fiery friend.

"So?"

My gaze ping-pongs between them, and I choose to remain

silent. They're capable of working this out, right?

"I have to get up early," Raven replies.

"That's a convenient excuse. Just toss the cakes in the oven and go back to bed," Addison suggests.

I hold up my hands, calling a timeout. "What the hell, Addy?"

"Not sure what you mean."

I raise my brows. "Your panties are in a seriously tight wad."

She settles back on the couch with a groan, tugging fistfuls of red hair in the process. "I'm an effing mess. Sorry for being a bitch," she whispers and looks between us.

"Oh, please. Like you have to apologize. We've been there." I rub her shoulder.

Raven nods. "Yeah, we wouldn't be women without mood swings. But what's the issue?"

Addison glares at the ceiling. "Where to begin? Dagos has been a madhouse with summer traffic. Shane keeps blowing me off. I got my period yesterday. And most recently, Tania told me she's moving out."

I wince at her itemized list. "Yikes, that's rough. What can we do to help?"

She blows out a frustrated breath. "I thought getting drunk sounded like a good idea."

"But the headache tomorrow will bring it all back," I point out.

"Ugh, you're being too logical."

"I'll be here all night." I laugh.

She sniffs. "I'll be all alone in this empty space soon."

I look around, trying to analyze the area from an outside perspective. The loft has an open concept layout with a ton of natural light. Addison has made sure every spot measures up to Pinterest perfection. She has at least ten inspiration boards dedicated to home decor. It's trendy-chic and screams of her personal style. She loves candles, and this week it smells like a tropical vacation. I'm not sure what Tania has contributed, but it can't be much.

I clear my throat. "Before Tania, you lived with Gia. This is clearly your place, Addy. Maybe you'd prefer having the place to yourself."

She sighs. "I enjoy having company."

"In that case, you have an adorable apartment right off Main Street. It won't be difficult to find someone," I tell her.

"But what if I don't like them?" There's a slight edge to her voice and I push the bottle closer. Addison laughs and gives herself a refill.

"You're a mess, love. Can't seem to make up your mind, huh?" I murmur and she nods.

"Do you need a roommate immediately? Or can you get by without one?" Raven asks.

Addison's hand seesaws back and forth. "It's tough to say. I could probably make due if needed. Splitting the bills in two is always nice, though."

Raven plops down on the couch. "Where's Tania going?"

Addison huffs. "Her boyfriend is finally ready to settle down so they're getting a place together."

"Well, that's great for her. She's been waiting for him to pull the trigger forever," I say.

"Yeah, I guess," she mutters.

"I feel like we're missing something. You're not happy for her?"

Addison tosses her hands up. "That's not it. I'm glad she's moving on and getting a happy ending. But now I have to search for a new roomie. Tania was low maintenance and really helpful. It's difficult finding that balanced relationship. Living with someone is so personal."

"Tell that to the residents of New York City," Raven mumbles. We turn and gape at her. "What? My mom and I stayed there for a few months while she dated some random dude. It's madness."

"Really?" I prop my foot on the coffee table.

Raven continues with, "It's crazy expensive. You can't find a spot to rent in the worst areas of the city. Get this—we found cockroaches in the shower one night."

I gasp. "Oh my gosh. That's so gross."

Addison gags. "I can't imagine my reaction to that."

Raven cringes. "Yep, it was bad. I couldn't fall asleep without picturing them crawling all over me. I'd fly out of bed screaming. We didn't stick around much longer after that." She shudders. "So yeah, no one can afford to be picky in the slightest. You'd have people lined around the block at a crack to live here with you."

"Never pegged you for a city girl," I say.

"I'm far from it. Not sure I ever belonged there. Don't get me wrong, it's a total trip with a lot of fantastic culture. It just wasn't meant for me."

I wrinkle my nose. "Yeah, I'll pass. It would be great for a vacation, but I couldn't hack it long term. That sounds like a constant ball of stress. Jeez, we're complaining about our shops being busy in our tiny town during summer. Could you imagine working in downtown metropolis? With the potential of roach infestation?"

"Not even a little bit," Addison says softly.

"Been there, done that," Raven adds.

Addison hums. "Either way, we're far from the Big Apple. The renter's market in Garden Grove is not stellar. I might be roomie-less for months. It's better than bugs, though."

Raven taps her chin. "Trey told me Shane is on the hunt. Something about his landlord being a dick. Blah, blah. I wasn't really listening, but maybe you should offer to let him move in."

Addison chokes on her mouthful of wine. "Great plan. I'll merge two of my problems into a bigger one."

"Shane has shown interest. What's the issue lately?" I ask.

"Lord only knows. He has great boyfriend potential, but damn. I've tried making it pretty obvious that I like him. He either doesn't get it or the feeling isn't mutual. I cannot wait around forever.

My lady bits are neglected as it is."

"Maybe this arrangement wouldn't be the worst thing," I press.

Addison squints at me. "I dunno. I've never lived with a guy, not to mention one I'm interested in. Do you think rooming with a man could work? If we're just friends?"

I think about her question for a moment. "I don't have experience with that, either. The boys in our dorm don't count."

"Don't look at me," Raven says. "Until Trey, the only guys I stayed with were my mom's boyfriends. I prefer to leave that part of history forgotten."

"Maybe this is a positive alternative. It might end up being the best of both worlds," I say.

Addison scoffs. "Doubtful. I'm not sure it's even an idea to entertain."

"Why not?" Raven asks.

"Because I like him, and he clearly doesn't care one way or another. Being around him constantly would be terrible," she grumbles.

I lift my chin, assessing her somber expression. "Really? I feel like the more you're exposed to him, the easier it would be to move on. You'll learn all about his worst habits and be totally turned off."

Addison waves me off. "Let's put a pin in this hairbrained idea." She takes a sip of wine. "Tell us what's new with Zeke."

"Oooh, yeah. I want some juicy updates," Raven joins in.

I bite my lip. "We've been having a lot of fun together."

Raven winks suggestively. "Guess you're outta that funk."

"You could say that."

"Is getting it on the regular fantastic or what?"

"Big time. Zeke can play my body like a perfectly tuned guitar. I've really missed having sex."

Addison's brow furrows. "Uh, okay? It hasn't been that long, right?"

I feel my cheeks burn but decide to hell with it. "Well, five years until like . . . ten days ago. But who's counting, right?"

Raven sputters. "W-what?"

I cluck my tongue. "I've always talked a big game, but it's bullshit. There's only been Zeke for me."

They're wearing matching expressions—hanging jaws and wide eyes. Addison chokes out a cough. "No shit? Wow."

"Uh huh. Zeke is on a mission to recreate some of our favorite teenage memories."

"Oh, no." Addison groans and covers her ears.

I toss a pillow at her. "Get your mind out of the gutter. It isn't all sexual."

She snorts. "Yeah, right."

I roll my eyes. "Whatever. Last weekend we picked fresh fruit, went kayaking, ate at our favorite diner, and made a bonfire. It was lovely."

They simultaneously exhale, long and whimsical. Addison rests her chin on a fist and says, "Lucky duck."

I giggle and my heart skips a beat thinking of him. "It's pretty damn romantic, if I do say so myself."

"I'd second that," Addison answers.

"Guess you're falling into old habits, easy peasy," Raven comments.

I smile, liking the sound of that. "Yeah, I suppose."

"I'm really happy for you, D. I know how much you've missed him," comes from Addison.

Raven leans in. "Are you sure he's going to stay in Garden Grove?"

I bob my head. "His boss was pretty reasonable last week when I stopped by the Roosters site. I think there's a decent possibility Zeke can stay without much trouble.

"How big of a chance?" Addison asks.

I take a healthy gulp of wine. "Enough that I'm not worrying about it right now. More of a cross that bridge when we get there sort of thing."

They both look at me, nodding their heads.

Raven says, "Good plan. Either way, there's a ton of building left to do."

Addison's eyes light up. "Oooh, speaking of the construction zone, were there hot guys everywhere? I haven't gone to inspect their work, if you know what I mean."

We all laugh at that.

"Who knows? All I see is Zeke," I tell her honestly.

Addison groans. "I'm jealous of all the magic you two are getting."

I give her a hug. "You'll find someone special if he isn't already around."

"Wish he'd hurry up," she gripes.

Raven bounces in her seat. "I have a great idea. Let's all go out dancing. Maybe to Cyclone? It's been ages since we've been there."

Addison makes an approving noise. "That could be interesting."

"It's a magical place." Raven sighs.

"Uh huh. We all have memories there," Addison says.

I bump my shoulder into hers. "Shane joined us last time."

"Precisely," she adds.

Raven taps on her phone before saying, "How about next Saturday? Looks like they have a band lined up. Guaranteed to be a fun time."

"And live music always draws a crowd. Maybe I can finally meet someone interested in me," Addison murmurs.

"This will take your mind off that laundry list of worries." I inject my voice with plenty of fluff.

She narrows her eyes at me. "I'll believe that when it happens."

"I'll hire a stripper if that'll make you smile," Raven suggests.

Addison's mouth curves slightly. "I might be desperate, but

there's a limit."

"I've got it!" I say. "Let's call Sam Walker."

The mention of Addison's high-school crush lifts her lips into a huge grin. "Yes, now we're talking. Do you think he has the same number?"

We all break out in a fit of giggles and open another bottle of wine. Cheers to all the second chances, right?

# TWENTY

## YOURS

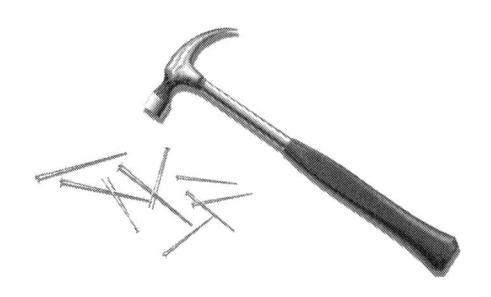

## ZEKE

THE MUTED LIGHTING IN THE restaurant offers subtle hints at some of Delilah's most tantalizing features. The dip of her cleavage. The slender column of her neck. The slight blush rising in her cheeks. I've just inhaled my steak dinner, but lust and desire for this woman still have me starving. I'm a fucking ravenous fiend for her, as always.

My muscles are tense while we wait for the check. Lava pools in my gut when Delilah nibbles on her bottom lip, peeking up at me through thick lashes. The shy smile she shoots across the table has me more than ready to get the hell out of here. If we hurry, I can be balls-deep in less than five minutes.

Delilah pats her flat stomach. "I'm so full. I couldn't eat another bite." The moan she tacks on eliminates any chance of lowering my erection, no matter how hard I think of puppies or grandmas. But her clean plate could work in my favor.

"So, no ice cream then?" I'm preparing to jump from my seat

upon her giving the all-clear.

She twists her mouth. "Let's not be too hasty. There's always space for ice cream."

My appetite for her grumbles a wordless curse, but I can be patient. At least, I think I can. I reach for her hand and press our palms flat together. "I've missed your sweet-tooth."

"Oh, yeah?" My gaze heats when she leans in and murmurs, "Why's that?"

"Dessert in the most important meal," I say. "It should always be . . . *savored*."

Delilah visibly shivers. "Maybe we should skip Cookies & Cream tonight."

I shake my head. "Let's share a cone. Whatever we don't finish, I'll lick off your skin."

"O-okay," she agrees.

As we exit the booth, I wrap an arm around her. "I'm going to tear your panties off with my teeth," I whisper. "I'll be enjoying a triple-scoop serving of you *real soon*."

Delilah stumbles against me. "Do we have to wait?" There's a slight whine in her voice.

"Delayed gratification, Trip," I murmur. And don't I fucking know it.

We cross the road toward Moo-Scoop, intertwined and huddling close. To anyone watching, there's no denying our late-evening plans. My chest threatens to crack open so all the pure joy can spill out. How is this my life?

I'm about to nibble along Delilah's neck when a pair of familiar faces appear in front of us. We freeze on the sidewalk as her parents move closer, wearing matching grins. My gaze bounces from Delilah to their welcoming expressions. For future reference, this is the ultimate boner-killer. It's a tad jarring going from extremely turned on to shutting down those thoughts entirely. Somehow, I manage to keep my shit together—at least I hope so.

"Well, well. If this isn't a blast from the past," her mother titters.

"Hello, Mrs. Sage," I greet, then hold a hand out to her father. "Mr. Sage."

"Oh, don't start with that nonsense, Zeke," her mother replies. "You should know better. We'll always be Sallie and Bill to you."

I smile at the sentiment and warmth roams up my neck. "If you insist."

They haven't changed much since I last saw them. Sallie's blonde hair has a bit more grey in it. Bill's stomach extends a tad further past his waist. But overall, they're the same loving people who helped me survive my teenage years.

As if hearing my thoughts, Sallie pats my jaw. "You'll always be like family."

Delilah hums in agreement. "That's very true."

"Are we turning back time?" Bill says and juts his chin toward the parlor.

I nod. "Something like that."

"Marlene keeps us informed on the Roosters' renovation. How's the building coming along this week?" Sallie asks.

Delilah groans at the mention of the gossip's name. I chuckle at her reaction.

"Oh, Delilah. She isn't so bad. If it wasn't for Marlene and Betty, we'd all be left in the dark," her mother scolds.

"Pretty sure we'd survive," Delilah replies.

"Think of how boring Garden Grove would be without those ladies. But when Marlene stirs up trouble, put your foot down," Sallie instructs.

"I've tried that," Delilah says.

Her mother tsks. "Be the bigger person."

I circle us back to Sallie's question. "The Roosters' rebuild is going well. Construction is on schedule, but there's been a few hiccups. We're currently framing the place."

Delilah's parents hum in understanding. Bill says, "I've driven by a time or two. Seems to be a lot of men working on the project."

I take a moment to think of how many we are. "Yeah, there's around twenty-five total. But that includes the specialties who only stick around for their portion. Devon employs ten of us year-round." I squeeze Delilah tighter when her body locks up. Before I can comment on it, Sallie speaks up.

"So, you're like Mr. Fix-It?"

I laugh, rocking on my heels. "I'd like to consider my skills a tad more primed than a regular handyman, but sure. I'm definitely capable of household repairs."

"He's quick too," Delilah chimes in. "My shelf broke at Jitters and he showed up thirty minutes later. Excellent customer service."

I snort and pinch her side. She yelps and retaliates, tickling my stomach. We exchange counter-attacks until someone clears their throat. Delilah straightens against me while I tuck my hands away. Her parents smile at us knowingly.

"Just like the old days," Bill says.

Sallie's jade eyes sparkle. "Exactly. And you're off the hook with Zeke around. He's taking over Delilah's repairs," she tells her husband.

Bill scrubs over his forehead with a chuckle. "Fine by me. I'm willing to bet you're far more capable with a hammer." I wave him off but know that's true. He gets credit for trying, but his craftsmanship always needed fine-tuning.

"Where are you living?" Sallie asks.

The truth is I've been shacking up with Delilah for several weeks, but they don't need to know that. "The crew is staying at The Mossy Den," I tell them instead. A slight omission won't hurt, right?

Delilah giggles, and her parents raise their brows. She gives me a side-eye and scratches her temple. "Oh-uh, have you seen that resort lately? Those cabins haven't improved, that's for sure. 1970 called and wants their shag carpet back."

Sallie cringes. "I was afraid of that. Maybe you can fix those up next, Zeke."

I rub the back of my neck. "Ah, maybe. Not sure what I'll be doing after this. Roosters will take months to finish, so there's no rush."

Bill nods. "Right. You're still young with plenty of options."

Sallie elbows him and huffs. "Anyway, you two need to join us for dinner sometime. I'll make lasagna. We need to catch up." She points at both of us.

The thought of facing my father's house is daunting, but I'd also love to revisit Delilah's childhood home. There are a lot of great memories in there. I tip my chin, looking into her gleaming greens, and find the answer. "We'd love to," I say.

"Oh, good. It'll be nice to enjoy a meal together," Sallie chirps.

Bill loops his arm around her shoulder. "We won't keep you. I'm sure you've got something far more exciting to do than stand on Main Street chatting with us."

We exchange hugs and a few more pleasantries before they wander off. Delilah sighs and links our fingers, tugging lightly. "They've missed you."

I kiss her forehead, my lips curling with glee. "I'm glad we bumped into them. Even if that was worse than a cold bucket of water dumping over me."

She gives me an exaggerated pout. "Are you chilly?"

"You can easily get me hot. There's no doubt about it."

Her free hand wanders until she's toying with the ends of my hair. "I think ice cream can wait."

I erase the space between us, my pulse already pumping faster. "Is that so?"

Delilah nods and leans up to whisper, "Absolutely."

With those words, I'm on the move and practically dragging her behind me. She giggles, and I pull harder. "I'm not getting enough urgency from you, Trip."

"Your stride is double mine. At this pace, I'll have to run to catch up."

I lead her around the building toward the staircase. "Ladies first," I purr.

Delilah's voice is all sass when she says, "Aren't you sweet."

"Trust me, this is one hundred percent for my benefit," I groan as she begins her ascend. My shorts get uncomfortably tight while more blood rushes south. I grasp her succulent ass, gripping and releasing with each slow step she takes.

She glances at me over her shoulder. "Keep doing that and we'll never make it inside."

I make a show of studying the empty alley to our left. "Nobody is around . . . yet."

Delilah shakes her head while rushing to the door. While she's opening the lock, my mouth gently assaults her neck. I suck and lick down her nape until she's melting against me.

"I love you, Trip," I murmur softly.

She sighs. "And I love you."

"I'm going to show you how much. Right now," I say and band my arms around her waist.

We step inside, her back to my front, walking as one. My fingers roam her sides, lightly brushing over her tits, and she's pushing forward for more.

"Don't worry, baby. I'll give you everything."

"Hurry," she whimpers. "It feels like this entire evening has been foreplay."

My palm slides across her stomach and cups her center, applying slight pressure.

"O-ohhh," Delilah moans.

"We're just getting started," I whisper along her jaw.

I guide us toward the bedroom, spinning her around before she touches the comforter. My thumb swipes strands of blonde from her eyes, and I bend closer. I'm no longer in a hurry, deciding to savor every moment. Our noses meet, gliding together in a different type of kiss, but just as powerful.

"You're gorgeous, Trip. My beautiful girl," I breathe across her blushing skin. My mouth seals over hers, locking us in a passionate embrace. I glide my tongue along the seam of her lips, and she opens for me with a whimper. I taste the essence that is purely Delilah. She's sugar-sweet and mine for the taking. Her chin lifts while I tilt my head, finding the perfect angle to bring us closer. Her nails spear into my scalp, the sharp tug pulling me under. I'm already lost in her, and this is only a kiss. We exchange air, my exhale becoming her inhale. I'm dizzy and high off her breath, but the cravings are never sated.

Delilah clings to me, her legs restless against mine. I could indulge on her mouth for hours without getting full, but my girl wants more. I break away slowly, sipping from her lips a bit longer. Lowering to my knees, I prepare to shower every inch of her with love.

I lift her dainty foot and rest the sole on my pec. "You're my forever." I place a delicate kiss on her ankle. "My always." My lips drift to her calf. "My future." I suck across her knee. "My happily ever after." I nuzzle her inner thigh. "My fairy tale ending." My mouth traces further up. "My existence." My touch lingers near her apex, pressing several kisses there. "Did I miss any?" I ask while lowering her leg.

Delilah stares down at me with tears swimming in her eyes. She cradles my jaw, and I lean into her warmth. "How about my one and only?"

I kiss her wrist. "That's an important one." My fingers reach under her skirt, lifting and seeking. "Have I told you lately how amazing sundresses are?"

She smirks. "You've mentioned it a time or two, in these situations."

I ease the hem over her ass and don't stop until the fabric is in a heap on the floor. For a moment, I silently admire her freshly exposed skin. Only a pink satin bra and matching panties cover Delilah's most intimate areas. After getting my visual fill, I continue on my journey, mapping out a few landmarks. Like the thin scar on her hip. The flat mole on her lower belly. A patch of freckles along her ribs that have faded over the years.

"Your skin is so soft, Trip. I hadn't felt velvet and satin against my palm for years. I never want to go without again." My voice is a plea as though she might vanish without a trace.

Delilah's fingers comb my hair. "You'll never have to, Zee."

I hug her middle, my ear nestling between her breasts. A strong and sure beat greets me, proving she's here with me. I want her with every cell of my being, but it's more than physical need. Devouring her body constantly consumes my thoughts, but worshipping her heart and mind are more vital. Delilah is my entire world, spinning on her own axis around me. I'm blessed to be in the same universe.

My cock twitches, signaling the incessant desire threatening to overtake me. I've kept us waiting long enough. True to my earlier words, I bite the silky edge of her panties. "Time for my dessert, baby."

# TWENTY-ONE

## LOVE

## DELILAH

I SHIVER AT ZEKE'S WORDS, my skin pebbling from the inferno blazing inside of me. He slowly drags my panties down and off, tossing the scrap of material over his shoulder. My grip on his hair tightens while I attempt to remain standing. My knees are ready to buckle under his sensual touch. Those skilled fingers skim up my legs, grazing over my ass and drifting along my back. He unhooks my bra with practiced precision, the clasp giving way without a fight. Zeke's blue eyes are liquid fire while he studies me, bare and exposed before him.

"Get on the bed." The command is a quiet growl, one I don't care to disobey.

I scurry onto the mattress, lying down while my lower belly tightens. I dig my fingers into the sheets, desperate for an anchor until he's with me. The sound of Zeke's belt and zipper makes me pant. He's standing at my feet like a marble statue, clad only in a tight pair of briefs. The sight of his enormous erection tenting the stretchy material is enough to have drool dribbling from my lips. I suck in sharply as my muscles quiver.

Zeke's gaze rakes over me with the patience of a trained hunter, taking time to explore every inch of my body. I feel like a feast he's about to consume. I spread my legs wider in invitation. He prowls closer, like a predator stalking his prey. I'll gladly let him eat me up.

"You want me, baby?" he rasps against my inner thigh.

"S-so much," I stammer as his touch wanders higher.

"Christ, I've missed you," Zeke groans. His finger traces my slit, and I gasp. "And you've missed me." There's no question in his tone.

"Yes," I confirm anyway. There's no denying how wet I am for him.

Zeke abandons my center, lazily moving along my squirming form, our skin sliding together. I arch up, his light dusting of chest hair tickling me. His mouth crashes onto mine, our tongues swirling in a twisted connection. My toes curl into the blanket before I edge them up his calves. He pulls away, tugging my bottom lip between his teeth.

"Where do you want me?" Zeke whispers against my raised chin. He exhales along my jaw, drawing my earlobe into his mouth. "Here?" I shudder at the hoarse tinge in his voice. Before I can answer, Zeke's lips are trailing down my neck and he nips at my collarbone. He licks my nipples, spoiling the tips with suction that has me clawing at his shoulders. "Or here?"

I moan and tug him closer, begging for more. "Please, Zee. Yes, yes."

My urging does the trick, and his hands slide down my sides. A coarse palm grazes against my lower belly, two fingers drifting lower. Zeke flicks my clit, and I jolt abruptly. His chuckle is dark and whooshes over my hyper-aware skin.

"Definitely here." His touch lowers until he's circling my entrance. "And here."

Feverish lust pounds in my core, and I'm not sure how much more of his teasing I can handle. "Y-yes, please." I already sound like a broken record.

Zeke blows across and around my waiting pussy, the whisper of air sparking an uncontrollable fever. My hips buck as I search for more. His rough palms scrape along my sensitive thighs, spreading me open wide for the taking. Without warning, he latches onto my clit and sucks *hard*.

"Holy fuck," I shriek and reach for his head. My nails scratch against his scalp, and he moans into me. The vibrations send me higher, the tingling of release already looming above me. I'm having difficulty keeping my eyes focused, everything is spinning against the onslaught. He presses a single digit into me, and the pleasure ratchets to "O-ohh, I'm almost there." The wail wheezes from my throat as I bend further toward him. Zeke pumps his finger in and out while attacking my clit with lashing licks. My hands go a bit numb and fire explodes from the very core of me. Prickles race along my legs while I wrap around him, never wanting this euphoria to end.

The waves crash over me, and I'm mewling, pleading for more but unable to handle another ripple. My chest rises and falls at an alarming rate as I step back from the peak. His tongue is giving gentle swipes to my slit while the aftershocks twitch through me.

Zeke props up on an elbow, shooting me a devilish smirk. "That might be a record." His voice is all cocky confidence and I swoon at the sound.

I bite my lip and nod. "You're a pro."

"Don't mind hearing that."

"Show me what else you've got," I murmur with my best come-hither expression.

Zeke sits back on his ankles and shows off the stacks of muscles lining his abdomen. I want to sink my teeth into his juicy flesh, but there's no time for that now. He hooks into the elastic of his briefs, shoving them down quickly. I swallow audibly as his dick bounces free.

*Good Lord, how does he fit?*

He settles on top of me, joining our lower halves in the most erotic way. Zeke enters me in a slow slide, taking his time to enjoy the snug pressure. We moan in unison, reveling in the feel of becoming one. He's so fucking big, it's still a shock after going too long without him. His hand searches for mine, and he glides our palms together. I sigh at the intimacy blanketing us.

"I'll never get used to this," Zeke whispers against my lips.

I kiss him softly. "Me neither."

His movements are languid and smooth. There's no hurry in this act. Our hips bump in an easy sway before rocking apart. I contract around him on each withdrawal, and he pushes deeper in response. He tweaks my nipples, tugging the peaks just right. Another orgasm flickers in the distance, taunting me to move faster, but I can't quite get there. There is too much emotion clogging my brain when he makes love to me this way.

My fingers trace along the familiar scars on his arm, new lines crossing the old. The messy pattern speaking of his painful history. My touch bumps along the raised edges, and Zeke grunts. I'm familiar with his torment and understand what he needs in this moment. I bend and replace each mark with a kiss.

Zeke sighs in relief. "I love you, Trip."

"I love you too."

He stills inside of me, leaning down to seal our mouths together. "How is it possible to love a person this much?"

"Because we were made for each other?" I swivel my pelvis. Zeke meets my request with several teasing strokes, never touching that spot I need.

"This is all so romantic," I murmur while he gently palms my breast. Zeke hums along my throat, and his cock finds purchase on the pleasure button that makes my eyes cross. "Right there," I encourage.

"I know what you need, baby. But building you up slowly makes it better."

"You're being so sweet," I purr.

"I bottled up the soft side for too long. Now it's pouring out."

My fingers wrap around his nape. "I don't mind the overflow. I love sex with you in every position. But changing it up mid-scene is always . . . *hot*," I whisper along his jaw.

Something ignites in Zeke's blue gaze, searing into me. I've flipped a switch inside of him, and a thrill zings through me. I involuntarily tighten around his thrusting dick, and he hisses.

"The lady gets what she wants," he says and pulls away to sit up. His hands grip the back of my knees, pushing up and out. My muscles stretch and burn from the position, but I'd never complain. I curve my spine, sending my breasts toward him. Zeke pistons in and out, his pace picking up speed with each drive. He powers forward and grinds against my clit, zapping me with a surge of electrical current.

He watches his cock enter me, groaning with each erotic shift. "You're so fucking sexy, baby."

I stare at his flexing biceps as he holds me in place. "I have the better view," I say on a breathy exhale.

"Agree to disagree," he growls with a hard thrust.

Zeke is so in tune with my body and every forceful plunge rockets me closer to the promised land. When his breathing picks up, I know he's getting more turned on. When he hits just the right spot, my back arches higher, seeking and reaching another hit of blissful pleasure.

"Flip over," Zeke suddenly rumbles.

My belly swoops at the demand, and I'm eager to follow his wishes. He guides me onto my hands and knees, pressing and lifting until I'm positioned to his liking. My shoulders are brushing against the mattress as I settle in. I raise my ass higher, and he tugs until our hips are notched together. There's no warning when he rams into me, not that I need it. I'm plenty primed and hovering over the breaking point.

Zeke doesn't ask permission with his next move—I wouldn't want him to. He understands what I need without me saying a word. His thumb slides along my crack, teasing and playing. He explores that forbidden area like so many times before. I squirm when he sucks that digit into his mouth and returns it to my puckered hole, rimming the edge. His strokes in and out of my pussy become lazy while he toys with my ass.

My moan is indecent when he sinks in, stretching me further. I'm so much fuller this way, and the pressure is more intense. Zeke presses deeper before dragging out, setting a slow rhythm. The addition of his finger heightens my pleasure tenfold. I get loopy off his touch, the way he worships my entire body.

"I won't last much longer like this," he whispers.

"Me either . . ." I wheeze.

"You've missed me back here, Trip."

I nod wildly, my hair whipping around me. "So much."

"You're starving for it." He groans and wiggles his finger further in.

"Uh-huh," I mumble incoherently.

I push my knees wider, lowering myself to get a better angle. Zeke shoves in without hesitation, taking advantage of what I'm offering. He invades and owns every part of my body. I'm soaring and sailing without a thought of anything else. All I feel is Zeke surrounding me.

Zeke's free hand delves between my legs, finding my clit. He's a master craftsman with those talented hands, and I'm the current project. He swipes once, twice, then I'm shattering into the white-hot atmosphere. I clench everywhere as the orgasm blasts through me. My legs shake from the overwhelming pleasure raining down on me.

With a deafening roar, Zeke finds his release, following me over the ledge. He collapses against me, and we sink onto the mattress, never separating for a second. We're a sweaty heap, but I've never been more comfortable. His bulky arms loop around my waist and pull me impossibly closer.

Once he's caught his breath, Zeke chuckles against my neck. I look at him over my shoulder with a raised brow.

He smirks. "Was that enough variety for you?"

I rub my temple. "Oh, yes. My head is still spinning."

"That good, huh?"

"I'm *very* satisfied, thank you very much."

"Hopefully not too worn out," Zeke murmurs and cups my breast.

I wiggle my butt against him and gasp when his dick twitches inside of me. "What the—? How are you still hard?"

He scoffs. "Because you're sexy as fuck."

"Good answer."

Zeke kisses my tattoo, something he does at every available opportunity. My belly swoops in the same way each time. His mouth moves up my neck, sucking along the sensitive skin. He begins pumping forward, entering me with shallow thrusts. "This round will be nice and slow, the whole way through."

I reach up and loop my arm around his neck, drawing him in. "That sounds perfect."

# TWENTY-TWO

## DANCE

## ZEKE

"THIS WILL BE SO FUN," Addison chirps from her corner of the backseat.

Raven twists around from the front toward us. "The club already posted a few pictures online. There's a huge crowd gathering for this band. Good call choosing Cyclone, Addy."

Her face is resting on the window when she mutters, "The real test is who'll be there waiting for me."

"You expecting someone?" I ask.

Addison leans forward to study me. "Not necessarily. Just . . . wishful thinking."

Trey snorts from behind the wheel and Raven shoves his shoulder. "What the fuck, Princess? I'm driving."

She scoffs. "Please. I hardly tapped you. Stop being rude."

"I make one little noise and get the fifth degree? That's bullshit," he says.

This is the point where I tune out. Delilah sits next to me, squished in the middle. Not sure she cares about the lack of space.

I definitely don't mind her pressed up against me. In my opinion, it doesn't get much better than having my girl stuck to me like glue. Aside from the clothing barriers. I'd rip off every scrap of fabric separating us before she could blink.

As the truck curves around a steep bend, Delilah slides even closer, practically sprawling across my lap. I have to bite back a moan begging to escape. I shift uncomfortably and try to alleviate the strain in my jeans. Finding relief is useless, so I give up the fight, sliding my hand higher on Delilah's bare thigh. She rewards me with a beaming smile, and I sigh. Too bad we're not alone.

As if listening to my thoughts, Trey says, "Still don't understand why we all had to ride together."

"Not sure what you're bitching about, Sollens. You've got all the leg room up there," I joke.

"He was hoping for a repeat performance," Delilah whispers from the corner of her mouth. Raven whips around with a finger against her lips. But it's no use, Trey hears loud and clear.

"Is nothing private between you girls?"

"Not a thing," Addison admits. Delilah and Raven nod in agreement. That's good to know.

"Whatever," Trey grumbles.

"And for your information," Raven adds, "carpooling is fun. Plus, it saves gas money."

"For who?" Trey asks.

"The rest of u-us," Delilah sing-songs.

I chuckle at her tone and wrap my arm around her. "Love you, Trippy girl."

"Ugh," Addison fusses. "Surrounded by effing soulmates. Save it for the bedroom, you two."

"The night is young," Raven assures.

Addison waves her off. "Yeah, yeah."

We pull into the jam-packed lot ten minutes later. In an unexpected show of manners, Trey drops us off at the door before searching for a spot. I grab Delilah's hand and help her out of the lifted pickup. She gives me a wink and leads us into the booming club. I've never been to Cyclone before tonight, but she seems to know her way around.

While my eyes adjust, all I see are bright strobe lights bouncing off the walls. The band is belting out a classic rock song, which makes me want to pour a little sugar all over Delilah. She swivels her hips and spins around me like an erotic ballerina.

I lick my lips and bend close. "Should we grab a drink before getting all worked up?" I motion toward the bar.

Delilah surveys the scene. "The lines are three or four people deep. Let's pass for now." Then she quirks a brow. "Unless you need something to loosen up."

I chuckle in her ear. "Hardly. I'll be putty in your hands, baby."

She purrs. "Oooh, I love the sound of that."

I smile against her silky skin, unfiltered happiness beaming down on us. Delilah laces our fingers and aims straight for the overflowing dancefloor. In every direction, bodies are gyrating and humping against one another. Why wait until later to blow off some steam?

I twirl Delilah in my arms and yank her into me. In this position, her ass is perfectly cradling my dick. I rock forward and she rolls back, our bodies finding a fluid rhythm. The music pounds from the speakers and encourages us to grind faster. We're surrounded by an endless sea of people, yet all I see and feel is Delilah.

I adore this woman.

My pulse leaps when her fingers crawl up my legs, not stopping until she's winding them around my neck. Delilah's head lolls on my shoulder and exposes her throat. I take advantage of the access, kissing and sucking along her neck. She bows against me, opening herself further to my wandering touch. I slide under her silky shirt and roam across the smooth expanse of her stomach.

Delilah's face turns into me so she can whisper directly in my ear. "I've missed this."

"Trip, baby," I groan. "You have no idea how much I've missed this."

Her torso vibrates with a laugh. "You always loved going clubbing in high school."

"How could I not? It's like fucking you with clothes on."

Delilah's dirty writhing is proving my point. "Dry-humping at its finest," she murmurs and bites my jaw.

We remain tangled through the first set of the band. They alternate between fast-paced jams and slow, seductive beats. The combination gives me nonstop opportunities to have my hands plastered all over Delilah. She's definitely taking advantage of our situation too, her suggestive moves driving me mad with need. I'm officially burning up, wearing lust like a winter coat during a heatwave.

I release a slow exhale when the live music cuts off for a set break. My brow is slick with sweat, and Delilah's skin is balmy. It's a fucking sauna and only getting hotter.

"Want something to drink? I'm fucking blazing," I say and tug at the collar of my tee.

Delilah nods. "Definitely."

"Come with me?" I suggest and hold my hand out.

She links her fingers with mine, but stays planted in place. I follow her line of sight and notice Addison standing nearby. Delilah nibbles on her bottom lip and keeps staring in her direction.

"What's wrong?" I ask.

"I'm worried about her," she says. Her shining green eyes meet mine. "Can you grab a few beers and meet me back here? I should talk to her." Delilah lifts her chin toward Addison.

I reluctantly agree, never pleased to let her go, especially in this capacity. I'm probably too obsessed, but who fucking cares. Delilah bounces up on her toes and kisses me. Our mouths meet for a fast moment before she breaks away.

"See you in a bit," she says with a wink.

I watch her approach Addison and the girls hug in greeting. Satisfied that she's not alone, I turn away and begin trudging toward the bar. I have a hard time believing this place isn't breaking maximum occupancy laws. A month ago, nothing could have convinced me to step foot in this joint. But Delilah has revived the old me. Instead of dread pooling in my gut, I'm loose and relaxed. Maybe dancing is a good way to blow off tension.

It feels like an hour passes before the bartender takes my order. He slams down three bottles without sparing me a glance. I pass him the cash and grab our drinks. Waiting in this never-ending line has stolen some of the calm I was enjoying, but the cold beer helps. Without further delay, I begin weaving through the throng to where Delilah and Addison are waiting. I'm about to offer up high-fives when the crowd parts and makes walking easier. But the relief is short lived.

I slam to a halt as some asshole puts his meaty paws on Delilah. White-hot rage consumes me while she shakes her head and struggles to get away. He's not taking the hint, but I'll be making it crystal clear. I blindly hand off the drinks to someone on my right and begin shoving my way toward Delilah. People in my path scurry so I'm sure my expression reflects the murderous fury flooding me. I've never felt such a driving force propelling me forward.

This shithead is messing with the wrong girl.

# TWENTY-THREE

## PUNISH

### DELILAH

"NO MEANS NO, JERK-OFF. LET the fuck go and get lost," I yell in this stranger's face. I try to rip my arm from his grasp, but he's locked around me.

His beady eyes slowly scan down my body. "I don't think so, sugar. You're coming with me." He licks his lips and yanks me closer.

I tumble into his chest on my wobbly heels. Stilettos were a bad choice. He smells like whiskey and fried food and vomit. I swallow the bile climbing my throat. My struggle continues, and I shove away, but he's holding on too tight. His arm cinches around my lower back like a metal band, and I scream to high heaven.

His vice grip loosens, and he appears distracted. For a moment, I think my tactics worked, and he's giving up. But then I catch him glaring over my shoulder. Without having to look, I know who's hovering there, and the panic bubbling in my belly fades.

"Hands. Off." Zeke's menacing tone carries over the music. I shiver at the powerful fierceness he exudes. Before I can blink, he's in front of me and in the stranger's space. The size difference between the two men is almost comical. Zeke could easily overpower this douchebag, but the other guy doesn't seem to care about self-preservation.

It's difficult to hear, but heated words are exchanged. The stranger pushes Zeke, and that sets off a chain reaction. Shit escalates in a blur of rapid motions, both men refusing to back down. Desperation strangles me. I need to stop them from fighting. I'm shielded from danger and don't see his elbow coming. Zeke's arm cocks back like a slingshot and blasts straight into my cheek.

"Mother fucking son of a bitch," I wail. Blinding pain sears bone-deep, the impact shocking and stealing my breath. My vision blurs with tears, and I blink them away. I'm clutching the tender spot when Zeke whips around to check on me. Horror widens his features, and he stares down at his trembling hands.

"Shit, Trip. A-are you okay?" He's about to touch my face but jerks away at the last second.

I touch around the sore area and hiss loudly. My left eye is watering, and I roll it around in the socket to alleviate the building pressure. Zeke studies my every move, silently appraising me between rapid blinks.

"I can't believe . . . Shit. I hit you."

"You didn't—"

"The fuck I didn't. Look at your face. There's already a bruise forming."

I force a smile in spite of the blistering heat covering my skin. "I wasn't paying enough attention. This was a total accident. It'll be gone in a few days."

Zeke's voice is agony wrapped in despair. "The swelling, maybe. But the significance is permanent."

"What?" I furrow my brows and wince.

"Dammit, you're in pain. I hurt you," he cries.

I shake my head. "No, it's all right. Don't look so worried.

See?" I lightly press against the tender area, and it's like a hot poker jabbing into me. "Ow, shit," I whimper.

That was the wrong thing to say.

The change in Zeke is immediate. A gust snuffs the light in his eyes. I watch as all traces of softness vanish from his broad build, and he turns into rock. His guard slams down with a deafening bang, my legs shaking from the imaginary force.

"Let's get you some ice," he clips. Without making contact, Zeke guides me to the bar. He's purposely keeping a safe distance, and an excruciating ache digs into my chest. I reach for his fingers, needing to be connected to him in this moment.

"I'm fine, Zee. It's already feeling better," I say. My entire face is throbbing, but a white lie in this situation is far less painful than witnessing him freeze me out. When my fingers brush his skin, Zeke's entire body tenses. He wrenches out of my light hold, and I stumble from the abrupt movement.

"Fuck," he roars and rips at his hair.

Fresh tears sting my eyes. "Zee? That was an accident. It's okay—"

He slashes the air with his hand. "The fuck it is. Just . . . no. We're not doing this here. Not now. You need to get ice on that." Zeke blindly gestures at my cheek, refusing to look at me.

A fissure cracks my heart at his standoffish behavior. I try to convince myself he just needs to cool off. Then we'll talk about this and be laughing by morning. But my gut sinks like a brick because I know Zeke better than that. He wouldn't act this way without a very serious reason.

*Shit.*

My mood spirals from there, low and lower yet. Reality bleeds into this nightmare and floats away in a cloudy puff. Ten minutes whip by in a fuzzy blur. I'm dazed, and stars twinkle on the edges of my vision. Suddenly we're buckling into the truck, but

I don't remember getting here. When I blink, we're on the road and heading home.

I rest a palm on my forehead. Dammit, I'm dizzy and disorientated. I adjust the bag of melting ice on my jaw and exhale slowly. Zeke is a stone pillar beside me, cold and stiff. He alternates between looking at the ceiling and burying his face between both palms. When he peeks out, his lashes are wet. All the air wheezes from my lungs. I hiccup on a strangled inhale, finding it difficult to breathe. Desperation to eliminate this frigid distance separating us propels through me. I shift to touch him, to soothe this unbearable ache, needing to feel his warmth under my palm. Zeke visibly flinches and leans away from my comfort. I clamp my jaw shut to trap the sob rising in me.

"Zee." His name is a desperate plea falling from my lips. "Please talk to me."

His only response is a barely-there jerk of his head. Once again shutting me down.

The pain in my face is long forgotten. All I can think about is losing this man. I absolutely refuse. Zeke stares straight ahead with a blank look, apparently not seeing anything.

"How're you feeling?" Addison's soft voice breaks the silence.

"I'm all right. It's not a huge deal," I murmur. I can downplay until my face is blue, but that won't change the fact that Zeke isn't handling this well. He won't even let me touch him. There's a big problem festering just below the surface. I shiver thinking about the conversation we'll have later.

Of course he's reading my thoughts. "You're not fucking okay. Don't pretend for my benefit," Zeke growls quietly.

"I'm really fine," I say softly and attempt to hold his hand again. He immediately snaps it out of reach. I don't bother concealing my defeated sigh. Addison rubs my shoulder, and I send her a wobbly smile.

We're all painfully silent for the remaining trip to Garden Grove. I can't help feeling this is some sort of peace before utter ruin.

I'm eager to assure Zeke that everything is good, but my stomach is twisted in knots. I'm worried he won't be easily convinced. When we pull into Trey's driveway, Zeke opens his door before the truck is in park. He's hauling ass away from me without a word. I slowly follow him to his pickup parked along the curb, sorrow weighing me down. Zeke tosses a glance behind him and realizes I'm there. He shuffles to a stop and faces me.

"What're you doing, Trip?

"Aren't we going to my place?"

He's shaking his head before I'm done talking. "You need to stay here with Raven and Addy."

"What? Why would I do that?"

"They'll keep an eye on you to make sure there's no concussion."

I frown. "That's silly. I'm—"

Zeke doesn't let me finish. "I know a thing or two about this type of abuse, Delilah. A concussion is very plausible." His expression is flat and lifeless.

"Abuse?" I whisper the word.

He's staring at his hands again, turning and flipping them rapidly, mumbling something unintelligible.

I eventually ask, "What?"

"I'm just like him," he mutters.

A sharp cramp squeezes my stomach, but I need clarification before assuming the worst. "Who?"

"My father." Zeke's despondent tone guts me.

I gasp and move toward him, but he stumbles away. I plead, "No, no, no. Don't ever compare yourself to him, Zee. You're nothing like him."

He holds up a violently shaking hand, glaring at it like the sight offends him. "But I am. Look what I did to you. I've always been terrified of turning into this type of monster. This is exactly why I stayed away all these years. I couldn't risk putting you in harm's way."

"Don't you dare, Zeke. This was a mistake," I say and gesture at my cheek.

He sucks in a choppy breath. "Yeah, it was. None of this should have happened. You've always been too good for me."

I gape at him. "What? No. That's not what—"

Zeke smirks sadly. "I get it, Delilah. His blood burns in my veins. I can't get rid of him. Why would you ever settle for a man like me?"

"You're so much better than him. He's a horrible human being, Zee. You're kind and sweet and the love of my life."

His bitter laugh is like a strike against my wounded face. "No, I'm not. Not anymore. I proved him right tonight. He'd always taunt me by saying I'd grow up to be just like him. Turns out he was right."

I can't hold back the tears, and they blur my vision. I angrily swipe the drops away. "Don't say shit like that, Zeke. It's not true. I know the real you, deep down, and this isn't him. Fight for us. *Please*."

"I did and look what happened."

"It was an accident!" I cry, desperately wanting to shake sense into him.

"Doesn't matter. I hurt you and that's what counts."

"You'd never lay a hand on me in anger. I know you wouldn't. You're upset, and I understand. But that doesn't mean you have to leave me here."

"I won't risk this happening again. You mean too much to me, Delilah. Letting you go will likely end me, but it's for the best."

I'm crying openly now while my heart is shattering. "Would you ever hurt me on purpose?"

His response is immediate. "I'd rather die."

I hold my arms out. "See? What's the issue?"

"Just look at your face! I hit you."

"Repeating that won't make it true. You were defending me."

"People won't see it that way."

"Who gives a shit what they think," I wail.

Zeke jabs a thumb into his chest. "Me. I've always known you deserve better. This proves it."

"Stop it. Stop this right now," I beg.

Zeke is crumbling before my eyes. His powerful frame is slumping in defeat. Torment is etched deep into his features. My fingers itch to smooth away the creases, but I'm sure he'd refuse to let me. He's breaking down. I need to be strong for us both. Arguing isn't solving anything. He needs to see reason, and that's not happening standing out here.

"Let's go home. We'll talk more about this in the morning," I say and reach out my hand for him to take.

He glances at my trembling fingers. "I don't belong there with you. Not after what I did."

"You're wrong. I love you, Zee. I need you with me. Always," I demand.

He's vehemently shaking his head. "I'm dangerous."

"No, you're most certainly not. Stop attacking yourself. I hate it," I tell him honestly.

His vacant blue stare veers off into the distance. "I'm so fucking sorry, Delilah."

"Why won't you look at me?"

"Because it hurts too much watching you cry."

I edge closer, and he doesn't move away. "I'll stop if you tell me everything will be okay between us."

"I can't do that," he replies softly.

Real fear takes root in my stomach and begins to grow. Zeke is serious about this. "Don't do this. I can't be without you."

He sniffs and rubs his eyes. "I can't handle the fact that your face is bruised because of me, Delilah. No matter the reason, I shouldn't have lost my temper. That fucker at the club was saying all these disgusting things about you. I couldn't stop thinking about him touching you. He pushed me too far, but it doesn't change shit. I've never hurt anyone before, not on purpose. But I wanted to pummel that guy."

"He would have deserved it. He's a creep preying on women. You were protecting me," I reiterate.

"And we see how that turned out."

I want to stomp my foot and yell. Instead, I take a calming breath. "Please stop aiming at that target. If you hadn't saved me—"

"But I didn't. I bashed my—"

I've had it with us going around in circles. I leap forward and wrap my arms around him. Zeke is a stiff board in my desperate hold, but after a few moments he relaxes into the embrace. For a few blissful moments, his hands drift up and down my back. All too soon he squeezes me and pulls away.

Zeke twirls a few strands of my hair. "I wish things were different."

"What do you mean?" I ask warily.

"I'd want nothing more than to be deserving of you. But I'm not." His voice is quaking, and the vibrations rattle my bones.

"N-no, Zee. Stop talking like this."

"It's the truth, Trip. I tried to avoid the inevitable, but my chances ran out."

He allows me to link our fingers. I lift my watery eyes to his. "We're meant to be together. There's no doubt in my mind or heart. I love you too much to ever give up."

"You'll have to believe for both of us. All my faith just ran out," Zeke admits solemnly.

"I'll never stop fighting for us," I promise him.

He brushes a thumb down my uninjured cheek. "My strong girl. It'll be better this way. One day, you'll see that."

I lean into his touch, but he quickly moves away.

"Why does this feel like goodbye?" I whisper.

He presses his lips to my forehead with a shuddering exhale. "Because it is."

Resignation slams down, and it's obvious Zeke is winning this round. No matter what I say, he's not taking me with him. I clear my throat and rasp, "All right. I'll stay with Raven and Addison. But this isn't the end of us."

"I can't offer you anything, Delilah."

I ignore his words. "Just don't keep me waiting five more years."

Zeke smirks sadly. "I'll always love you, Trip."

"That's what I'm hoping for because I'll never stop loving you."

He presses his velvet lips against mine for a couple beats. I greedily inhale his woodsy scent, wanting to commit this moment to memory. Zeke slowly pulls away, as if ending our kiss is painful. It sure feels that way to me.

"Will I see you tomorrow?" I try to inject positivity in my voice.

He shrugs, and that's all the answer I get. Zeke gets in his truck and drives away. I watch his taillights fade, my tears blurring them into a blotchy mass of red. A soul-deep burn strikes and spreads while I worry about him not stopping at the county line.

# TWENTY-FOUR

## SABOTAGE

## ZEKE

AS THE VEIL OF SLEEP whisks away, the first thing I notice is the searing pain in my neck and shoulders. After scrubbing the gunk from my eyes, I quickly remember why. I spent the night cramped in the cab of my pickup.

There was nowhere worth going so after cruising aimlessly, I parked in a deserted lot at the outskirts of town. I gingerly sit up and contemplate my next move. Ditching Garden Grove without a backward glance sounds appealing, but I'm not a fucking coward. I've already committed enough crimes against Delilah and this town. I won't add more to that rap sheet by abandoning my responsibilities and job. Devon has never let me down so no matter what, I'll pull through and finish this project.

My worst fears warped into reality when I struck Delilah. That bruise might not leave a lasting mark, but I'll always see the harm I caused. She wasn't mad, which confused me at first. I've come to the realization that she was in shock yesterday. The full impact of what I've done hadn't set in. I'm sure she's singing a different tune now.

I recall the hurt flaring in Delilah's eyes. I'd ignored it. I couldn't let her seep through the cracks and see my weakness. I refuse to budge on that. I'm lost and broken and only bring destruction.

But dammit, I want her. The battle flares to life, both sides demanding and unforgiving. I feel ripped in half and utterly destroyed. There's no walking away from Delilah unscathed.

A ping calls out into the silence around me. I've lost track of how many times Delilah has texted or called. The notifications sound like static at this point, similar to the dull buzz in my brain. To add insult to injury, I grab my phone off the dashboard. I scroll through her messages and read a few of my favorites from last night.

TRIP: THE SHEETS ARE COLD WITHOUT YOU BESIDE ME. I MISS YOUR WARMTH.

TRIP: I MISS YOUR GOODNIGHT KISSES.

TRIP: I MISS YOU CUDDLING WITH ME.

TRIP: I MISS YOU, ZEE. PLEASE CALL ME.

Then I see the one Delilah just sent.

TRIP: WHERE ARE YOU, ZEE? I NEED TO SEE YOU. I LOVE YOU. COME BACK TO ME.

I wipe the moisture from my eyes. Imagining her upset over me is worse than brass knuckles to the kidneys. Why doesn't she hate me? She's trying to console me, the one who struck her face. What the hell? Delilah can try excusing my behavior, but I know the truth. I hurt the only person who's ever truly loved me.

Being away from her is going to hurt so fucking bad. But this is the price I must pay.

Even with miles between us, Delilah hears my need for her. Another alert sounds and I glance at the screen.

TRIP: WHY WON'T YOU ANSWER? YOU BETTER NOT BE SITTING AROUND, TAKING THE BLAME. YOU'RE A GOOD MAN, ZEE. THE BEST

I've ever known. The only one for me. Remember? You can't leave me.

Maybe Delilah expects me to flee like the unreliable loser I am. That would explain why she's blowing up my cell. She won't have to worry about me hounding her for a second—no, scratch that—a third fucking chance. I'll keep my distance for real this time. I won't be dragging her down with me.

Delilah needs a good man who will treat her right. I gulp down the acid burning my throat. Thinking of her with someone else is the worst type of torture, but that's all I deserve. I've ruined us permanently with no hope of redemption. After the dust has cleared, I'll visit her and end things for good. I'll make sure she moves on. I don't want her clinging to an ounce of false possibility or belief this can work out for us. We're done and it's all my fault.

I groan and bang my head against the steering wheel. The sharp blow temporarily distracts me from the shitstorm my life has once again become. Not that I'm surprised. I'm destined for nothing except swinging a hammer and building other people's dreams.

Thank fuck it's the weekend so there's no work. I can wallow in my well-deserved misery alone. An idea pokes at my foggy brain, and I blink rapidly to clear the cobwebs. I'll head to the gym and beat my own ass, or find someone to do it for me. There will be plenty of takers for how I treated Delilah. I bet an angry mob is already forming on Main Street.

I crank my pickup to life, and the engine turns over without pause. Trey worked magic on this rust-bucket, just like he boasted about. Fucker wouldn't even let me pay him. Bertha's like-new condition is one more thing Delilah helped with. I can't escape her, even in my own damn truck.

My thoughts grow darker and grimmer, a black cloud swooping in and stealing any signs of light. I'm sure Delilah is crying to her friends about what an asshole I turned out to be. She's probably regretting the weeks she wasted on me. She's probably cursing my name and never wants to see me again.

*Fucking stupid shit.*

I punch the steering wheel repeatedly. How the fuck did this happen? How could I do this to Delilah? I hit my temple, again and again, barely seeing the road in front of me. If I crash into a tree, the world will be a better place. But there's other people around to worry about. All I need right now is to hurt someone else. Dammit, on top of everything, I'm a reckless idiot.

I slam to a stop along the curb, get my bag stashed under the seat, and jog the rest of the way. The concrete building beckons me and speaks to my toxic mind. I'll take care of the crazy shit spinning inside of me soon enough.

I step through the doors and immediately gag. It smells like piss and sweat, which goes great with my mood. This gym is exactly that, straightforward with no frills or fancy shit. Just a place to pump iron, or in my case work out until I'm in a comatose state.

I overload the bench press and get moving. I quickly lose track of reps, the motions a rapid blur. Soon enough my arms are numb, but I keep pushing, determined to force out every last ounce of breath from my pathetic lungs. I feel blisters forming on my palms, but that doesn't hinder me. I go until there's nothing left.

My mind is empty and drained. Fire races across every inch of my skin. My heart is pounding too fast, yet I feel sluggish. A hollow beat echoes through my chest and lulls me into a false sense of peace. My eyes burn, it physically hurts to keep them open. Maybe the fight will be over soon.

I'm barely conscious when someone moves toward me on the mat. I hardly notice since my body has effectively been pushed to the point of collapse. Fingers snap in my face, and I flinch but can't move otherwise. The person claps several times, and I manage to peel my heavy lids opens. Ryan is there, hovering over me with concern marring his features.

"Thank fuck," he says. "For a second, I thought you were dead."

My mouth isn't functioning. Probably due to my jaw being full of lead. I rotate it back and forth until the joint clicks. "Nah, not yet," I rasp.

"The fuck you doing? Trying to kill yourself?"

I shift slightly and hiss out a stilted breath. "That'd be fine. Save people a lot of trouble."

"And why is that?"

"Word hasn't spread? That's surprising."

"Considering I have no clue what you're talking about, I'd say the secret is still locked up."

White spots dance in my vision, and I blink too slowly. Ryan shakes my shoulder. "Stay awake, man."

I force my eyes wide, which only seems to be a sliver. "Sorry," I mumble.

He scans the rest of me. "Dude, your hands are fucked."

I snort. "Good. I should cut them off for the pain they've caused."

"That's melodramatic as fuck. What the hell is going on?"

I lick my chapped lips and don't think twice about spilling the truth. "I hit Delilah last night."

His face screws up into an odd expression. "You? I find that extremely hard to believe. You're a fucking teddy bear when it comes to that woman."

I attempt to shrug. "Guess not, huh?"

Ryan lifts his brows. "Tell me what went down. Paint the scene for me."

"What more to do you need to know? We went to Cyclone. Some asshat was trying to force himself on Delilah. I was putting a stop to it and clipped her instead."

"So, it was an accident," he states.

"You sound like her. Doesn't matter either way. That bruise on her cheek is from me."

"Damn, that's messed up."

A choking sound bubbles from my throat. "Glad you're on the same page. I'm a fucking monster."

He scoffs. "Don't be a dumbass. You're taking blame for a legit mistake while protecting her. That's what you were doing, right? Defending her honor? That's more your style."

"I was trying until my elbow rammed into her. And that's the indisputable fact. She's hurt because of me."

Ryan widens his stance above me. "When she finds out how you're coping, it won't end well."

"Good thing she won't hear about this. We're no longer together."

Ryan gapes at me. "What's that bullshit you're spewing?"

"There's no way I'd risk Delilah's safety, ever again. I'm obviously a loose cannon."

"Uh-huh. There's definitely a few screws loose up there." He flicks my forehead. I don't even flinch.

"Fuck off. You know what I mean," I say with zero room for argument.

Ryan goes quiet for a minute. He clears his throat and fidgets with imaginary lint. Eventually he grows the balls to ask, "Is this because of your father?"

"Ding-ding," I announce.

He squats down to my level. "You're not him, Zeke. Far fucking from it. We've talked about this so many times. I always figured you saw the differences."

"Used to believe that. Not anymore."

"You're on a spiral, huh?"

"I'm not lounging on this disgusting mat for my health," I snap.

"Get the fuck up so we can fix this." Ryan holds out a hand, but I wave him off.

I struggle to sit up, every exhausted muscle screaming in protest. "I'm not your problem. You don't wanna be caught around town with the likes of me. This is my fucking cross to bear."

"Stop tearing yourself down, man. No one would believe you'd hurt Delilah on purpose. I'm not sure why you're taking this so damn hard."

I use every remaining reserve stored in my broken body to yell, "I fucking hit her!"

He doesn't flinch from my outrage, which only causes my blood to boil hotter. My chest is rising and falling rapidly, completely out of control. I suddenly feel like the walls are closing in on me, and there isn't enough oxygen. I claw at my neck, begging for a decent breath.

In the back on my mind, I hear Ryan murmuring but can't make out the syllables. He places a cool cloth over my forehead, and the relief is instant. My skin sizzles before the fire recedes completely. I pant for a few moments and try to collect my sloppy thoughts.

"You good?" Ryan asks and removes the towel.

I give a jerky nod. "For now."

"It's gonna be okay. You'll see," he assures.

I don't have any fight left to keep up with him. "How'd you find me?"

Ryan lets me off the hook. "Saw that heap of rusted metal down the block. Process of elimination. Figured you weren't antique-shopping or buying women's clothes."

"You've always been a smartass."

"I'll take that as a compliment coming from you."

I move to stand, and he helps stabilize my wobbling legs. "Thanks," I mutter.

"Damn glad I showed up before you caused serious damage. Your palms are torn to shreds," he says and inspects the massacre again.

I flip them out of sight. "I hardly feel it." And that's the truth. I'm just an empty shell.

"You'll have to skip work for a few days. No way you can wield any tools in this condition."

"I'll manage."

"Always the fucking tough guy. Lean on me for today, yeah?" His eyes shine with empathy and I'm too tired to resist.

"Whatever."

"We'll rehydrate and eat," he begins. He continues talking when I try interrupting. "Somewhere quiet without any gossiping hens."

"Yeah, all right."

Ryan coughs into the collar of his shirt. "First, let's get you in the shower."

"Why bother?" I mumble but begin stumbling toward the locker room.

He chuckles. "I might not be leaving your sorry ass, but you fucking stink."

# TWENTY-FIVE

## GOSSIP

## DELILAH

I APPRAISE MY APPEARANCE IN the mirror, tilting this way and that. No matter what angle I turn, the bruise still shines. The injured skin is fading into a greenish-yellow blotch, but visible none the less. With a lengthy sigh, I stow away my suffocating sadness and leave the bathroom. The time has come to face another day of sympathetic looks and persistent questions.

With a roll of my shoulders, I drag-ass down the hall and settle behind the counter. Jitters will be bustling with customers soon. My belly swoops thinking about a certain someone walking through those doors. I immediately scold myself for grasping onto that possibility. It's most likely not going to happen, and my tattered heart can't handle more disappointment.

It's been days since the incident at Cyclone, and I haven't heard a peep from Zeke. I'm becoming increasingly more desperate with each passing moment. It's embarrassing to admit I've gone full out stalker mode a few times. But what's a girl supposed to do? Driving by Roosters to see if his truck is there isn't so bad.

Thankfully, Bertha has been sitting pretty along the street each time so I haven't lost my shit. But the truth is almost worse.

Zeke is purposely ignoring me, which cuts deeper each time I let my mind wander there. At least he hasn't left Garden Grove, I remind myself. His close proximity is definitely something I'm holding onto until we see each other again. I'm forcing myself to give Zeke time to figure shit out on his own. A week seems like a reasonable amount, right? If he hasn't called or messaged me by then, I'll be paying him a special visit.

The chime sounds, signaling my first caffeine seeker. I plaster on a fake smile with a warm greeting to waiting on my lips. But the expression falls flat when I notice who's strutting toward me.

"Good morning, Delilah," Marlene sings.

I slump against the register. "Hello to you. How's Wednesday so far?" What are the chances I can distract her from more obvious topics?

Her face wrinkles with a wide grin. "Peter comes home tomorrow. We're having a gathering to celebrate."

I nod at the mention of her oldest grandson. "He hasn't visited Garden Grove in quite a while. What's the occasion?"

Marlene's features beam bright and I almost shield my eyes. "His wife, Becky, is expecting. I'm going to be a great-grandmother. Can you believe that?"

"Wow, congratulations. That's wonderful news," I tell her honestly. Maybe this will keep her preoccupied for years to come.

"Thank you. We're all very excited."

"You should ask Raven to bake a gender-reveal cake," I suggest.

Marlene sucks in a startled breath. "Oh, my. I never considered that. Do you think she'd be willing?"

"Absolutely. That girl loves specialty projects."

"That's a great idea, Delilah. I'll talk to Peter and Becky, see what they say."

I give her a genuine smile, pleasantly surprised she hasn't

brought up my—

"You need better makeup, dear," she suddenly whispers.

Ah, there's the Marlene I barely tolerate. I decide to play dumb, for entertainment's sake. "What do you mean?"

"No need to pretend with me, sweetie. The mark is clear on your cheek."

I scowl, not appreciating her assumptions one bit. "I hope you're not implying—"

"Hush now. It's all right. Don't bother making excuses on my account," Marlene says. She leans across the counter, and I get a lungful of her signature floral perfume. I try not to breathe while she murmurs, "I always worried about that boy, but he seemed to really love you."

I bristle at her placating tone, immediately stepping up to Zeke's defense. "He would never hurt me, and I don't appreciate you jumping to conclusions."

She tilts her head, sending her grey curls bouncing. "No? Then tell me what happened."

For a brief moment, I contemplate spinning a wild lie. But what would that really accomplish? My mind reels, and I decide to tell the truth. Hey, there's a slim chance Marlene will spread the real story.

I lick my dry lips. "We were at a bar—"

She tsks. "Those drunk dens are nothing but trouble."

I grind my molars at being cut off again. "As I was saying, there was a man trying to take advantage of me. Zeke stepped in and saved me. He accidentally elbowed me in the process. It definitely wasn't intentional."

"Men and their egos. How typical," she scoffs. "Zeke lost his temper and took it out on you."

Didn't she hear a word I said?

"W-what?" I sputter. "No, not at all." I curl my hands into fists and silently release a string of curses. It's judgements like these that have Zeke believing he's a monster. My bitch-meter cranks up to high and there's no more biting my tongue.

I point at her and growl, "Don't you dare, Marlene. I swear on the deed of this store, Zeke was only protecting me. The end. You better not tell anyone otherwise. That'd be the worst type of injustice."

She pats my arm. "That's what they all say, honey. His dad beat on his mom, you know. That anger can run in the genes. I dated a man with a real short trigger. If you ever—"

I slash through the air, having quite enough of her garbage. "No. Zeke isn't like that. He would never hurt me."

Marlene's expression turns somber. "He already did."

I want to stomp my foot and demand she listen to me. How am I supposed to convince Zeke that this was a minor mishap when she's dragging his name through the mud? Thunder cracks in my veins, and I try to rein in the desire to throttle her. After taking a deep breath, I feel marginally cooler.

"He's one of the good guys, Marlene. Please never say otherwise."

She rolls her eyes and huffs. "We'll see what everyone else—"

I slam my palm on the glass between us. "I've had enough. If you're going to keep bad-mouthing my boyfriend, please leave my shop. I don't want your business. Or need it for that matter."

Marlene gapes at me. "Well, I've never been talked to in such a way. Your mother—"

"Her mother what?" The interruption calls from beside us.

I startle at seeing my mom waiting there, arms crossed and ready for battle. How did she sneak in without me noticing? Air whooshes from me in a hurry, and I slump against the counter. This is an interesting turn of events.

My mom clears her throat and moves closer. "I raised my daughter to be a strong and honest woman, Marlene. Are you calling her a liar?"

The old woman's lips pucker. "Not exactly, but look what that man did to Delilah. And she's trying to defend him."

"Oh, I didn't realize you were there when this happened. Did you have a front-row seat?"

Marlene blinks her clumpy lashes. "Sallie, that's ridiculous. I wouldn't be caught dead in those nightclubs your daughter hangs around."

"Exactly. You didn't see the man threatening Delilah, trying to drag her away. You weren't a witness to Zeke standing up for her. You don't know how that bruise got on her cheek," my mother states coolly.

Marlene glowers. "And I take it from all that you were in attendance?"

My mom comes behind the counter to stand by me, and I'm thankful for her support. "I wasn't and never claimed otherwise. I'm choosing to believe Delilah and the truth she told me. Considering, after all, she was there and it happened to *her*. Zeke is a wonderful young man. My daughter cares a great deal for him, as do I. Listening to you speak ill of him, trashing his character this way, makes me sick."

"How did this get turned around on me? I'm under attack all of a sudden," the older woman says.

My mother leans forward, propping a hand on her hip. "Marlene, I appreciate your tales as much as the next gal. But this is straight slander, and I need to intervene. Accidents happen. You know that just like everyone else. Zeke would never hit Delilah on purpose so get your facts straight. Harmless gossip is one thing, but this is a man's integrity and reputation we're talking about."

I want to pump the air at my mom's warrior ability. Marlene's mouth opens and closes several times without a word. I'm certain she's about to turn and walk away, but no—she continues hovering. My mom reaches for one of her wrinkled hands and gives it a rub.

"I think that's enough for now, yes? No hard feelings on our side. We know you're always trying to do right for this town. Just remember to give folks a chance to explain," my mother soothes.

The older woman nods slowly before lifting her eyes to me. "I'm sorry for being rash, Delilah. You let Zeke know I apologize to him as well. I'll be calling Raven about that cake."

I give her a soft smile. "Thank you, Marlene. It's all right. My attitude could have been a bit nicer."

She inspects her immaculate manicure. "I'd act the same way if someone talked poorly about my Wally. I wasn't acting very ladylike, dear. I should probably be better about giving the benefit of the doubt."

"I appreciate that," I say.

Marlene fiddles with a stack of napkins in front of her. "I was steamrolling all over the place and not listening to you. Wally says I have a habit of doing that. Guess it's time to pay more attention."

My mom and I share a knowing smile in regards to Marlene's husband. He's the only one who manages to corral her crazy jabbering. Out of love, of course.

"Everything is fine and dandy between us. Don't worry a pretty hair on your head. I expect to see you Friday for the usual," I supply softly.

She fluffs those grey curls in response. "I'm seeing the errors of my ways, scattering all about. Thank you for the kindness. You're very forgiving, Delilah." Marlene glances at my mom. "You've raised her right, Sallie."

My mother wraps her arm around me. "She's my favorite oldest daughter."

A snort escapes me, immediately followed by a choked sob. I fan my eyes, getting overly emotional during this gush-fest. I'm usually not a big crier, but the last month has been a rollercoaster. Ever since Zeke arrived in Garden Grove, the waterworks won't quit.

"Well, I better get going. There's a lot of planning to do," Marlene chirps in her typical upbeat tone.

I offer a small wave. "Extend our congratulations to Peter and Becky."

My mom grins widely. "See you at tea on Thursday, Marlene."

With that, Marlene sashays out in a cloud of sickly-sweet perfume. I collapse against my mother, feeling deflated before eight o'clock in the morning. Her head rests on top of mine, and we spend a moment in quiet comfort.

"Thanks for coming to my rescue, Momma," I murmur against her shoulder.

"That's what I'm here for, sweetie."

"And dang, you're feisty. She didn't see that sassy-sass coming."

My mom's chest shakes with a laugh. "Sometimes we all need a refresher on how to mind our manners. Even ladies like Marlene. And Zeke is like the son I never had. He's mine to protect, too."

Emotion stings my eyes, and I bat the tears away. "I'm such a mess over all this. He won't talk to me. I've tried, but he won't answer. The last thing he said was goodbye, and it sounded so permanent. Why does he think I deserve better? He's all I want," I weep.

She combs through my hair. "Shh, shh, sweetie. Give Zeke time. That boy can't stay away from you for long."

"B-but he did before," I say.

"That involved far more than just your relationship. And he explained all that, right?" I nod quickly, and she continues. "He'll come around eventually. He's gotta fight off these bad feelings first."

"How can Zeke believe he's capable of actually hurting me? That would never happen. I feel it here," I say and press against my chest.

"He grew up in a different environment, D. Remember that. We don't understand everything he's been through. But he's stronger in spite of it all. I know he is."

"H-have you seen him around town this week?"

"No, but that isn't a huge surprise. I went almost a month before seeing him out and about with you. He's probably not in the best place. And I'm not talking about The Mossy Den," she laughs quietly and I hiccup a sad giggle.

"I love him so much. Why won't he talk to me?"

"Sometimes the damage runs real deep, beyond where anyone can reach. But Zeke isn't lost. You'll get to him. Or maybe he's planning to stop by any minute."

I blow out a long exhale. "Yeah, but he was pretty serious about staying away. I'm not feeling very confident."

She rubs my arm, shaking me out of the stupor. "Dry your tears, sweetie. It's all going to work out exactly as it should. Enough sadness for one day. Let's focus on something positive. How about I make you some coffee?"

I roll my watery eyes. "That's my job."

"Well, then. I'll have a large hazelnut with extra whipped cream," she orders and bumps her hip into mine.

I scrub over my blotchy face and force the storm clouds away. I'll obsess over all this later. "Coming right up, Momma Bear."

She hums at the nickname and begins wiping off the display case. "What else can I do to help around here?"

I shrug while measuring out the grounds. "Just sit and relax. The rush won't start for another thirty minutes."

"Like clockwork?"

I lift my lips in a half-smile. "Predictable Garden Grove."

She makes a noise of agreement. "No truer words. Speaking of, did you hear about Polly's latest mix-up?"

I shake my head and laugh. "This should be good."

# TWENTY-SIX

## VISIT

## ZEKE

PENT-UP FRUSTRATION THRASHES LIKE AN angry sea, and I force more effort into expelling all of it. My biceps complain when I swing the hammer wide, smashing the nail clear through the board. I rip at the wood, splitting it off the beam with a brutal crack. I throw the broken piece away and grab another to destroy. I'm on a direct course of tearing all our progress down, just to rebuild all over again.

"What the fuck are you doing?" Devon bellows from behind me.

I don't spare him a glance. I raise my fist to strike dead center.

"Zeke, I'm talking to you!"

"And I hear you. Just don't care," I spit and punch the wood again.

He grips my shoulder and yanks me away from the destruction I'm creating. A pile of ruined tools and equipment rest at my feet, a gravesite of sorts. My focus settles on the heap of damage, and chaos gains strength inside of me.

"Look at me," Devon demands. I swing my glare his way. "I've let your surly attitude go for long enough so knock it off. Maybe you need some time off," he suggests.

"No way," I clip. "I need this job to stay sane."

Devon levels his gaze at me. "You call this sane?" He gestures around us before pointing at me. "Look at your fucking hands. You're not even wearing gloves. There's blood everywhere, Zeke. How am I supposed to react to your careless behavior?"

I shrug. "Look the other way."

He grunts and gives me a rough shake. "Snap the fuck outta this . . . whatever you wanna call it. You're a good worker, but this shit won't be tolerated."

"Or what?" I challenge while wiping my palms on a dirty towel. The abused skin burns, but I hardly feel it.

Devon juts his chin out, meeting my furious stare. "I don't wanna fire you, but I will if it comes to that. I can't have unstable people on this crew causing liabilities. We talked about this when you first started. There's been no trouble since so don't go backwards, kid."

My breathing is erratic, and I pant uselessly. "This isn't like that."

"No? Then tell me what's eating your ass."

"I'm fine."

"Stop lying, Zeke. Anyone in a twenty-mile radius can tell you're not okay."

I exhale and try to cool down. "I'm having a bad week."

Devon hoots. "You can say that again. What happened? Is Lewis bothering you?"

"No, he's not a problem. I can handle him."

He studies me silently. "Is this about your girl?"

I grind my teeth and growl, "Don't mention her."

"Ah, I see. That explains a lot," Devon says and crosses his arms.

"You don't know shit."

"Better watch it, Zeke. You're skating on damn thin ice."

I rein it in, hoping he'll leave me be. "I'm sorry for the mess. Dock my wages or whatever."

"That's not my concern. I'm worried about your wellbeing. Take the afternoon off and screw your head on straight. Pretty sure a doctor should look at your hands too. Come back on Monday ready to actually work. Got it?"

I open my mouth to argue but think better of it. Losing my job will drive me over the edge, and I'm not quite ready for that. My gut churns while I stew in his unyielding presence. Devon's expression remains neutral as he waits me out. I offer a jerky nod and storm off without a word.

Delilah's beautiful face filters into my thoughts. A flicker of joy prods at me until her bruise comes into view. My head hangs in shame as I trudge along the sidewalk. I'm fucking everything up. Was an alternative ending ever possible?

I'm a few feet from my pickup when *he* calls out.

"Hey, boy."

The fire blazing across my skin instantly turns to ice. I'm being punished for hurting Delilah. I deserve the shit-cannon my life has become. Crap just keeps pouring down in a relentless stream. I don't turn around, not ready to face the monster breathing down my neck. Guess he got tired of haunting me from afar.

"What? No warm welcome?" He limps around my left side, and I almost stagger at the sight of him.

What the fuck? I barely recognize this man.

Malcom Kruegan was always a frightening darkness. An enforcer of immoral justice with an arsenal of weapons.

This person in front of me is nothing more than mottled flesh and crippled limbs. He smells putrid, like spoiled waste, and I fight the urge to cover my nose.

"How'd you know where I was?" I hate the slight tremble in my voice.

"Your ugly truck sticks out like a sore thumb. Always hated that piece of garbage."

His gaunt complexion and hunched posture are the lasting effects of tough years. No surprise there. I want to avert my eyes from his evil grin, but that would be showing the weakness he feeds off.

I clench my jaw, greeting his malice with my own. "It's reliable, which is a lot more than I can say about certain people in my life."

His lip curls into a sneer. "We already done with the pleasantries?"

"I prefer to dump the garbage before it stinks up the place. Speaking of, you look like shit."

"Yeah? Well, you look like a felon." He gestures to my busted-up knuckles and disheveled appearance. "And that's no way to address your dear, old dad," he tacks on for fun.

"Get fucking real. You've never been a real dad. Especially after Mom—"

"Don't you dare, son."

Him cutting me off gets my blood pumping hot again. "Pretty sure the years of you telling me what to do are long gone."

"That might be the case. You better still respect her memory by leaving it resting in peace."

I scoff. "Because you've respected her wishes by taking care of me?"

He shuffles toward me and wags an unsteady finger in my face. "You're such a little punk. If I wasn't desperate, I'd keep pretending you were dead, too."

Being this close is like suffering his cruel abuse all over again. My healed bones cry out with the memory of breaking, and I wince. He's relying on the fear I always carried with me. I doubt he'd bother raising a hand to me in this condition, though. It would be laughable to see him try. I shove the shadows away and flatten my expression into concrete.

"So, I'm guessing there's a reason for this delightful reunion," I say.

My father rolls his bloodshot eyes. "Way to go, genius. You solved the puzzle. I need money, a lot of it. Got myself into hot water and gotta bail out."

"What kind of trouble?" Not sure why I bother asking.

"The less you know, the better. That way if the cops come sniffing around, you won't be lying."

I let out a humorless chuckle. "That almost makes it seem like you care."

"Don't fool yourself, son. I don't want you leading them to me."

"Sorry to disappoint, but I'm broke." I have plenty saved. He's not touching a dime of it.

He squints and tilts his head. "Wonder what would happen if I ask that pretty girlfriend you've got? She'd fork some over. Especially if I say you're in trouble."

The threat of Delilah getting dragged anywhere near him is enough to make me foam at the mouth.

"Don't even think of her, you piece of shit."

Too late, I realize he's found a new weakness. My only one. Using Delilah is the lowest blow and proves his thoughtlessness. I don't want to imagine the scare tactics he'd use on her.

"Might have to if you insist on being difficult. You've got a fancy gig here. Must be pulling in some decent coin," he says and motions toward Roosters.

I rely on the truth, hoping it saves me. "Well, that won't get you far. We're not dating anymore."

"Is that so? Wonder why," he muses with a tap to his chin.

"None of your fucking business."

"But it is. Nice thing about Garden Grove is everyone knows everything. I've only been around a day and caught up on the latest quick. Even gutter rats like me hear the whispers of what you did. Was it nice smacking her around? Make you feel like a big man? Suppose I taught you well."

I have half a mind to dig out my hammer and use it on his skull. But I'm better than him. It's time to fucking prove it. "I'm nothing like you."

His rotting teeth are on full display when he smiles. "No? We share quite a few characteristics. Might even admit I'm a tad proud."

"You're a sick fuck."

"Name calling won't help you or Delilah, Zeke." He leans in, trying to intimidate me. "How're your ribs holding up? The wounds always manage to heal, right? I wouldn't worry too much about your precious honey. She'll come crawling back."

Bile rises up my throat at his implication. I swallow the acid with an audible gulp. "You disgust me."

He shrugs off my insult. "Give me the money, or I'll find it elsewhere."

My mind whirls with possibilities, but I can only think of Delilah. "You're gonna stay away from her." There's no question in my statement.

He holds his arms out. "You gonna make me?" I don't move, and he laughs. "You've always been a wimpy pansy. Bet you can't even look in the mirror. She probably hits harder than you."

His taunt drives a stake straight to my heart. I was scared of this man, went far out of my way to avoid any interaction. But what the fuck? Gasoline floods my veins and he's striking a match. I roll my shoulders back and widen my stance. With startling clarity, I realize that all the fear I once felt for this man has dried up. I'm younger. I'm stronger than him, and I'm much bigger.

Why the hell would I cower?

"This is exactly what you've always done. Shame me and soil my mind with your bullshit. But we're nothing alike. You're a vindictive bully, and I'm ashamed of you."

He stares at me, seeming to decay more before my eyes. This decrepit state almost has me pitying him, but I douse that reaction.

My backbone is a titanium rod as I stand tall and proud. I replay all the hits and whippings, nights of nursing injuries, of cursing my existence. This man deserves a beating, but I won't stoop to that level. My father will get what's coming to him soon enough.

"You're a haggard old man, begging for change like an addict. But instead of being a decent human being and asking for it, you threaten me. I shouldn't be surprised, though. This is who you are." I expel the poison from my lungs and take a fresh breath.

"You about done with the tantrum? I don't need to witness your fucking awakening. Just hand over the cash," he spits.

I take another calming inhale, picturing Delilah. "If I do this, we'll never hear from you again?"

His beady gaze gleams with victory, and he nods. He's pummeling me once again, without laying a finger on my body. But this is a battle I don't mind losing. I'll easily cave when it comes to keeping Delilah protected. Paying him off is the easy solution.

I walk to the passenger door and open the glovebox. Without hesitation, I write a check with far too many zeros. Everything inside of me rebels at the idea of handing over this much to him. What he doesn't know is I'd offer double this amount to keep Delilah away from him.

I smile at that, awareness smacks me in the back of the head. I've always been comparing myself to this man. Constantly terrified of turning into him. But his visit has taught me a valuable lesson. I'll never be like him, and that's because of Delilah.

"What the fuck are you grinning about?"

This was the wake-up call I needed. "You can take my money,

terrorize me, but I come out the winner."

He rips the check from between my fingers. A smarmy grin curls his lips when he catches sight of the amount. "Whatever makes you feel better, son. I hold all the power, just like always."

"You have nothing. You're alone with nobody loving you. I hope you're happy taking from me."

"Love? What a joke. You're such a prideful, sniveling shit. Got too much of your momma. Fucking soft and sensitive. You'll never be worth anything," he stabs.

"Let's be honest, your opinion means nothing. The bar has been set pretty damn low. Regardless, I don't care what you think. Never have."

"Yeah, yeah. Pleasure doing business with you," he says with a salute.

"Afraid I can't agree. I don't plan to ever see you again."

"That can be arranged. Unless—"

"Nothing. This town won't be victim of your presence ever again. Otherwise I won't be as forgiving next time."

He scowls but doesn't say anything else. I give him a final look, wishing there was a single moment between us not full of hate. But I come up empty handed. With a spring in my step, I hop in the truck and take off without thinking twice.

My father can eat my dust.

A pure sense of ease lifts me up for what feels like the first time. I'm finally ready.

# TWENTY-SEVEN

## CLEANSE

## DELILAH

I SETTLE DEEPER IN THE tub, letting the lavender salts and bubbles relax my muscles. This has been a hellish week for a laundry list of reasons. Zeke refusing to speak to me is by far the worst one. I snivel into my glass and take a greedy gulp. At least it's Friday night so I can soak as long as my little heart desires.

My toe jiggles the faucet, and a stream of hot water pours out. I'll probably lie in here for hours . . . or until my skin is wrinkled like a raisin. The grip on my emotional control is a ticking bomb. Each second is a challenge held together by fierce determination and fraying hope. But any moment now, I'm going to collapse into an ugly-crying puddle and never get up.

I could call Raven. She's more than likely with Trey, though, and I don't want to interrupt their romantic evening with a bawlfest. Her reliable shoulder is probably still soggy from my last shed tears. Addison is working at Dagos, and I could drag my ass out to visit her. But the weekend crowd is rowdy and my fragile stability isn't up for that. I'm so drained and just . . . tired.

Looks like wallowing by myself is all the action for this evening.

Normally I don't mind living alone. I enjoy having my own space and being the master in command. There's plenty of perks, right? I can walk around naked, blab to myself without being judged, and binge on the cheesiest Netflix shows. I'd give all those up in a snap, though. They won't keep me warm at night. Maybe I should get a dog . . .

"Great idea, D. That will solve everything. Or how about not," I mutter.

Only silence greets me, which doesn't help my pathetic pity-party. I bang my head against the wall, wishing for a certain growly timbre to interject. I glance at the door and buzz my lips.

"Don't worry, Trip. We'll be right as rain soon enough," I say in a purposely deep voice.

Ugh, I'm a loser.

I smack my forehead and sit up. It's time for an intervention . . . of the ice cream variety. I ease out of the claw-footed relaxation station and stand on wobbly legs. I stumble toward the vanity and shake off the dizzy spell. Maybe I overindulged a smidge—on wine and bubbles. It's easy to lose track of time in porcelain monstrosities fit for two.

A broken sob hurdles up my throat when I see Zeke's toothbrush. It was a dream having him here each night, cover-hog or not. I wonder what he's doing tonight.

I shake off that train of thought, knowing it will lead to more suffering.

Instead, I focus on my foggy appearance. The bruise on my cheek is barely a blemish, which should help my case tomorrow. With a confident nod, I slather on some moisturizer and wrangle up the strength to comb my hair. The persistent cramp in my chest has eased slightly and I'm calling that a win.

I slip into my favorite pajamas, grab a carton of Rocky Road, and plop onto the couch. After clicking through numerous channels, my brain returns to a numb state. Losing the will to care, I land on *Friends* and stretch out across the cushions. My feet shuffle against the opposite armrest, and the empty space is magnetized. I miss Zeke letting me lounge on his lap as if there wasn't another spot to sit.

Why am I insisting on this torture?

I should probably recruit backup to keep my willpower intact. I'm just a sad sack of lonely, liable to make bad decisions. I take another useless glance around my loft for any potential distractions. These are moments when nosey neighbors would be appreciated. My weary limbs beg for bed, but I'm too wired. I chew on a nail and think about my big plans. I shake out my hands and mentally list all the things to do. Tomorrow I commence Operation Smother Zeke With Love. He's going to hear me out one way or another.

I reach for my phone and open the string of unanswered messages I've sent. My fingers hover over the keys. To ease my weeping heart, I'll send him a preview of what to expect. I groan and fling an arm over my face.

Dammit, I'm so weak.

But one more sappy text won't hurt.

D: THIS WEEK WITHOUT YOU HAS TAUGHT ME A LOT. MOST IMPORTANTLY? I CAN'T LIVE WITHOUT YOU. I ACTUALLY REFUSE TO. I'M YOURS IN EVERY SENSE. DON'T ASSUME I'LL EVER BE MOVING ON. I'LL ALWAYS LOVE YOU, ZEE.

I roll my eyes, but the weight on me feels lighter. Guess that counts for something. Restlessness swoops in, and I stand up. All the oxygen gets sucked from the room when I peer down at me cell. Three dots appear on the screen, indicating he's typing. My legs tremble and demand movement. I begin pacing in circles while holding my breath. When the alert sounds, the tears begin to flow.

Zee: 🖤

I blink at the screen through blurry eyes. On any other occasion, receiving a single emoji in response wouldn't be cause for celebration. But this is totally different. I've gotten nothing but radio silence from this man for six days. That tiny heart might as well be a five-page manifesto.

Without a word, Zeke soothes my worries. He's granted me the key to unwind the knots twisting me up. Confidence scrubs off all the doubt clinging to me. He's still mine, isn't he? But how am I supposed to wait twelve hours to prove it?

Renewed faith infuses me, and I shimmy around the room. After a few spins, I'm wide awake and totally rejuvenated. I waffle between pouring another drink or doing something more productive . . . like read a smutty romance. My inner fangirl squeals with her choice. I'm about to go in search of my Kindle when a heavy knock calls out from the foyer. I furrow my brows and glance at the clock. Who the hell is dropping by—unannounced—at ten o'clock?

I consider not answering, but that's plain rude. Plus, it would drive me semi-bonkers to never know who's there. A little peek into the peephole will ease my curiosity, if nothing else.

I slink across the carpet with measured steps. I press my palms to the wood, hop up on tippy-toes, and almost fall backward after getting a good look. An embarrassingly loud gasp escapes me, and I slap a palm over my mouth.

# TWENTY-EIGHT

## BEAR

## ZEKE

THE METAL STAIRCASE IS NEARLY impossible to navigate in the pitch dark. I glance up and make a mental note to replace the busted bulbs. Maybe this is a sign that I should wait until morning. It's late, and Delilah is probably out having fun. Why did I spend so long fucking around and second-guessing this decision again?

I shove the excuses away. If she's here, Delilah will be happy to see me. She practically invited me over with that most recent text, right? If I wasn't already on my way, those words would have made me haul ass here. I climb the final step and pause on her stoop, taking a deep breath for courage.

I'm over this fucking day, but the night is only getting started. My palms are sweaty as I knock on Delilah's door. I'm jumpy and edgy as hell, but there's no doubt left in my mind. This is the right decision. I press on my thumping chest, trying to slow the erratic rhythm that wants to break out.

The door swings open, and my mind wipes clean. Any reason to not be standing *right here* in this exact moment vanishes. Delilah is a fucking vision.

Her blonde hair is damp and loosely braided. I want to free those twisted pieces and run my fingers through the soft waves. There's no makeup on her face so every freckle is on full display. Evidence of the bruise lingers on her cheek, and I wince. Delilah blinks rapidly, drawing attention to her red-rimmed gaze. Her imploring greens search my blues for answers, and the impact of everything at once staggers me. My exhale sputters as I lean against the wall for support. What does this beauty possibly see in me?

Delilah appears to be holding back for my benefit. Or give me the chance to react first? Her hands are twitching, and she's practically bouncing in place. I move to tug her toward me but stop short. I feel my eyes widening when I see what she's wearing.

"Holy shit, you still have my shirt?"

She glances down at the faded bear and traces the words. "How could I get rid of this punny gem? You've always been a BEARY good listener, Zee." Delilah pauses and glances up through wet lashes. "I needed to feel close to you."

I take a step forward. She's not done, though. Delilah reaches under the neckline and pulls out a familiar silver chain. My breathing stalls on a gasp. "My mother's r-ring?"

She nods, fiddling with the shiny metal. "I always keep it close to me."

I rub at my heating face, cracking at the seams. This girl has the power to bring me to my knees. Delilah lifts her arms out to me, offering comfort. I collapse into her embrace with a long groan, letting go of every last insecurity. I wrap around her like ivy, pulling and tightening until my body surrounds hers completely. There's no space between us, and never will be if I have any control over it.

I nuzzle Delilah's hair, inhaling deeply with a sigh. "I missed you, Trip. So damn much, baby girl."

She shivers and I grip her harder on instinct. Her voice is a warble when she murmurs, "I missed you so much. I c-can't believe you're here."

"Nowhere else I'd be, ever again. Promise." I whisper the conviction against her skin, needing to brand the words there permanently.

"Love isn't supposed to hurt so much," she sniffles.

"That's the proof we're real, Trip. A little low makes the high even stronger."

Her fingers dig into my shoulders. "Let's only go up from now on."

"That's the plan."

"Good, because I've missed your arms around me."

I flex and manage to bring us closer. "We fit perfectly."

Delilah trembles again. She shuffles backward, and I follow seamlessly, keeping us locked as one. I leave my pain and suffering outside under the inky dark sky. Only love and compassion join us inside. Without looking, she leads us to the couch, and I settle her on my lap. Exactly where she belongs. I'm going to tell her anything and everything, whatever she needs to hear so we can move forward. The past can't be haunting our future for another moment.

But first . . .

"I can't live without you either," I confess.

Delilah lifts her face from the crook of my neck. She smiles wide, and any trace of sadness is gone. "I'm glad—"

I rush to continue, wanting to explain. "From your last message. I wanted to tell you in person and was on my way already. I'm sorry for keeping you waiting, Trip."

She cradles my bearded jaw and brushes our lips together. "You're here now."

"Maybe I don't deserve you. Hell, I know that's the truth. But I can't stay away. If you need space, I'll be a silent warrior, hiding in the shadows. I can try to keep my distance—"

"Please don't," Delilah begs. "I never wanted you to leave in the first place."

Ten tons of bricks fall off my conscience. "Thank you for that," I say in a long breath.

She giggles and kisses me. "I'd track you down, Zee. Don't tempt me."

My thumb traces her bottom lip. "I've been an idiot and couldn't see what's been clear in front of me. You've always been the answer, my solution for everything. I never should have doubted that." I hold up my less damaged palm, and she aligns hers with mine. "We belong together, baby. Our paths merged the day I moved to town. We're never meant to be apart."

"And we won't be," she continues for me.

"Ever again," I finish.

"So, tell me what happened to change your tune. I'm glad you read my texts, but those aren't the reason. You were already on the way."

I nod, squeezing my eyes shut for a quick moment. "Ah, well . . . my dad came around."

"What?" Delilah sits up so fast she almost tumbles off my legs.

I tighten my grip around her, just in case. "Yeah, it was quite a fucking shock."

"Oh my gosh. When?"

"This afternoon. Devon sent me home early because I was wrecking shit, myself included." I raise my busted-up hand, and Delilah sucks in sharply. "Sweet old pops must have been lurking nearby. He was ready and waiting to descend on me."

Her eyes are wide while she listens intently. "Wow, I can't even imagine. Are you okay?"

I shrug. "It was terrifying at first, seeing the man responsible for so much abuse. But he isn't intimidating anymore. All of a sudden, a lever flipped, and the fear was gone, you know?

Suddenly, I couldn't understand why I was ever scared of him to begin with. My father is a monster who preys on weakness. I didn't show any. Well, until . . . uh," I trail off, not wanting to admit the extent of his visit.

"What? Tell me," Delilah urges.

My gut clenches and roils. I lay her head on my chest, nervous she'll leap away. I need to feel her against me in this moment. "He wanted money and was willing to get it by any means necessary. When I refused, he threatened you." I gulp down the residual anger toward him, focusing on the warmth in my arms. "I gave him a check without thinking twice. You're all I need. He can have my money."

Delilah shifts slightly and looks up at me. Tears glisten in her eyes before she wipes them away. When she swipes at my cheeks, I realize I'm crying with her. This woman slays me with a single touch. She'll always be the better end of any deal.

I blink slowly, and more drops make a path down my face. "I should have fought for you all along. For myself. I'm not him, I'm very aware of that now. But damn, his hate was powerful. It's not anymore because I'm stronger now. I chose love, and you, over all else."

Delilah's throat bobs with a heavy swallow. "I love you like crazy. You're a good man, Zee. The very best person I know." When I try to interrupt, she silences me with a finger to my lips. "Thank you for always protecting me."

I wheeze out a stifled sob, releasing all that overflowing emotion in earnest. I rest my forehead along hers and whisper, "I love you."

Our mouths meet and part, fusing us together. I groan into the kiss and press deeper. Delilah's tongue slides against mine, and my dick twitches in hunger. But we aren't finished yet. I break away and blow lightly against her exaggerated pout.

"You'll never be in danger, Trip. I'll always keep you safe," I say.

She nods, our noses brushing with the movement. "My own personal bodyguard."

I groan. "I like the sound of that."

Delilah clears her throat and pulls back to stare at me. "So, where is he now?"

"He's gone for good. If he dares to show his face again, I won't hesitate to destroy him."

"He'd deserve it, but don't you dare," she says.

"Nah, just kidding. I'd call the cops. He was dumb enough to share there's trouble following him."

Delilah relaxes into me. "Are you relieved?"

I take a moment to think about that. "Sure, of course. But mostly I'm glad to just . . . move on. This feels like the beginning of my real life. Does that make sense?"

"Uh-huh," she says and bites her lip.

I lean in and lick along the place she's biting. "It all revolves around you."

"I accept the center position of your world," she murmurs.

Signature dimples dent Delilah's cheeks, and damn, those tiny divots do something wild to me. I suck on the left, then right, and back again. My palm drifts up her leg and under the tattered hem of her shirt. My exploration comes to an abrupt halt.

"Christ, Trip. You're naked under here?" I roam her bare thighs and hips, all the way up her back. "That's so fucking sexy," I moan. My cock agrees, pulsing behind the zipper of my jeans.

"Yes," Delilah purrs. "Hmm, it's hot in here. Maybe I should take this bad-boy off?"

I glance at the vintage tee. "You wearing that has always been a turn-on. But in this instance, I'd have to agree."

She wiggles on my lap, and I hiss. With a giggle, Delilah darts out of my hold and scampers across the room. I willingly follow, possibly leaving a trail of drool in my wake. She's waiting near the bed, completely naked. The silver ring rests between her tits, rising and falling with rapid breaths. My mind whirls with possibilities, and I stash those away.

I reach back and rip the shirt over my head. With a few jerky tugs, I shed my pants and briefs. The need grows and expands inside of me while I stalk closer, erasing the space between us. It's like this every time I'm around Delilah. Each moment with her is a gift, and I cherish every breath.

We crash together in a burst of need. In a single beat, I hoist Delilah up, spin around, and sit on the mattress. She straddles me and shifts until her slit rubs all over my dick. My hands roam up her bare back, and I draw her tighter against me. I make good on my earlier desire and undo the tie of her braid. My fingers comb out her satin locks before bunching the strands in a fist, tugging and beckoning.

I cup her jaw and tilt until my lips lightly graze along hers. Our breath mingles and blends, a preview for what's to come. Delilah shivers and inches closer, peeking her tongue out. The wet heat of her mouth makes me moan, and I don't hold back another moment. The time for teasing is over.

I thrust up, entering her in a long stroke. Delilah's mouth opens on a soundless moan, and I match her expression. Each time is like diving straight into the purest form of bliss. Sunny warmth blankets me, and we stretch further into the heat. My skin tingles while my blood pumps hotter. Her palms skate along my arms, finding purchase on my shoulders for leverage. Delilah matches my slow rhythm, grinding down when I push up. Our bodies mesh and press, bonding two halves into one whole.

A gorgeous flush races up Delilah's neck, and my eyes track the color. One of my hands remains buried in her hair, the other clutches her ass. I roll her hips along mine, punching up for adding impact. She expels a garbled whine that feeds my need, and I work faster at making her split apart. My fingers untangle from her silky waves, making a slow trail down. I thumb her rosy nipple, and it peaks under my attention.

"Yes, more," Delilah whispers.

I move to the other side, giving the same affection. "Your body was made for mine," I rumble.

"D-don't stop," she pleads.

"I never will," I promise.

Delilah is the only one who reaches me, and I've never been more grateful. I'm a grumpy bastard with calloused hands and a tortured soul, but she soothes me. When she places a single kiss on my chest, over my heart, a vibration buzzes inside—I'm the one she wants. Her delicate touch across my neck and jaw tell me I'm worthy. She loops me into an intimate hug that shows me how she's never letting go. The shimmer in her mossy eyes and those dimples in her cheeks say I'm making my girl happy. *Me.* No one else, not ever. I'm the only one who gets this from her.

I'm a lucky son of a bitch who almost missed out on all of this.

"You feel that?" I murmur against her cheek.

Delilah's movements pause with mine. "Us," she answers.

I hum in agreement, sucking down the column of her throat. "The booming in my veins is for you."

"The pounding in my soul belongs to you," she whispers against me.

"The words curling off my tongue are yours."

Delilah finds room to scoot in tighter. "The fibers and molecules buried under my skin thrive because of you."

I cover her lips with mine, sealing eternity between us. "And the rest of these days are ours."

# TWENTY-NINE

## TOGETHER

## DELILAH

I SNUGGLE DEEPER INTO ZEKE'S embrace, feeling more comfortable and protected than ever. Post-coital cuddling is mandatory. Mostly because Zeke is so damn good at it. My ass is nestled against his groin, and the rest of our bodies are entangled in a human web. Nothing could separate us right now.

Well, almost nothing.

He begins kissing along my shoulder blade, murmuring sweet words between each touch. I hum in contentment and get swept away in the moment. I bend my neck forward, granting him more access. Zeke obliges with a sultry moan and adds a few nips for good measure. This man is trying to stake some serious claim, and I'm his field.

"Let's get married."

My lazy eyes pop wide open when his words slam into me. I take an extra moment to process, almost positive it was a figment of my imagination.

"Would you like that?" Zeke continues. "You'd be the most

beautiful bride in the world."

If I'd been standing in this moment, my knees would give out. In my current horizontal position, all synapses fire at once, and an impending system overload is gaining momentum.

"Uhhh," I manage to shutter. He can't see the shock exploding across my features and I'm thankful for that. I need another moment to collect myself and determine if this is actually happening. I could be dreaming, right?

Zeke presses on my arm, encouraging me to roll over. I do and settle on my hip, getting an up-close and personal look at the genuine honesty streaming from his expression. Guess that rules out the potential of me still sleeping. But this is all walking the line of fantasy territory.

A stupid-huge smile stretches my lips, and I'm not trying to hide it. "You're serious?"

He wears a matching grin. "Can you blame me? I've wanted to marry you from the moment we met. When you tripped into me, this was a done deal. Just took a bit longer to get here."

Tears spring to my eyes, and I cup his cheek. "Really?" The awe in my voice echoes around the room.

"Do you doubt my love for you?" Zeke asks and dusts his nose along mine.

"Never."

"So, why all the questions? That's my job in this scenario," he laughs.

My pulse races out of control, and I'm suddenly a bit dizzy. "Have you been planning this? Do you have a . . ."

My words fade when he picks up the ring dangling around my neck. "Have I told you the entire story behind this?" Zeke toys with the silver circle, tugging lightly on the chain.

"Wasn't this your mother's wedding band?"

He shakes his head. "No. It belonged to her mother, and her grandma before that."

"Oh," I say simply and stare at the significance glinting in his palm.

"You know what else?" Zeke murmurs into my ear.

I shiver slightly and lean closer. "What?"

"She would want you to have it."

I furrow my brow. "Okay . . . ?"

He chuckles at my expression. "I'm getting there, Trip."

"I didn't tell you to hurry."

His finger brushes my temple. "Your wheels are spinning fast."

"Well, duh. This is kind of a huge moment."

"Right, okay. When my mom was dying, she gave me her ring. With her final breaths, she told me to save it for the woman I wanted to spend forever with. When I placed it around your neck all those years ago, it wasn't just to keep you safe. I was claiming you, Trip. You've just been wearing it wrong," Zeke explains softly.

My exhale is choppy as I try holding the tears back. A few slide down my face, but he catches the drops with his thumb. He lifts my hair and unfastens the lock, sliding the band off the silver string. Zeke kisses me sweetly, and my toes curl against his. I glance up through hooded lids, elation bursting across my skin like happily dancing feet.

He reaches for my left hand, clutching it in a trembling grasp. "You've always been mine, Trip. I'll never be a rich man, but so long as you're by my side, I'll be wealthy in love. I'll always be yours."

"And I'll always be yours," I say.

He cuts me a scolding look, but it's all fluff.

"Sorry," I whisper, and feel my lips curve with a grin.

"As I was saying, we've always been destined for this. Let's make it forever, okay? Delilah Marie Sage, will you be my wife?"

My vision is cloudy, and I'm nodding like a bobblehead. "Yes! Yes, yes, yes!"

Zeke's chest vibrates with laughter. "What was that?"

I nudge him playfully. "Yes, yes, yes, yes!" I punctuate each agreement with a wet peck on his face. He leans into my touch each time, and I love his constant need for more.

He slides the ring onto my finger, and I sigh at the weight that's always been missing there.

"It fits perfectly," he murmurs.

I hold up my hand for inspection. "Did you expect otherwise?"

Zeke clucks his tongue. "Not from us."

His arms loop around my waist, tugging me on top of him. We lie quietly for a moment, reveling in the future before us. His nails trace up and down my back while I draw lazy circles on his bicep.

He breaks the silence by asking, "Do you wanna hear my backup proposal spiel?"

I prop my chin on his sternum. "Of course."

"Knock, knock," he starts.

I giggle. "Was this a real possibility?"

Zeke pinches my thigh. "Play along."

"Who's there?"

"Will."

"Will who?"

"Will you marry me, Trippy girl?"

Butterflies swoop and flutter in my stomach. "Aww, that's adorable."

He winks. "I'm romantic like that."

"I would have said yes either way."

"That's what I was banking on."

"I've been Zeed," I say in a whimsy lilt as I slink higher up his torso.

Zeke's head bobs slightly. "What was that? Are you turning my name into a verb?"

I wiggle my brows. "Sure did."

"What's the definition? I've taken care of you? Bowled you

over? Worshiped every inch of your body?" he murmurs into my neck.

I pretend to think about it. "You've checked all my boxes."

His tongue peeks out, dragging a line along my jaw. "Hmm, might be my new favorite word."

"Mine too."

After a few quiet beats, Zeke asks, "Do you have any plans today, or are you all mine?"

"Oh!" I exclaim and sit up.

Zeke's blue eyes expand and he jerks forward. "What's wrong?"

I push him down and settle back against him. "I got an idea. We need to have an engagement announcement."

He laughs. "Now?"

I bop his nose. "No, smarty-pants. But how about tonight? Just our nearest and dearest."

Zeke licks his lips, and my focus zooms in on his mouth. "Whatever my future wifey wants, she gets."

Oh, I definitely love the sound of that.

# THIRTY

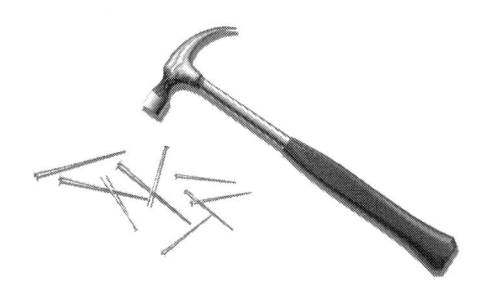

## BONDS

## ZEKE

"WELL, YOU TWO HAD QUITE a whirlwind this week," Raven comments from across the table.

Delilah's eyes sparkle. "It's ending on an epic high note."

She hasn't stopped smiling all day, and damn, that makes me feel good. I've been resisting the very real urge to pound my chest like a barbarian. Even my cheeks are a bit sore from grinning nonstop. Having Delilah agree to spend her life with me has sent me soaring into the starry atmosphere. Not sure I'll ever come back down to reality.

Raven and Addison are already going overboard with planning. They're blabbering about wedding dates and venues while my girl nods, just enjoying the ride. I take a sip of beer and just watch them, more than content to have a front-row seat of her pure joy. Delilah shows off her silver band like it's a five-carat solitaire from Tiffany's.

Yes, I looked. Hell no can I ever afford it.

Not that I really would've gone down that route. My mother's ring was made to fit Delilah's finger. This occasion has been in the making since we were twelve. Somehow my momma knew from her place in the clouds. Guess she never stopped guiding me to the right path.

Trey taps his bottle against mine. "Congrats, Krue. I'm glad you're making an honest woman outta her."

I snort. "Thanks, Sollens. I appreciate that." And I'm not lying. We've managed to form some sort of . . . truce.

"So, what happens now?"

I tilt my head and look at him. "What do you mean?"

"Where are you living?"

"With Delilah."

"What're you doing for work?"

I glare at him. "I'm part of the crew building Roosters. We've discussed this."

Trey waves my words away. "After that."

I scratch my scalp. "Uh, there's at least six months left on the Roosters project. After that? I'll figure something out."

"You glad to be back in Garden Grove?"

"Extremely," I say and rub Delilah's back. She sucks on her bottom lip and bats those extra-long lashes. Damn, I'm sunk.

Trey clears his throat. "What about your truck? That pile of rust is bound to die soon. I would know." He smirks, and I cock a brow. Where the hell is he going with this?

"And that is any of your concern because . . . ?"

He shrugs, and his rapid-fire questioning come to a pause. Apparently, he's collected all the necessary intel. Did Raven put him up to this? Trey couldn't give a shit about my career objectives.

We all order another round when the server stops by. I relax on my stool and glance around the table. Our usual five gathered at Dagos to celebrate. It's still setting in that I'm part of the equation. Delilah's parents should be here shortly too. I invited Ryan, and he's stopping by after work. We'll make an impressive bunch. Crazy to say, right?

I squint at the far-end corner. There's a new guy joining us tonight. Apparently, Shane works with Trey and is the source of Addison's recent mood swings. That's what Delilah told me anyway. I'm no expert, but they seem to be getting along fine. Shane's arm is resting on the back of Addy's chair, and she laughs far too loudly when he makes a joke. She's telling him something about cockroaches in New York City. But it's none of my business.

The scent of popcorn permeates the air, and my stomach grumbles. Delilah smirks at me. "Should I get us some?"

"What did I do to deserve you?" I question in all seriousness.

She shuffles over until her ass is balancing on both of our seats. "I could ask the exact same thing."

"Pretty sure we both know which way the scale is tipping when it comes to our balance."

Delilah shakes her head. "Don't point out my downfalls at our engagement party. It's not super nice."

"Right, that's exactly what would happen."

She winks and shifts to get up until Raven sets a heaping bowl of buttery goodness in front of us. This bar makes the best popcorn. I grab a handful and get munching.

"Thanks, Raven," I say around another mouthful.

Delilah sends her an air-kiss. "You're the bestest."

She slashes the air with her palm. "Please. You two have barely come up for air. The least I could do is provide sustenance."

"I'm surprised you detached from Trey's mouth long enough to notice," Delilah says.

"Good comeback," Raven spouts and returns to her seat.

I toss a kernel in Delilah's waiting mouth, and she pays back the favor. We go back and forth before realizing everyone is staring at us.

"What?" she asks the group between chews.

"Wow, you guys are just . . . so adorable." Addison is the one to pipe up.

"Uh-huh," Raven replies. "Save some romance for the honeymoon. Jeez."

I push some stray hairs away from Delilah's face. My thumb traces from her temple to chin, and she shivers. "We're just getting started," I murmur to her, but everyone hears me.

They share a collective sigh, like I've given them the solution for finding happily ever after. Maybe I have. I certainly know that's what Delilah is for me. I grip her knee and squeeze gently, hitting her ticklish spot. She laughs and pushes at me, preparing to counterattack. I block her and lace our fingers together.

Delilah winks at me and says, "You win this round."

She rests her head on my shoulder and blows out a long exhale. I look around at all the smiling faces. Everyone seems so giddy. Clinking glasses in toasts, sharing exuberant stories, and whipping up fresh ideas for whatever comes next. Only joy and happiness exist in this realm. The bliss is so thick that it bubbles over and spreads to the tables around us. It's intoxicating. Overwhelming too. I've never had a place to truly call home. But this feels an awful lot like that . . .

I scrunch my forehead. This is my life?

The stirrings of doubt creep in, muttering filth and spewing hate. I don't deserve to be here. I'm an imposter trying to fit in, but no one seems to notice. It's temporary—this disguise won't last. I gulp, my throat bobbing with the effort. Mended pieces of my confidence threaten to break apart and spill all over the floor.

I glance at Delilah, desperately needing an anchor, and she's right there, beaming at me. Slowly, the toxins evaporate as if the poison was never there.

This is my life.

And this time, there's no question about it.

# EPILOGUE

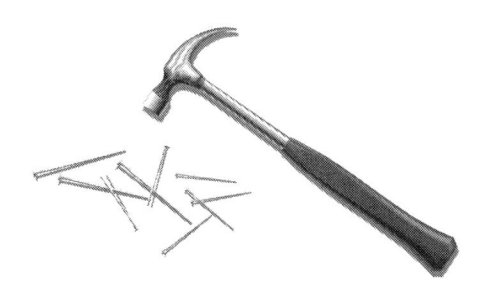

## NEXT

## ZEKE

DELILAH'S HEELS CLICK ON THE sidewalk as we stroll toward Roosters. A cool breeze picks up, and she burrows against my chest, snuggling closer to block the wind. It's been an unseasonably warm spring, but there's a bite in the air this afternoon. My arm tightens around her, and we hustle to the entrance. I yank on the heavy door and usher Delilah forward.

Her steps falter on the shiny stone floor. "Oooh," she whistles. "This is super fancy. But I think you did too good, Zee."

I chuckle. "What's that mean?"

Delilah rubs the chill from her bare arms. "I feel like we're in a swanky, big city restaurant. Did we leave Garden Grove without me realizing it?"

"A vacation without leaving the comfort of your town," I say. "That can be another selling point."

"Yeah, I like the thought of that."

I glance around, taking stock of the new and improved Roosters. The interior is old news to me considering this is where I've been spending over forty hours each week. But from a fresh perspective, comparing this to the before version must be a shock. The tables and high-tops are a mixture of different color wood, creating a pattern around the room. Black chairs and stools give people a spot to sit. Exposed beams show off the industrial-style ceiling. Numerous chrome lamps dangle from black cables, lighting up the joint just right. There are minimal decorations adorning the walls, just a few pieces from local artists. Natural brick pillars add to the understated-yet-upscale appeal.

But none of that steals the show.

I follow Delilah's line of sight, noticing what holds her attention. "The bar is beautiful . . . and seriously massive. What is it made out of?"

With a palm to her lower back, I steer us that way. "It's a concrete composite that's been buffed until it's silky smooth. All these,"—I drift my fingers along the side—"are hand-placed mosaic tiles and rocks. That took almost a month, I swear. I'll keep coming here just to appreciate all my hard work on this beast."

Delilah mirrors my movements. "Well, it's stunning. The entire set up is amazing. Mary Sue and Bob must be pleased."

The beaming owners wave from across the room, and I return the gesture. "I'd like to think so."

Not to brag, but we surpassed their expectations by a thousand miles. They told us so. To make matters even better, we finished ahead of schedule. That gives them extra time to fuss over minor details and ensure absolute perfection. It's been a pleasure building their dream, and they're all about showing gratitude. The happy couple invited the crew for this little gathering as a token of their appreciation. We're celebrating the end of construction together before everyone moves on.

Mary Sue and Bob will be plenty busy running Roosters.

Devon and the guys are leaving tomorrow, off to the next site.

And I'm exactly where I want to be.

Aside from being jobless, that is. My chest gets tight when the telltale dread takes shape. How will I support myself and this gorgeous girl next to me? I'll run into a few snags when my savings dry up for sure. Delilah shifts into me, wrapping herself around my torso, and my worry fades away. I'll figure work shit out later.

"How's my favorite foreman?" Devon booms behind me.

I turn to face him. "You looking in a mirror?"

He laughs. "Always so humble. Never lose that humor."

"Lewis will fill in the gaps."

Devon snorts. "Unlikely, but he'll have to do. Glad your better half is here. Maybe she'll keep you in line," he says and gives Delilah a wink.

She giggles and elbows me. "He's got a mind of his own."

"Ah, cute. You two are ganging up on me."

Devon jabs my arm. "I'll be gone by morning. There's only precious hours left to ruffle those pretty feathers of yours."

I roll my eyes. He's always been supportive but enjoys tossing out plenty of barbs. Especially since I've become more . . . civil. I can take a joke and roll with the punches far easier these days.

"Are you going far?" Delilah asks.

He nods. "Two hundred miles south. You won't see me around these parts for a while."

I jut my chin at him. "What's the gig?"

Devon raises his brow. "Interested? You can bring a plus-one."

"Maybe next time," I tell him.

"I'm gonna miss you on the crew, Zeke. You're a good worker. Whatever you decide to do, I'm confident you'll succeed."

My head lifts a little higher, and I can breathe a tad easier. "Thanks, boss. I appreciate that."

"Ah, not your boss anymore. You're a free agent."

I chuckle. "Guess so. That doesn't sound too bad. Maybe I'll do my own thing. Be a solo contractor."

"I'd hire you," Delilah cuts in from beside me.

I glance down into her honest eyes. "Yeah?"

She squeezes me, nuzzling into my neck. "I'd be crazy not to. I bet a lot of people would take you up on it."

I shrug. "That might be a possibility."

"You keep prodding at The Mossy Den's owners. When they're ready to renovate, call me. I'll slap you back on my payroll in a heartbeat. I'll cut you in on a higher commission," Devon offers.

"Don't mind that one bit," I reply.

Devon salutes Bob and Mary Sue, signaling he'll be over in a moment. "We can be partners from afar. Take care of yourself, Zeke. And your lady." He holds a hand out to me, and we shake on it.

"Thanks, Devon. Same to you. I'm sure we'll see you around."

"We appreciate everything," Delilah says.

He waves us off. "Enjoy the honeymoon, love birds."

After he ambles off, I scoop Delilah up and plop her on the bar. She makes room for me between her thighs. Her fingers wander up and down my side, tracing the ink hidden there. I'm not sure my girl realizes how often her touch settles on this spot. Not that I'm complaining.

I love Delilah's hands on me all the damn time. It's a feeling that intensifies with each passing second. And the fact she loves her mark on my skin? That drives me absolutely wild. I shift closer so her palm presses harder into my ribs. Delilah bites her lip, sending me a knowing look.

"You're so sexy," I tell her.

Her tongue peeks out. "Have I told you this tattoo is a serious turn-on?"

I groan and bump my hips into her legs. "Not nearly enough."

Delilah leans in and kisses along my jaw. "I get so hot thinking about our names intersecting and blending together. I'll never get enough."

My mouth waters, and I'm suddenly starving. "You wanna

see it, baby?"

Her hair tickles when she shifts against me. "Remember what happened last time you showed it to me in public?"

"I haven't showed you the bathrooms yet. They're real spacious," I say.

She shivers. "Is that so?"

I begin tugging at the hem of my shirt, but she stops me. I lift a brow in question.

"I'm capable of waiting until this party is over," Delilah teases.

"What if I'm not?"

"I lavished that spot with extra attention not even two hours ago."

I spread her thighs and rock forward. "Doesn't matter, Trip. I'm always ready for more."

Delilah moans quietly and shakes her head. "Pretty sure Mary Sue and Bob weren't expecting their bar to get christened tonight."

I chuckle and back off. "It'd make a great story, though."

"No doubt about that. Let's give it a few more minutes." She winks, and her focus flickers away.

Delilah is watching something over my shoulder, and I follow her gaze. She's focusing on one of the many high-def flat screens mounted to the far wall.

"They're showing barrel racing. Dagos rarely broadcasts this channel," she explains.

A laugh rumbles from my chest. "You'd make a sexy cowgirl, wrapped in all that country. I'll take you to a rodeo, wifey."

She playfully bumps into me. "A real one? Or will you be starring as the bucking bronco, hubby?"

"Why not both?" I moan into her ear, and Delilah smiles against my cheek. We got hitched two weeks ago in the sand of our secluded beach spot. The ceremony was small and intimate, exactly how we imagined it. I'm still floating in the clouds. I can still feel the freezing spring water lapping at my ankles while we promised each other forever. It was the perfect day, just like each one I spend with her.

She toys with the band on my finger, an exact match to hers. "Always everything."

"I love you, Trip."

"And I love you, Zee."

I hum softly, never tiring of those words. "Wanna check out the patio?"

Delilah pulls away and squints at me. "In this weather?"

"I'll keep you warm, baby."

"That sounds promising."

"And there's a few hidden corners, close to the massive firepit."

She scoots to the counter's edge. "Well, in that case, we have a deal. Lead the way, Mister Kruegan."

I spin around, offering her my back. "Your chariot awaits, Missus Kruegan. Now boarding for a happily ever after."

# DELETED SCENES

## TRIP

## DELILAH

WE'RE GETTING NEW NEIGHBORS AGAIN.

I'm currently watching a moving truck pull up to the house. The sides are plastered with advertisements for hourly rates and I recognize the brand from a television commercial. I guess these folks rented the vehicle and are handling things on their own. I stare from my perch, silently wondering if they'll need help. My parents aren't home and I should probably ask permission first. Waltzing next door to introduce myself doesn't sound super-safe.

A bored sigh escapes my throat, which causes my lips to flap from the exasperated effort. Being twelve really sucks, especially in this small town. I rest my chin along the wall as I continue spying on the people we'll soon share a yard with. An older man is behind the wheel and he's all I can see from here. Disappointment rattles around in my head and I sink deeper into the plush cushions. Would it be too much to hope for a kid my age? It sure would be nice to have another friend around here. My foot taps rapidly while I consider the options.

Should I stay or go?

Just as my internal debate gains momentum, a boy hops out from the truck's backseat. My heart instantly takes off at a fast gallop and I stare with newfound interest. I can hardly contain the excited butterflies swarming around my stomach. I press my face against the cool glass and get a closer look. My wish might be finally coming true.

*Holy buckets, I think he's around my age . . . and really freaking hot.*

With sun-tanned skin and dark brown hair, he's a bright spot in the dull surroundings of this town. Forget all that nonsense about waiting until later to offer a helping hand. I'm ready to lend all my fingers and toes without skipping a beat. I'd be giving off a horrible impression by continuing to sit and do nothing.

Let's be honest.

My decision was made once that cute kid appeared on the pavement. But I'm trying to ease the pit of guilt when considering going against my parents' rules. They'll understand once I provide my iron-clad explanation. There's no denying love at first sight.

I skip over to the hallway mirror to appraise my appearance. Thankfully I'm already wearing my favorite jeans that fit around my butt just right. My pink shirt isn't anything special, but it'll do for now. I don't want to waste precious moments obsessing over the perfect outfit. My blonde hair is hanging in loose waves that shine in the overhead lighting. No need for a brush. I twist this way and that, double-checking everything. I bite my bottom lip before giving my reflection a shrug.

*Good enough for now, I suppose.*

My fingers shake as I walk toward my entryway. I stretch them wide, forcing steadiness into my bones. A blast of blistering heat immediately seeps into my skin after opening the door. I step outside and sweat immediately forms along the base of my neck. I quickly hop down the porch steps and stroll along the stone path leading across my front yard.

A hint of nauseous taunts me and I swallow repeatedly. What am I so scared of? He's just a random dude. But the closer I get to this guy, the dryer my mouth becomes. Maybe I should have chugged a few glasses of water. But then I'd have to pee. I don't want to interrupt the conversation we might be having if nature calls. I clench my hands into fists before quickly releasing them. Anxiety hovers around me like a heavy blanket. I reach the edge of my lawn, take in a lungful of steamy air, and cross onto their property.

The boy is alone, kicking rocks into the street. I'm not sure where the older man went, but he's not important. I only have eyes for one guy, and eagerly scan him from head to toe. My sandals swish in the grass, sliding against the too-long blades. Suddenly I'm falling, my foot lodging into a hidden hole. When I stumble, a startled squeak escapes my parched throat. The most gorgeous face I've ever seen whips in my direction.

Even though my leg is throbbing, it seems like I'm floating. Did I crack my skull on something? But no, it's him. The crystal-clear blue of his eyes soaks into me, soothing all worry away. I almost fell on my butt while trying to rush over to meet him, but none of that registers. I'm lost in a cloudless sky with a dopey smile lifting my lips. With a sigh, I decide to forget everything else.

Wait, what's my name again? Shoot. That's kind of important.

My gawking is all fine and dandy, until I notice his reaction.

The cute jerk is laughing at me, which releases the hold on my nerves. All at once, mortification threatens to drown me and I choke on thin-air. I dip my face, cutting off the connection between us. I roll my aching ankle, and shuffle out of the grassy danger zone. My face is burning hotter than the heatwave. I'm sure my cheeks are bright red. I take a few moments to collect myself, and get on solid ground, before glancing back up in his direction.

His brilliant blues are full of humor and delight as he continues cackling at my expense.

I want to stomp my uninjured foot and demand he stop, but the words won't surface. My brain has short-circuited and gone all fuzzy because the vision of this kid smiling is screwing with me. He's so hot that I'll let this little rude incident slide.

Through his nonstop chuckling, he manages to bust out a jumbled, "Nice trip."

*What the eff?*

I see how he wants to play this and I can definitely dish it out.

"Oh yeah? Well, nice shirt." I grin and pop out my hip for added sass.

He glances down at the ridiculously huge bear wearing sunglasses. The design is plastered across the front, definitely hard to miss. *I'm Bearly Listening* is scrawled under the image and I have to keep my giggle on lockdown.

But my amusement quickly fades.

The gray fabric is stretched tight over his chest and muscles bulge from the short sleeves. How is he so ripped? All the kids from school look like toothpicks compared to this guy. His biceps are seriously chiseled. My heart speeds up into a full sprint being so close to his hotness.

His laughter cuts off, and he flips his hair in that ultra-cool boys are doing now.

"Whatever, Trip. You can't distract me from your epic-fail and graceful moves." He shoots me a cocky smirk.

Gosh, he's hilarious. And extremely good looking. I definitely need to know him better.

So, that's exactly what I do.

# #2

# ANAL

## DELILAH

I BEND INTO DOWNWARD DOG, enjoying the twinge in my muscles from this pose.

A low groan rumbles from behind me. I peek between my stretched legs to find Zeke standing there, getting a great view of my butt.

"Watching you exercise is the sexiest fucking way to pass time. I'm not sure how to feel about this sorry scrap of material, though." He snaps the spandex around my thigh.

"You don't like them?"

"That's not the issue. It's that every other man gets a full view of your ass." He makes a show of adjusting himself. "You wear these in public?"

I wait a few beats, letting him sweat it out for a moment. I send him a wink. "No, they're only for you."

"Teasing me?"

"Uh-huh."

"Do you want me to fuck you, Trip? All you gotta do is ask."

"This is more fun."

"Oh, yeah?" Zeke's fingers dip under my waistband, exploring and searching. I hold the position, allowing him to cop all the feels. "You miss me?" he asks.

"Always."

"Here?" He circles my back entrance. I shiver.

"Yes."

Zeke groans, spanking me lightly. "Hold that thought."

He's gone and back before I can comment. When I look at him again, he's naked and his dick is slick with lube.

"Someone's in a hurry," I say.

"I like to think of it as prepared. And optimistic." Zeke points to the bed. "Up you go."

There's no hesitation from me—following his command requires zero effort. I get situated on my hands and knees with electric desire coursing through me. His touch is barely a skim as he wanders up my inner thighs. He peels off my too-tight shorts and sucks in a breath.

"Naughty girl. No panties?"

I shake my head against the pillow. "Why bother?"

"I like your style. Now ditch the bra."

I struggle out of the constricting straps and toss the material away. Zeke's touch returns to my ass. He gently pulls my cheeks apart so I'm on full display. I spread my legs wider and shift lower, exposing myself to him. He hisses at my movements.

"You know what I want, Trip?"

"Yes. I want the same thing."

"Are you feeling empty?" His palms drifts along my lower back.

I tremble. "So much."

I'm already panting, needing this more than I realized. We've crossed all our previous boundaries except this one.

"Shh, baby. Relax," he coaxes.

The hum of a vibrator breaks into the silence.

*Where the hell did that come from?*

Zeke brings the pulsing toy to my clit, rounding in slow circles. His free hand reaches for one of mine, placing my fingers on his working ones. We swap places so I'm in charge, sliding the small bullet back and forth. I'm getting lost in the waves of pleasure when he begins stroking down my lubed crack.

I'm so slippery and slick—everywhere.

"You been thinking about me back here?" Zeke asks, circling my tight hole again.

"Heck yeah."

I hear the telltale click of a bottle and bite my lip on a groan. Cool drops hit my over-sensitized skin and I lurch forward. He smooths the liquid around my back entrance, but it's only a tease. His finger is there, probing and spanning and getting ready. He dips into me, the slight pressure sending sparks along my skin.

"So tight, baby. I've gotta stretch you all over again."

"Yes, please," I beg. The preparation is my favorite part. Each drive and push will send me deeper into heady lust.

He spins his finger around and down, the sting intensifying along with my need. He knows what to do to drive me crazy. As I circle my bundle of nerves, he's working my ass just right.

I twist my head to the side, breathing hard. "Please, I want you."

"Be patient," Zeke demands. There's more drizzle and wetness, more frustratingly slow strokes.

"Never," I moan, arching closer.

"I love your desperation. Do you trust me?"

"I only trust you."

"Love that even more. But still?"

I push back, silently urging him on. "Yes."

One finger turns into two and he scissors them apart. My legs shake and I almost collapse onto the bed. But his digits are slippery and easily slide into me. Over and again, on a smooth cycle that's hypnotizing me.

"Holy shit," I groan.

"That's my girl. Opening up for me. You want me to fuck your ass?"

My hips buck, pushing him deeper. "So much. Please, yes."

Another finger goes in, followed by more lube. My hole is tight and resistant to the additional intrusion, but I acclimate easily enough. His fingers pump in and out, slowly building me up with the humming on my clit. I'm humping the air, seeking more and he gives it. He twists and swirls, making more room. I'm drooling for his dick, wanting to be split in half. I crave him there, in my most forbidden area.

"Fuck me," I plead.

"You gotta let me do this or my cock will never fit."

I try, breathing out slowly. All three fingers work in unison to drag me closer to the edge and I groan in relief. There's a pinch as he wedges in further.

"That's right, baby. Just like that." He shoves in and out while I rock into his touch, asking for more.

"You excited?"

"Uh huh."

"You always loved this."

"I've missed it."

"Me too."

I feel Zeke jerking his shaft, and I want to touch him. I want him inside of me. I manage to widen my knees further, giving him the green light. His fingers move faster, in and out. He's pumping his arm harder with labored breaths.

I moan and pant, desperate for more. "I'm ready."

"You sure?"

"Yes."

His fingers leave me and I rub my clit faster, an orgasm looming right before me. The head of his massive dick is kissing my rim, a warning of sorts. Ready or not, here we go.

I feel his tip lining up with my hole. I blow out a breath and let my muscles relax. There's no stopping the slight quiver in my limbs.

"Are you nervous?" he purrs.

"Maybe a little."

"Why?"

"Because it's been five years."

"So? It'll be like riding a bike." He prods me lightly and I bite my lip.

"Doubtful. Your cock is huge."

Zeke chuckles. "You sound the same as back then."

"Yeah, well, she knew the truth."

"We'll go slow. I know how to take care of you. We taught each other."

"We did."

The time for talk is over. Zeke eases in, sinking slowly and easily enough. I hiss at the sting, but push into his forward flow. When he breaches deeper, the burn lashes through my middle. I hiss as the air whooshes from my lungs. The flames are incinerating me, threatening to boil my insides. When he presses further, the pressure doubles. Zeke's palm smooths my ass cheek, a bit sticky from the lube. He grips my hips and tilts me up, positioning me just right. The move drives him in and I cry out.

Zeke stills. "Should I stop?"

I shake my head. "No, I'm fine. It'll get better."

"You sure?" He starts to pull away and I grip his leg.

"I want this."

My encouragement works and he begins moving again. Just an inch, but it feels like I'm being torn apart. My mouth opens with a silent scream, then Zeke pops through the restrictive ring. I widen my knees again, lowering further onto the mattress and giving him a better angle. This isn't our first time, but it's been quite a while. He glides forward, the bulbous steel entering me with a blooming force.

"Shit," I hiss and squeeze my eyes shut.

"Okay?" Zeke's fingers sweep across my lower back.

"Yes, keep going."

A quiet click and more lube drips down. He slides in a bit and pulls back, letting me adjust to him. I push the vibrator harder against my clit and stars dance in my vision.

"Talk to me, Trip."

"It's good. I just have to get used to this again."

Zeke withdraws further, then thrusts deeper than before. My ass is searing from the size of him, but my core heats with the beginning of utter ecstasy. The pleasure floods over me and I quiver against him. All discomfort recedes as my body lights up with a different type of heat.

I tremble in his grip. "Oh, oh, yeah."

He prods further, listening to my desire. "You feel this? That's us, baby."

"It is, so much."

Then Zeke is fully seated and I'm stretched to the max. One arm bands around my waist and he hauls me up against him. My back meets his chest and I moan when he hits even deeper. In this position, I have the power. He takes control of the vibrator and I start to move in his lap. I impale myself on his dick, up and down, my movements fluid.

"Your ass is so sexy. So fucking tight," he whispers along my jaw. Zeke circles the bullet faster against me and I get a little dizzy.

I shift forward before lowering, swiveling my hips. "Just like that. I'm gonna come soon."

"You love my cock in your ass, and I love being buried here. It's so fucking hot how you stretch for me."

I look at him over my shoulder and he's watching our connection.

"Not gonna last much longer, Trip. You feel too good," he groans. "Fuck, I've missed this." He grips my thigh and shoves up into me.

I rock into the vibrations, ready to tumble off the cliff. "Oh, Zee. I'm right there."

"Yeah? Gonna come?"

"Uh huh."

"Thank fuck, me too. I'm gonna fill your ass with every drop. How does that sound?"

# SNEAK PEEK of LASS

What's next? How does Addison and Shane sound?

"Hey, cutie. Welcome to Dagos. What can I get for you?"

I just stare at her angelic face, lost in a fog of red hair, brown freckles, and green eyes. The beauty waves in front of my face.

"Are you okay?"

I swallow once, then again.

She giggles. "Cat got your tongue?"

I manage to find my voice. "S-something like that."

> Be on the lookout for LASS,
> a swoony roommates-to-lovers
> romance, in early 2019.

Read on for an excerpt of GENT, available now.

# PROLOGUE

## MOVE

## RAVEN

*AM I CRAZY?*

As I cross the Stockton county line, my heart leaps into my throat. I'm not typically nervous, but this is big. Huge, really. Life changing and all that. Moving clear across the state seems extreme, right? It totally is, but this is happening. *Tonight.* I've never visited this city before, but in a few hours, it will be my home. Talk about taking a chance.

I'm worrying myself into an ulcer, and for no reason. Delilah wouldn't steer me wrong, or offer false promises, yet doubt continues to plague me.

What if everyone hates me? Or Delilah decides I suck at baking? What if I make a fool of myself?

This is the type of impulsive decision I was subjected to growing up. My mother made one hasty choice after another, dragging me along for the bumpy ride. The thought stops me cold.

*Oh, Lord. Am I acting like her?*

The idea makes me sick to my stomach, and I reject it immediately. She'd never live in a small town, unless there was a damn good reason. Like meeting her next Mr. Right Now. I shudder thinking of her current flavor of the month. They're overseas living in a gorgeous villa off the Mediterranean. He's twice her age with a bank account busting at the seams. My mother swears up and down his money isn't the reason she loves him. Too bad I don't believe her.

Restless energy courses through my veins as I fiddle with the radio. I wish that audiobook had been a bit longer. It was a stellar distraction from the chaos buzzing through me. Getting lost in a sappy romance gives everything a rosy hue. Once they all lived happily ever after, the panic of my situation filtered in. Living in the pages of a love story would be far easier.

My eyes quickly land on the gift from Delilah. The bright pink apron lays spread across the front seat, like a constant presence reminding me of what's ahead. Master Baker is embroidered across the front. It makes me laugh each time, and this moment isn't different. As my giggle dies off, the view from my windshield looks brighter than ever.

I change the station and a slow country tune fills the speakers, calming my racing pulse. This sounds like sweet haven, which is exactly what I need to hear. I'm digging in and grabbing the happy place buried in my soul.

This is my choice. I'm controlling my future. Confidence replaces the doubt as my foot presses harder on the accelerator. I'll finally be planting roots. Everything will go perfectly. Yeah, I've got to stop overthinking this because the time is now. My hands twist on the steering wheel, and I exhale slowly. I've been waiting for this my entire life. I'm ready.

My headlights flash across a sign welcoming me to Garden

Grove, and giddy nerves attack my gut.

Their slogan feels like arms wrapping me in a warm hug. I smile and repeat the words silently.

*Where everyone belongs.*

That sounds just right, like Goldilocks. Ready or not Garden Grove, here I come.

# ONE

## MA'AM

### TREY

"DID YOU HEAR WHAT I said?"

At her question, my gaze shifts to connect with the woman's stare. She's an unfamiliar face, probably lured into town by the specialty shops off Main Street. Sitting closer than socially acceptable, she's almost stuck on me. The bar is crowded tonight, though. I let the proximity slide, but her attempt at conversation is pushing it too far.

I came to Dagos for a few beers after work, not to engage in chit-chat. Usually I won't hesitate sampling fresh meat, gladly gobble up what's being offered, but not today. Try as she might, this chick is striking out with me. I have zero intentions of giving her the quick fuck she's been practically begging for since sitting down.

I clear my throat. "Ma'am, I'm not interested."

"Excuse me?" she says as her eyes widen. "Ma'am? That's what you call a grandmother. Do I look old to you?"

The dial on her annoying meter cranks up a few notches. I'm not stupid enough to fall into her trap, but still bite my tongue to keep the insults from barreling out.

I quickly scan her pinched face, covered with powdery shit likely meant to hide her age. I was trying to be polite by using a respectful term, but she's clearly not the type. I rub my forehead while blowing out a breath, frustration already building like a storm cloud.

"I mean no offense," I grind out between clenched teeth, "but I'm spending the evening solo. Cheers." I raise my bottle in a lame-ass salute.

The yappy broad huffs and rolls her eyes. It seems she might spit more crap my way, but then her attention darts to a man across the room. She eagerly slips off the stool, nearly spilling her drink with the jerky movements. She glances back at me, shooting daggers from her eyes.

"Asshole," she shoots over her shoulder before sauntering off.

*Good fucking riddance.*

I lift the nearly empty beer to my lips, but a burst of laughter interrupts me.

"Wow. You sure know how to pick 'em. How are you still single with suave moves like that?"

"Not you too," I mutter without turning around, recognizing the raspy voice immediately. "Was the entire female race set on driving me fucking crazy?" My chin tilts skyward as I silently ask for patience . . . or a fucking break. Neither will come for me.

"Would it kill you to be nice?" Addison rests her arms against the bar next to me.

I puff air through my clenched teeth. "Most likely. And I was nice. I called her ma'am."

"You know girls hate that," she shoots back. "It's a dig more than anything and makes us feel old. Might as well call her a raging bitch or wrinkled hag."

"Those names seem more appropriate. Thanks," I chuckle but there's no humor behind it.

"Don't start, Trey. You know I'm right."

"I'm not saying shit. Just thinking I might use those instead."

"You're impossible."

"That's the point."

"What-ev-er," Addison singsongs while glancing around. "Where's Jack?"

"Still at the shop."

"Burning the midnight oil?"

"In more ways than one. Had a rough day."

She tilts her head and gives me a once-over. "You too?"

"Don't I always?"

"Meh, I suppose. You're always a grump so it's tough to tell the difference."

"And here I thought we were exchanging pleasantries."

"You and pleasant will never go together." Addison hitches a thumb over her shoulder. "Running off that lovely lady is a prime example."

I grunt and shake my head. "She deserved it for being so desperate."

She snorts and elbows me. "Why are you such a dick? All that handsome is going to such shameful waste. You need to find someone to treat right."

Peering at Addison, all toned limbs and tan skin, I consider a quick fuck after all. I grip the cool bottle, picturing her soft flesh giving in to me.

"Why haven't we ever—"

"No way. I know that look," she says. "I see you give women those bedroom eyes every Friday night only to watch them turn cold the following morning. I haven't fallen for them yet and I don't plan to start."

Just like that, our breezy banter slams to a halt. Tension strains my shoulders after being cut off. *Again.* What is it with chicks bulldozing me tonight?

Having Addison call me out does nothing to help my mood, but it's no surprise she sees straight through me. Although I've known her since kindergarten, it still pisses me off. Moments like this make living in a small-town suffocating. There's nothing and no one new around here. I know useless shit about everyone from Garden Grove, whether I want to or not.

I roll my neck and restore my typical look of indifference. "I never get any complaints. Your loss, Addy."

Addison shakes her head. "So fucking cocky. I ain't giving you any ass, but how 'bout another?" She asks and gestures to my beer.

I grumble, "That'd be great," without looking back at her.

Addison just stands there so I give in and glance over. Her arms are crossed as she raises a slim brow my way, seemingly waiting for . . .

"Please," I grit. The irritation from earlier whooshes in my ears and I'm ready to get gone.

*Right after this drink.*

She snickers and says, "That's better. We'll make a gentleman of you soon."

"Don't hold your breath, *ma'am*."

Addison gasps and flames rise in her hazel eyes.

Before she digs into me, I add, "Chill out. I'm just fucking with you. But seriously, get back to work. I'm thirsty."

"You really are an asshole," she says while patting my cheek with more force than necessary. I'm sure she'd love to slap the shit out of me but won't risk getting in trouble for it. She shakes her head and turns away, strutting off to serve other waiting customers.

My eyes lock on her swaying hips, losing myself in the rhythm of her movement for a moment. No harm in looking, right?

Sweet-smelling perfume wafts in as the abandoned stool next to me shifts slightly.

"Is this seat taken?"

The notes are soft but rise above the booming noise in the space. The feminine lilt of her voice snakes around before I feel a twisting in my gut. I quickly shove that fluffy shit away. My jaw ticks while I ignore her heavenly scent closing in around me.

"Don't even bother," I growl loud enough for her to hear.

"Excuse me?"

Disbelief colors her voice and I can't help swiveling toward her.

*Holy shit.*

Bottomless blue eyes greet me, sparkling with fierce emotion. The glittering sapphires are hypnotizing, the type of pull any man would fall victim to.

*Except me.*

I manage to break out of my trance and scan the rest of her features. Golden waves frame her face, the long locks shimmering in the bright lights. Her skin is clear of makeup, giving her a natural glow that I rarely see on the women around here. That caked-on crap always looks like a shield, hiding secrets and truths, like the ballsy bimbo from earlier. Nothing like this stunner in front of me. She's on a whole new level.

She's open to me, hiding nothing at all, which I'm realizing is a huge fucking turn-on. My hips shift slightly to alleviate the sudden pressure rising in my jeans, but it's pointless. My dick is definitely taking notice of all she has to offer.

Maybe I'm not meant to spend the night alone. This newbie is definitely worth changing plans for.

My gaze wanders lazily along her slender figure, outwardly showing minimal interest while my pulse pounds erratically. Why am I having such a strong reaction to her? With an innocent look and a few words, she's screwing with my mojo like a voodoo witch.

*What makes her so damn special?*

She's just another woman, looking for an easy lay, and I'm the biggest target. This stranger probably heard about me from locals like Addison and came over to try her luck. My body is betraying me by falling under her spell, but I see the threat like a neon sign. I'm not letting her sink those perfectly painted nails into me.

Her flawless face dips into my line of sight, and our eyes clash. I blink and take a clarifying breath as determination to get rid of her barrels through me.

"Listen, babe—"

She holds up her hand like a stop sign and for some reason, having her interrupt doesn't bother me.

"Did you just *babe* me?" Her question is all sass.

"Sure did, sweetheart. Call 'em like I see 'em. Don't pretend to be offended. We both know why you're over here talking to me."

Her face turns an adorable shade of pink. "First, stop with the nicknames. Second, are you for real? What the hell is wrong with you?"

"I don't see any issue. You're the one disrupting my quiet evening."

"What the . . . I mean, seriously? I want to sit down and this is the only available spot. You honestly think I came over here to hit on you?"

Her ridiculous question doesn't deserve a response. My glare matches hers as I silently explain my opinion on the matter. My expression must tell her everything she needs to know.

"Wow, you're an asshole."

"You're the third woman to call me that tonight. Be careful, I might get a complex."

"Aw, poor baby. I'd hate to dent your fragile ego," she snips with a curl in her lip.

"There's nothing fragile about me. Don't worry. I'm hard and solid. Wanna feel?" I ask and pat my abs.

She nods to my hands. "No, thanks. I'd hate for you to rub off on me."

"Does the grease under my nails bother you? Princess is afraid of getting a little dirty?"

"Do you get a rise out of being mean?"

I lean against the bar and cross my arms. "I don't get many complaints. You're not from around here, so I'll fill you in—the ladies love me."

"Pretty sure I saw Barbie McCleveage storm off after chatting with you. She didn't look too satisfied."

"Now who's using nicknames? Jealous much?"

"Hardly," she huffs.

I smirk before checking out her rack, being extremely obvious about it. Pushing her buttons takes away the tension from earlier, replacing it with a surprising ease. Fighting with her is the most nonsexual fun I've had with a woman in a long time. Wonder how she'd react if I called her ma'am.

"All right, all right. You've broken me down. I was set on not having any company tonight, but for you, I'll make an exception. If you insist on standing here, blabbing away, I've got far better uses for that luscious mouth. My place isn't too far away," I suggest while waggling my brows. My behavior is over the top, but what can I say? She's bringing out the best in me.

Her lips part in shock. This stranger just stares at me, and I'm sure she's about to turn away . . . or slap me. Either way, mission accomplished.

But this chick is full of surprises.

She raises her chin and says, "You're pathetic, and I see straight through your bullshit. I've dealt with guys like you my entire life—dime a dozen playboys looking to score. Having a place to sit isn't worth being ridiculed."

I keep my face void of emotion but my blood is boiling. "Why are you still here then?"

"I have no idea." She rests a palm on her forehead, looking bewildered and sexy as fuck. "I don't want to surrender so easily, but just . . . forget it. You're clearly used to getting what you want. I'd hate to be another tally in your win column."

I chuckle, the sound dark like a rumble. "No truer words. I'm a fucking winner. Since you're not interested in my *cocky bullshit*, let's make a deal. I was here first so go find someone else to harass."

A dimple dents her cheek as she smiles, but the expression looks weak. The fire in her eyes extinguishes as she mutters, "A real man wouldn't hesitate before offering an empty seat to a lady. My mistake."

I'm the one forcing her away, but for some messed up reason, the distress creasing her face is a punch to the gut. So, I offer some parting words for her to remember me by.

"I never claimed to be a gentleman, Princess."

GENT is available now

# ACKNOWLEDGMENTS

I'M NOT SUPPOSED TO HAVE favorites, but Zeke and Delilah stole my heart. MISS holds a very special place inside of me. I really hope you loved their story.

This journey as an author has been a nonstop adventure and I have so many tour guides to thank. I have so many incredible people in my corner and I'm extremely grateful. First and foremost and always, I owe everything to my husband. He is the most supportive and incredible man. I wouldn't be able to follow my writing dreams without him.

To all the readers and reviewers and bloggers, you all rock! The hours and dedication you show to this community never ceases to amaze me. Thank you for the constant support, messages, shares, encouragement, and love. I can't extend enough gratitude but know how much I appreciate each one of you!

To Talia, my extremely talented cover designer and close friend. I'm forever in your debt. You're incredible and wonderful and fabulous. We'll meet one day soon! I hope the cockroaches never stop by for another visit.

To Sunniva, my gracious editor and outstanding author friend. I'm so thankful for all you do, without hesitation. I'd be lost without you.

To Michelle, my go-to pal and reliable confidant. Thank you for always offering up kind words when I need them most. Our crazy brainstorming will make us rich one day! Fingers crossed I'll be seeing you next year.

To Anne, my hilarious relief when life is too much. Your words mean so much to me. The stories you share can never be replaced. Thanks for being there!

To Ace, my constant and genuine friend. Not only do I love your books, but I love you. I'm grateful for your support. I'll never forget everything you've done for me.

To Tijuana, my super-duper princess and beta extraordinaire. Thank you for being a shoulder for me to blabber all over. You never complain about my crazy. You're the greatest and I'm so thankful to call you friend. Thanks for being so dedicated and caring.

To Sarah, my outstanding beta/blogger/reviewer friend. I don't know how you do it all and I'm in awe of you. Thank you for making my books better and being there with suggestions. I appreciate all you do!

To Melissa, my newfound friend and beta. Thank you for the lovely feedback and being willing to read my books. I greatly appreciate your guidance and support!

To Kate, my sweet and generous friend. You're so amazing and talented. I love your words, graphics, and talent. Thank you for always being there!

To Tia, my super sweet and lovely ally. I'd be lost without your support and encouragement. Thank you for always offering me the greatest words that I need to hear.

To Nicole, my driven and caring friend. You're an inspiration. Thank you for being so helpful and willing to lend a hand. You rock!

To Suzie, my voice of reason when I need it most. You are the kindest and always leave me smiling. Thank you!

To Victoria, my longest-standing author buddy. I'm grateful for our friendship and your sweet words.

To Lauren, my dependable and selfless friend. I never have to worry about you being there. That means more than words can describe.

To Leigh, my inspiration and driving force. You are the sweetest and give me so much confidence with a few simple words. I can't wait to hang out in Vegas for some Shen-anigans!

To Megan, Shauna, and Jacqueline, my fierce trio. I couldn't do this without you ladies. Thank you for the encouragement, shares, love, and for being great friends. You're fabulous!

To Cindy, my friend with all the sweet words. Thank you for sharing them with me.

To Candi, my extraordinary PR professional. You seriously knock my socks off with everything you accomplish in a day. I'm amazed by you. Thank you, thank you, thank you for everything. I'll never be able to say it enough.

To the ladies of Give Me Books, thank you for being extremely reliable and dependable. I love working with you!

To Sara, the very talented photographer who shot the image of Alex and Carolyn. Thank you for giving me a beautiful cover photo for this story.

To Crystal and Maggie for taking a chance on a new author back then. I'll never ever forget your willingness to help me out. I love you both!

To my Hotties, the greatest reader group of all time. I'm so thankful to each one of you for taking this journey with me. I appreciate you and the dedication you show to our community. I love our special place on social media!

To the Harloe's Review Crew, thank you so very much for wanting to read and review my words. You're the bestest and I'm forever grateful.

To the 60K in 30 ladies, thank you for keeping me on track and making sure I met the deadline. You all give me plenty of laughs of love.

To my fellow DND authors, I owe you all a huge hug for all the motivation and support. I love our little family and would be lost without your encouragement.

To The Squad, you're all lovely and fantastic and beyond words phenomenal. Nicole, Jane, Jess, JL, Kim, Liv, Paige, Meg,

Ava, and Brooke rule for always!

To Bobbie for always proofing and providing extra support.

To Eva for the gorgeous teasers and GIF.

To Alexandra for the hilarious dolphin story.

To Tim for creating my book trailer for MISS.

A huge thank you to Christine with Type A Formatting for always making my books beautiful.

And last but certainly not least, a huge shout out to YOU for reading MISS. I'll never be able to say it enough how much that means to me. Just continue loving books and reading for me, okay? You've made me a very, very happy author!

# ABOUT THE AUTHOR

HARLOE RAE IS A MINNESOTA gal with a serious addiction to romance. She's always chasing an epic happily ever after.

When she's not buried in the writing cave, Harloe can be found hanging with her hubby and son. If the weather permits, she loves being lakeside or out in the country with her horses.

Harloe is the author of Redefining Us, Forget You Not, Watch Me Follow, GENT, and MISS. These titles are available on Amazon.

Find all the latest on her site :
*www.harloe-rae.blog*

*Join her newsletter at http://bit.ly/HarloesList*

*Join her reader group, Harloe's Hotties,*
*at www.facebook.com/harloehotties*

# ALSO BY HARLOE RAE

REDEFINING US
A standalone friends to lovers, military romance.

*In order to truly save him, I need to redefine us.*
Xander Dixon was my best friend.
Loyal and dependable.
A brave warrior.
A permanent presence in my life until that fateful day he boarded a plane headed overseas.
Xander's unwelcome silence haunted me for three years . . .
Until he suddenly resurfaces.
Blinded by misplaced fury.
Trapped in a pool of darkness.
Unable to escape the perpetual pain.
Though it would be easy to walk away, I refuse to give up on him.
I want to know his misery and torment, so I can rescue him.
Then Xander will finally be mine.

FORGET YOU NOT
A standalone sweet second chance, military romance.

I didn't believe in love at first sight until Lark stood before me.
Pretty sure I would have married her on the spot.
Too bad fate had other plans.
Duty called and I had to answer—no matter the consequences.
There wasn't a chance for goodbye, but I'd never forget her.
Time has a way of creating change—but only on the surface.

Even after all these years, I know Lark is mine.
I belong to her just the same.
The moment I see her again, it's a done deal.
All I've got to do is convince her this is forever.
She can push but I'll only pull harder.
I'm not letting our second chance slip away.

## WATCH ME FOLLOW
A standalone stalker, double virgin romance.

*Creep. Freak. Crazy Eyes.*
I've heard it all.

Over the years, they've slammed me with every demeaning name in the book.

Their taunts warped me like a steady stream of poison.

Anger replaced anxiety as I started believing the cruelty spat my way.

Until she showed up and changed everything.

Lennon Bennett is pure innocence—warm sunshine breaking apart my stormy existence.

She's everything good and maybe I can be too.

For her. With her. Because of her.

Lennon doesn't know I'm beckoned closer with each breath.

She isn't aware that I'm completely consumed with her.

It's become my sole purpose to protect her, by any means necessary.

But if she discovers the depth of my obsession, it will be the end of me.

So, I remain in the shadows.

Waiting. Watching. Wanting.

She'll be my first. My last. My only.

Printed in Poland
by Amazon Fulfillment
Poland Sp. z o.o., Wrocław